# Arcaneus

## Chronicles of Datch

By David Hallam

ISBN: **978-1-917238-16-8**

# DEDICATION

For my wonderful daughter Emma.

## ACKNOWLEDGMENTS

I want to say thank you to all the staff in my local public house for putting up with me sitting in the corner typing away on my laptop.

I would also like to thank Jeff and Mick for all their hard work in proving that I can't spell or type any better than I could teach an elephant to tap dance. Thanks for the proof reading, guys!

# The Tour

Datch stood looking at the luggage. They used to just have a rucksack, now he was looking at three suitcases. Yes, they were going to be away for three months but the Raven did have the systems to clean clothes. Also, they were staying in a lot of very expensive hotels that would be more than happy to do your laundry if you asked them to. He sighed and started to take them out to the Raven. It had been two Bellatrixian years (Four Earth years) since they finished school and had already completed three galactic tours. This was number four.

Carina was now living with him and they had their own home. It was still at his dad's ranch but his dad had helped them convert the old barn into a two-bedroom house and they even had their own small garden. This gave them their own space but they still spent a lot of their down time round the pool with Datch's mum and dad.

Carina came down the stairs humming to herself.

"There is another bag on our bed upstairs. I'll fetch it down in a minute."

"Ok. Babes." He said taking the second case out of the door.

The Raven was sitting on its landing pad which Datch and his dad had built to save on storage costs as keeping the Raven at a space port was very expensive. During the last two years they had spent a lot of time in the Raven and Datch was now getting very good at flying her. He had got a lot of practice in with all the travelling they had been doing.

Finally, he got all the cases into the Raven. He headed down the ramp and over to the pool. Carina was sitting in one of the sun loungers with a drink. The rest of The Pack would be arriving soon. Datch went inside and fetched a drink before coming out to wait for them to turn up.

Tansya came walking over and sat in one of the chairs next to them.

“Hi mum.” Datch said as she sat down.

“Hi Datch.” She had a swallow of her drink and then asked.

“What time you setting off?”

“When the others are all here, I expect. We have a three day trip ahead of us before planet fall.”

“Where are you heading first?”

“The Cervantes system, we have five gigs in that system. Three on Cervantes four and two on Cervantes five.”

“I hope you’ve got your coats, Cervantes five is a bit on the cold side.”

“Yes, I’ve put them in the suitcase.” Said Carina.

“Oh, that’s why we have three!” Said Datch suddenly realising why there were more than normal.

Just then there was the sound of approaching bikes. Datch looked up.

“Here comes Tish and Dapo.” he said getting up and heading over to the Raven.

They landed at the back of the ship and got off the bikes. Datch helped them take their bikes inside the ship and unload their luggage. Ten minutes later they were sitting next to the pool chilling with a drink and discussing the trip. It wasn’t long before the bikers with Hagger and Rosey arrived and after stowing their bikes and luggage they came and joined them at the pool. Last to arrive was Jep and Timbo on the Timbo Machine.

Timbo was their road crew manager. The Pack had sorted out a custom bike for him as he was on the large side. In fact, he was built like a house and every bit of it was muscle. Because of this his bike was big. It had extra thrusters for stability and an extra seat at the back for Timbo's partner. Then came the extra-large storage boxes on either side. One of which had a built-in chiller for keeping things cool, mainly beer. The bike was so big it could easily have been confused with a pickup truck. Timbo liked to have things just in case and as such brought everything with him. That was why he was very good as a road crew manager, that and the fact that no one would ever say no to him, due to his size. They put the Timbo machine in the hold and sorted their rooms out before coming back out to join the others next to the pool.

"Ok. Looks like we're all set." Said Datch, "Let's have one more drink and then get going. We have two hundred and eighty-two light years to cover."

He got up and headed into the bar via the veranda. Inside his dad was sitting looking at a bot that had been behaving erratically. Datch walked over to him. His dad looked up as he approached.

"Hi Dad, we're going after this drink."

"Ok, Datch. Have you done a full system check on the Raven?"

"Yes. I did it this morning, It's all good."

"Great, I'll come over in a minute. I just need to put this back together."

"Ok."

Tank came walking in with Jep.

"Hi Dechow."

"Hi guys, I'll be with you in a minute."

He poked the bot with a screwdriver and there was a bang and a small cloud of smoke came out of it.

"Crap!" he said.

He looked at the smoking remains of a circuit board and put the screwdriver down. He got up and headed around the back of the Bar.

"So, what can I do you for you folks?"

"I'll have a Grucks please as I'm driving and Carina would like a starburst, please?" Asked Datch.

"And you guys?"

"We would like six Bellatrixian ales, Two old man's boots with Grucks and ice and a large Grucks and a white wine for Tish."

"OK, coming up."

Dechow started to pull drinks and place them on trays ready for them to take out.

"Datch, before you head off can you just check with your mum as we were talking about a holiday."

"Ok. I think we'll all need a break after this trip. But we have told Jim we'll do four gigs at the Barber's when we get back and we have two gigs down south as well. I'll make sure we keep the following three weeks free."

"That sounds good."

He finished pulling the beers, then made Carina's Traxsent starburst and one for Tansya as well.

They picked up the drinks and headed out to the pool.

Datch sat down and handed Carina her drink.

"Ok folks. Has everyone got their coats?"

There was a general round of nodding.

"Good. Well, here's to The Pack's 4th galactic tour!"

They all lifted their glasses and took a drink.

Afterwards Tansya turned to Datch.

"Have you got any breaks on the way?" she asked.

"Yes, we have a three-week break after the gigs in the Tancanar star system before we need to go to Serpentis. It's a bit too far out to come back so we're just going to hang out on Tancanar 4 at a beach resort and see some of the sights."

"Sounds like you have got it all worked out."

"Yes, it took a bit of planning though." Said Fred.

"I bet!"

They chatted a bit more before it was time to go. They all said their goodbyes and headed to the Raven. Five minutes later they were sitting in the cockpit. Datch sat in the pilot's seat and did the pre-flight checks with Clax before bringing the thrusters online and starting the main engines.

"Everyone ready?" he said looking round.

They all nodded. Datch turned to the front and activated his headset.

"Yuland City control, this is the starship Raven. We are ready for lift off on route to the Cervantes star system"

The comms burst into life.

“Raven. This Yuland City control, you’re clear to lift off. Head on a vector of 259.7 by 197.2. Please be aware you will be joining heavy traffic 15km out on your left.”

“Thanks, Yuland City. Will advise on reaching orbit.”

Datch pulled back on the flight controls and dust was blown into the air as the Raven left the ground. He pointed her nose skyward and increased thrust.

Tansya and Dechow watch as the Raven headed into the clouds and vanished out of sight.

“Well, I don’t know about you but I fancy another beer now we have the place to ourselves.”

“Yes, me too.”

They both laughed and headed into the bar.

As the Raven climbed into the upper atmosphere the sky started to darken and one of the orbiting space stations started to appear to the south. Then the sky turned to black and the star appeared.

“Yuland City control. This is the Raven, orbit reached, heading for clear space before entering interspace.”

“Have a safe trip Raven, Yuland City control out.”

Datch banked the ship away from the main stream of traffic and headed into empty space. As he did, he accelerated and once he was clear of the shipping lanes he turned to the others.

“Here we go folks! Computer lay in a course for the Cervantes system, interspace factor fifteen. Give a one-hour alarm before arrival.”

“Course laid in. Journey time will be 3.4 days.”

“Engage!”

The stars in front of them winked out and then started to flicker.

“Ok folks, let’s go play solar ball!” Said Datch getting up from the seat.”

“You folks can, I’m heading to the bar.” Said Tank.

“Sounds like a plan Tank. I’ve got that new movie we were talking about watching.” added Peebop.

With that they all split up. The bikers, Jep and Timbo headed to the rec room come bar and the rest went to the hold to play solar ball.

# Tancanar

After five weeks, six planetary systems and twenty-five gigs they arrived at Tancanar 4. It had been a busy few weeks and they were looking forward to a break. Only one more gig and they could relax for three weeks before heading to Olympus, the capital of the IPSF, via the Serpentis star system.

The Pack sat in their dressing room getting ready for the gig. The hosts had supplied a lot of food and drinks along with various gifts to remind them to come back and see them. The previous night's gig had been a great success and they had packed out a hundred-thousand-seat stadium and tonight was no different with all the tickets sold out.

"So, what we doing first when we get to the resort?" asked Dapo.

"I'm going for a swim in the sea." Said Carina.

"I'm with you on that." added Rosey.

Before anyone else could answer there was a knock at the door.

"Yes?" Said Fred.

The door opened and a security guard stood in the doorway.

"I have a letter for Datch."

Datch got up and walked over to him.

"Here you are, Sir." He said handing Datch the envelope.

"Thank you." Said Datch taking it.

"You're welcome, Sir."

The guard left closing the door on the way out.

The letter was in a plain envelope and had 'To Datch and The Pack' written by hand on the front. Datch looked at it. He had got one the previous night. He opened it and read it.

"That's odd." he said.

"What is?" Asked Carina.

"The letter, I had one handed to me yesterday. It says the same thing and its hand written."

"Hand written, what does it say?"

He read the letter out.

"To Datch and The Pack. Sorry to bother you but I have no one to turn to. My planet of Arcaneus has been taken over by monsters from the nearby star system of Plantar. They are a barbaric race enslaving our planet. We were just about to join the IPSF but they invaded before we could sign the treaty. I have heard of your great deeds. Saving your president and bringing Welly Four into the light. Please can you help me get my father and the ruling council to safety so that they may save our planet. I've tried other people but no one wants to know. Please help me. I fear for my dad's life. Please if you can help, meet me after the concert in the Jaffar Bar in Forge Street. Signed Gilla."

Datch stopped and looked at the others.

"I see what you mean. Very strange."

"I'm not surprised no one will help, Plantar was rejected from joining the IPSF for being too violent. They are a bunch of thugs." Said Clax.

Datch sat pondering the letter.

"Datch, what are you thinking?" Said Fred noticing the look on Datch's face.

"I think we should meet her."

"Are you sure?"

"Yes, I think we should hear her out if nothing else. I might be able to get Don to help."

He looked around at the others, they were all looking at him. Carina stood up.

"Well, I think we should help if we can. I'm with Datch." she said.

The others all nodded and they called Timbo to sort out some transport to the bar.

The gig was a big success again. They had come up with a set of dance routines that made the most out of their aura's and caused them to interact with each other making quite a light show. They did three encores before they finally left the stage and the whole audience left with sparkles of green circling their heads and big smiles on their faces.

Timbo came to The Pack's dressing room and told them a limo was waiting for them along with two security guards. He was going to be coming as well. They left the stadium and headed to the Jaffar Bar in Forge Street.

Forge Street was dark and dimly lit. It was also in a quiet area of the city. The Jaffar Bar was small by city standards and was painted brown with a number of brass lights illuminating the front of it. It looked quite old with wooden beams running across the front and a little wooden sign hanging outside that was blowing backwards and forwards in the wind. Timbo walked inside first to look around before sticking his head back out the door. He nodded and they followed him in.

The bar had both a bar and lounge. They opted for the lounge as it had carpet on the floor. There were one or two people drinking but it was not that busy. The Pack took over four of the tables which was basically, half the room. Timbo went and got a round of drinks for everyone and they sat drinking them. It was quite a nice little bar and had a lot of character with some scenic pictures on the walls along with nice subtle lighting. The bar had a number of fake stuffed animals along the top of it and the barman was currently chatting to one of the locals.

The Pack had just got their second drink when the door opened and a woman walked in. She was tall with a slim build, she had dark brown hair, blue piercing eyes and was wearing a red dress with a pink jacket. She looked around twenty years old and had a scruffiness about her. She looked over at them and smiled.

“Do you think she is the one?” Asked Tank.

“I don’t know?” Replied Datch watching the woman.

“Well as we are all staring at her, I have a feeling she will be leaving if she’s not.” added Clax.

The woman went to the bar and ordered a drink and paid for it using the local currency. She turned and smiled at them and started to walk over. The two security guards stood up and she stopped. She looked at them and then at Datch.

“I’m Gilla. I sent the letter.”

Datch stood up.

“Ok, let her come over.” he said.

The two guards stood slightly to the side so that she could pass. She walked over to the table with Datch.

“Thank you for coming. I didn’t know if you would get the letters.”

“Yes, we did.” Said Datch, “Please sit down.” He gestured to the chair in front of her.

“I am really sorry to bother you but I don’t know who to turn to.”

“That’s ok, please let me introduce myself. I’m Datch, this is Carina, Dapo, Tish, Hagger, Rosey, Tank, Clax, Jep, Peebop, Fred and Timbo.”

They all said hello and then Datch turned her.

“So, what is this all about?” he asked.

“As I said in the letter, I am from the planet of Arcaneus three. I was smuggled off the planet by friends of my father after the Plantars invaded. My dad is leader of the ruling council who were ready to sign the treaty with the IPSF. The Plantars didn’t want us to become part of the IPSF and took over the planet. They are now strip mining our planet for the precious metals and anyone who stands up to them is taken off and never seen again.”

“Have you tried talking to the IPSF?” Asked Fred.

“Yes, but they say as the treaty wasn’t signed, they can’t do anything.”

“What about your dad’s friends, can’t they get your dad off the planet?”

She looked down at her drink.

“Their ship was destroyed on the way back to try and rescue them. Someone had tipped off the Plantars to what the ship was doing.”

“So, what do you want us to do?”

“Help save my mum and dad.”

The Pack sat looking at each other. It was a while before anyone spoke.

"I suppose we could use the scattering field to get there." Said Datch slightly concerned.

"Are you mad? If we get caught, they will kill us!" Said Clax.

Datch looked at Gilla, he could tell she was scared.

"Hmm... Gilla, do you have a place to stay?"

"Not really, I have been sleeping in an empty building just outside of the city."

"Ok... Why don't you stay with us for a bit?"

"I don't want to impose."

"Look, just stay with us until I talk to some of our friends and I'll see if I can get you some help."

"Are you sure?"

Datch looked at the others. They nodded one after another.

"Yes, we're sure."

"Ok. Thank you."

"Do you have any bags?"

"Just a rucksack and that's hidden in the building."

"If you tell this officer where it is, he will fetch it for you. Have you eaten yet?"

"No, not for a couple of days. I'm having to be careful of my funds. My dad's friends gave me some credits to keep me going until they brought my mum and dad to me. I've only got a few hundred left."

"Well, we haven't had dinner yet so let's finish these drinks and go get some food."

"Ok. Thank you."

"So, what's your world like?" Asked Carina.

"It's a bit warmer than this one and has lots of lush green forests. I live," she paused, "used to live in the capital city with my mum and dad." She looked very sad.

"And you will again." Said Datch.

She talked more about how her world used to be and how the Plantars had taken the world from them. They had been a peaceful race and only had a limited military. The Plantars had pretty much walked strait in with very little resistance. There had been a few attempts to stop them but they had over whelming forces and had crushed the military in a matter of days. Then anyone who spoke out against them would either be executed on the spot or would be taken away and never seen again.

The planet Arcaneus three was rich in rare elements that were used for interspace drives and various other high-tech systems. They had been about to sign a treaty with the IPSF which would have given them access to the interstellar markets and would have made the planet very rich. It would also have cut the trading route to the Plantar system which would have put a stop to any chance of them expanding out of their star system as they needed the raw materials for their ships.

The party moved to a restaurant in an up market part of town and a member of security was sent for Gilla's bag. The Pack had told her to have what she wanted and not to worry about the bill. Gilla was very hungry and had soon demolished the starter and main course.

"I can't thank you enough for this." She said putting the last bit of Weega in her mouth.

"You're welcome. After what you have been through you deserve a good meal." Said Datch.

"Yes," Said Rosey, "No one should be forced out of their home."

"So, tonight you will be with us at the Tiger Palace. I have called ahead and sorted a room for you. Then tomorrow we are heading to a private resort on the equatorial island of Diamar. I'll contact our friends tomorrow when we get there."

"Thank you. You don't know what this means to me."

The rest of The Pack looked at Datch. He knew what they were thinking, but at the same time he wanted to help.

"Well, let's order the sweets. Ice-cream everyone?"

"Yes please!" Said Hagger.

"Ice-cream?" Gilla asked.

"Yes. Ice-cream!"

Datch waved at one of the waiters and he came over.

"Chocolate Ice-cream all round!"

"Certainly, Sir."

The next morning Datch slowly opened his eyes and was greeted with the view of the back of Carina's head. He lay there for a while thinking about Gilla and what she had told them. After a few minutes laying there he lifted himself up and kissed Carina on the shoulder. She turned to look at him.

"Morning lover." she said.

"Morning babes." he said and got out of bed.

"Are you ok?"

"Yes, I was just thinking about Gilla and her problem."

"And?"

"I want to help and rescue her dad."

"Well, hopefully Don can pull some strings?"

"Yes, but I have a bad feeling that Don won't be able to help."

"At least you're trying."

Datch sighed.

"Yes… but I don't like the idea of Gilla losing her mum and dad."

"I'm sure someone will help."

"Hmm..."

"Let's go and get some breakfast." she said.

They got dressed and headed to the restaurant.

Two hours later they were on their way to the Raven in a shuttle. Gilla was looking much more relaxed now and was chatting with everyone.

They arrived at the landing area and exited the shuttle. The Raven had been refuelled and the systems had all been checked.

"Welcome to the Raven." Said Datch walking up the ramp.

"Wow, this is an impressive ship. Is it yours?"

"Yes, I own it."

They walked inside and he showed her to one of the spare rooms.

“If you put your stuff in here, we’ll be taking off in about five minutes.”

“Thanks.” She put her bag on the bed and followed Datch up to the cockpit. Datch pointed to a seat near the back.

“You can have that seat there if that’s ok?”

“Sure. Thanks.”

Datch headed to the pilot’s seat and sat down. One by one the others came in and took their seats.

Clax came over and sat next to Datch.

“Think we’re good.” he said.

Datch pressed a few buttons and the ship powered up. He put on his headset and brought the ships thrusters to standby.

“Tancanar Control, this is the Raven. Requesting flight path to Diamar island resort near the equator. Also, we would like automated launch and city clearance please?”

“Good morning, Raven. Heavy traffic at the moment. Please hover at two hundred meters and lock on to beacon 22374. Auto clearance will take you away from main orbital traffic and you will then be clear to navigate.”

“Thanks, Tancanar Control. Locking on to Beacon and ascending to two hundred meters.”

Datch increased thrust and the Raven lifted off. He put the Raven in hover and instructed the computer to lock on to the beacon. The Raven hung in the air for about two minutes before it turned and accelerated. The ship started to gain height and then levelled off at five thousand meters. The sky was very busy with a lot of ships taking off or landing. They were following a freighter heading for orbit. The Raven started to turn away from the main stream of traffic heading to the right of the city.

"Raven, this is Tancanar Control. Please be advised the beacon will terminate in 1 minute. You're cleared for a flight path at 15,000 metres on vector 10.9 by 251.1. Cruising speed 10,000KMPH."

"Thanks, Tancanar Control. Programming course and speed into the navigation control."

Datch rested his hands to the controls and waited.

"Raven, this is Tancanar Control. Raven is yours. Please contact Diamar control and have a safe trip."

"Thanks, Tancanar Control, Raven out."

Datch increased thrust and the Raven headed to the thin outer atmosphere. Datch contacted Diamar control and within a few minutes they were heading down towards the surface. The whole trip only lasted 20 minutes and then they were over the island. The Island was split up into private villa's each with their own landing pad and staff to make sure your stay was perfect. Along the shoreline there were a number of small villages with restaurants and bars. According to the planetary guide each of the restaurants had a different theme and catered for all races.

Diamar Resort Control directed them to the correct landing pad and they touched down in amongst the palm trees next to their own private villa.

The rear of the Raven opened and Datch came walking down with Carina followed by the rest of The Pack. Standing at edge of the landing pad were two ladies and a man. Datch and Carina walked over to them.

"Good morning, Sir. Welcome to Diamar Resort. My name is Peter, I am your Concierge for the length of your stay. If you need anything at all please just ask."

"Thank you, Peter, I'm Datch and this is my partner, Carina."

"Pleased to meet you both. This is Jana your maid and this is Filis your chef. If we have missed any of the food you like please let her know and she will make sure it's on hand for you."

"Thank you." Datch said as the others came walking over.

There was a round of introductions as everyone was introduced to the staff after which, they were then shown around the villa. Peter had already got a large table for them to sit at. It was apparently on a list somewhere. After being shown to their rooms they headed out to the pool area.

Peter was standing discreetly near the outdoor bar. Datch walked over to him.

"Hi Peter. Any chance of a barbeque this evening. We sort of fancy a few steaks and that sort of thing if that's ok?"

"Certainly sir, would you like fresh bread and salad with it?"

"Yes. That sounds good. Thanks. I just need to attend to a few things onboard the Raven, I'll be back shortly."

"Thank you, Sir. I'll get straight on it."

Datch headed to the Raven to make some calls.

Fifteen minutes later he came back and headed to the others near the pool.

"So?" Said Carina turning around.

"I've sent messages to Coola, Widfab and Don. It's going to take a day at least before we get a response. It's going to take two days for Don to get the message so he must be a long way off."

“What did you tell them?”

“I just said that we had the daughter of the Arcaneus president with us and she had told us that they wanted to sign the treaty but they needed help to escape their planet to do it. I asked if there was there anything they could do to help.”

“Sounds good.” she said.

Datch turned towards the pool and called Gilla over. When she arrived Datch repeated to her what was going on. Afterwards the party started and Peter and Filis got the barbeque fired up. Datch and Carina headed to the pool along with half of The Pack.

The next couple of days were spent getting to know Gilla and a bit of sightseeing. The sea was warm with crystal clear water. They hired a small boat and went sailing around the island. Then on day three, Datch called everyone together around the table.

“Thanks all, I’ve had all the responses back and it’s not good news. Don can’t intervene as they are not members of the IPSF. Coola has tried diplomatic channels but so far has had no joy as the Plantars are blocking all forms of communication. And Widfab said he would love to help but it’s a very long way away and they currently only have one interstellar destroyer which is very busy helping to sort out a very large galactic party they are having and asked have we had thought about singing to them?”

They all looked at him. There was a long pause before anyone spoke.

“So, no then!” Said Gilla and burst into tears.

The others all looked at each other. They all liked Gilla. She was a fun-loving person and very easy to get on with. They all felt sorry for her. They comforted her and told her not to worry they would think of something. After about five minutes Datch spoke.

“Gilla, we all need to talk. Would you mind leaving us for a few minutes?”

“Ok.” She said still sniffling. She got up and headed inside.

After she had gone Datch turned to the others.

“What do you think folks. We can’t just let her lose her family. I think we should get her mum and dad if no one else.”

“You know we could all die if we do this, don’t you? And more to the point we’ll stay dead.” Said Clax.

“Yes, I understand. But we need to help.”

“Well, I suppose if we used the scattering field and the same trick as the pirates used to leave Bellatrix five, we might get in and out unseen.” Said Hagger.

“Yes, but we would still need to get to her parents and smuggle them out.” Said Fred.

Datch thought about it.

“OK, look. If we can sort the getting to her mum and dad bit out then who is in? and don’t feel you need to go.”

He looked around the table, Hagger put his hand up followed by Rosey and Dapo, then Carina, Tish and Timbo. the bikers looked at each other.

“We must be mad you know that!” Said Fred.

Datch laughed.

“Well, maybe, but at least it will be fun.”

Jep looked at the others.

“Fun is not the word I would use but what the hell.”

“Babes, can you fetch Gilla?” Datch asked.

Carina got up and went to fetch her. When she came back Datch stood up.

“Gilla, we have decided to help you to get your mum and dad to safety.”

“Thank you, thank you!” she said starting to smile again.

“But we need some information first.”

“Yes, like we need to know where they are and how to get to them without being seen.” Said Fred.

“Yes. We don’t want to get shot.” Added Tank.

Gilla looked at them.

“Well, I was smuggled out of the tunnels under the city and then we walked into the toxic hills where the ship was hidden.”

“Toxic hills?”

“Yes, the hills where the old mines are.”

“What sort of mines?”

“They had radioactive ore in them. No one goes there because of it. They’re deserted these days as most of the material has been mined out.”

Clax thought for a while.

“I see what they did. Landing their ship in a radiation zone would stop the orbital sensors seeing them. The Plantars’ tech is very old and can’t see clearly into radiation. They would be invisible.”

“How long could the Raven stay there?”

“With its shielding, years!” Said Clax.

“So, we know where to land. What next?”

“We head across the fields and into the caves.” Said Gilla.

“Ok, But then what?”

“Yes, how are we going to get to your dad?” Asked Fred.

“There is a cellar in the bottom of the house that leads to the tunnels, If I go, I can get him to come down to us.”

“Hmm… what if he’s being guarded?” Asked Tank.

“I don’t know?”

“We’ll have to improvise.” Said Hagger.

“OK, I’m going to send a message to Don when we take off telling him what we are doing.” Said Datch.

“You know he’s not going to like that, don’t you? he’s going to be pretty mad!” Said Fred.

“I’m counting on it.” Said Datch grinning.

They all looked at him. Now they knew that things were going to get interesting. The grin said it all.

“So, let’s chill tomorrow and then head to Arcaneus the following day, At maximum speed it’s about two days travel.”

“Peter, Beers all around please.” Said Tank.

# Arcaneus

Datch sat in the Raven looking out of the cockpit window. Carina came in and sat next to him.

“Are you really sure about this?” She asked.

Datch could tell even she had doubts. He did too. This time there was no back up, no army coming to save them. If this plan failed it could mean their deaths. He sighed.

“No. But we have to try. I Love you babes.”

“I love you too.”

“I think sometimes you just have to do things and hope.”

The others started to fill the seats behind.

“Ok, looks like it’s time to go.”

Carina kissed him and went and sat in her chair.

When everyone had sat down Datch turned to them.

“Ok, last chance! If you have any second thoughts now’s the time to get off.”

They all looked back at him. Then Fred spoke.

“Datch, we are The Pack! Now let’s get moving before we all change our minds.”

Datch turned and brought the thrusters online.

“Diamar control, this is the Raven, heading for a bit of sightseeing in a couple of nearby star systems. Requesting free space exit.”

“Hello Raven, cleared for launch. Head on vector 342.2 by 272.1 have a nice trip.”

"Thanks, Diamar control. Raven out."

Datch increased thrust and the Raven took to the sky accelerating up through the atmosphere. The sky turned from blue to black and then they were in space. Datch flew the ship to an empty bit of space before engaging the interspace drive.

"Computer set course for Arcaneus three."

"Warning! Arcaneus is contested space do you wish to continue?"

"Engage interspace drive. Inform me when we enter contested space and engage the scattering field."

"Alarm has been set. Scattering field will be activated on entering contested space."

The stars outside winked out and then started to flicker.

"Well. I need a beer!" Said Datch getting up.

"I think we all do." Said Fred.

"Speak for yourself. I need some Old Man's Boots." Said Hagger.

They all got up and went to the rec room.

"I've been doing some research and have downloaded some maps that I found from before the invasion. I think we should take a look now before we have too much to drink and Gilla can update us on any changes." Said Datch.

"Sounds like a plan." Added Clax.

They all sat down in the rec room and after everyone had got a drink, Datch turned the vid on. He tapped a few buttons on his vid com and an aerial map appeared showing the mine area. The area was very barren with large black areas where waste ore had been dumped. There were a number of old tumbled down buildings and a disused rail track leading towards the city. Datch turned to Gilla.

"Which way did you come from the city?"

"Err..." she looked closely at the map, "I think it was here." She pointed to a bit of the map. "Then I think we went over these fields and through the old mine workings to that flat area there. Yes there. That was where the ship was."

Datch looked at it. "Hmm... Well, what if we park the Raven here," he said pointing to a large black bit. "We can use that gully running down there to stay hidden. The scattering field should keep the Raven hidden from their sensors. At their level of tech, they have no chance of seeing through it. If anything, it will blend into the background radiation. Only if someone goes there will it be seen."

"No one will go there. The radiation and toxic minerals keep everyone away." Said Gilla.

"Ok, so I take it the reason you went across the fields was to keep under cover?"

"Yes, the railway lines take you past a cave exit but you can easily be seen. So, the fields are best."

"Ok, so where is the cave entrance?"

"Can you zoom in here?"

Datch did and there was an old building with a tumbled down wall.

"You see the side of the wall there; it fell into one of the caves a few years ago. The hole is under that wood."

"Do the Plantars have patrols?" Asked Fred.

"They do in the city. But there is nothing out near the mines to look for or to protect. They are far too busy making sure my people behave themselves and do as they are told. I don't think they have that many troops on the planet."

"They did take over your planet."

"Yes, but we didn't have much of an army, just a few thousand men over the whole planet. We never had need for an army."

"Hmm… so do you know your way through the caves?"

"Sort of, I left little marks on the way out because I wanted to find my way back if anything happened."

"Ok, so we can get in," Said Tank, "What about getting your mum and dad out, won't they be watched?"

"I don't know. We were being made to stay in our home and my dad was only let out to broadcast to the people when the Plantars wanted him too."

"OK, that might help." Said Fred.

Datch looked at the ships clock.

"When is it night there?"

"Err… I'm not sure, I left fifteen days ago and it was at night. So, maybe now ish."

Datch turned back to the vid.

"Computer. Show the Arcaneus system."

The computer displayed a star system with seven planets. The first two were just rocky worlds with no atmosphere. The third was Gilla's home world and had two moons, one of which had a methane atmosphere. The rest were gas giants apart for the outer most one that wasn't much more than a very large frozen rock. Datch sat looking at it for a minute.

"Hmm, if we come out of interspace behind the moon just above its atmosphere. It should be enough to hide us from any ships." He paused. "Then we wait till dark and head for the planet. If we use the interspace drive on a short burst we should pop out in the upper atmosphere. We just need to time it right so we're above the mines and can drop straight down unseen."

He looked at Clax.

"It might work. With the scattering field their sensors shouldn't pick us up. But it's going to take both of us to get it down undetected." he said.

"Gilla, how long will it take to get to your mum and dad?" Asked Fred.

"If we don't get held up, maybe eight hours."

"That means we'll get there just before day break." Said Tank.

"Fred, do you still have your little toy?" asked Datch.

"Yes, it's in my room. Why?"

"We could send it in the house first to check for guards or cameras. We don't want them to know we've been there until we're on the way out of the star system."

"I can put it on quiet mode so it won't get noticed."

"OK, so we sort of have a plan." Said Clax.

"Let's chill out for a bit and have a think about what we're going to do. If anyone has any doubts or ideas then we'll go through them tomorrow. Computer. I need another beer." Said Datch.

The unit in the corner made a humming noise and a beer appeared through a flap. Datch walked over, picked it up and took a drink.

“Ah… that’s better.” he said.

The others all followed suit and then the younger members all went to play Solar Ball in the cargo bay.

The following day they all had a nap in the afternoon to get ready for the evening activities. Afterwards they all had a big meal and dressed in black. That is apart from Hagger, Rosey, Tank, Clax, Jep and Peebop. They were staying behind in the Raven in case things went wrong and they needed to go for help or get the Raven out of there fast if it was discovered.

The warning alarm went off. Datch and Clax got up and headed to the cockpit.

Datch sat down and pulled up the long-range tactical view. The Raven had been a criminal’s ship before Datch was given it and as such, it had a few extra bits that most ships didn’t have. Such as the tactical systems, four pulse canons and of course the scattering field which Datch had kept so they could stay out of sight when flying past worlds with security risks. They were no match for a big ship but they should put a big dent in a small fighter or pursuit craft.

The tactical plot of the Arcaneus system took a few minutes to come up. It showed two large ships in orbit around Arcaneus three, four medium size freighters, three of which were leaving the star system and one on approach to the planet. There were also two small scout ships flying what looked like patrols to the outer parts of the system. They were more than likely checking for unwanted ships coming into the system. Datch checked the scattering field was functioning normally and brought the weapons systems online. Clax sat down next to him.

“Are you ready for this?” He asked.

“No, but we need to do it. No one else will help them.” Said Datch.

"I suppose." He paused, "Well, if any ship can do it, it's this one. Are all the weapon systems and defence shielding, ok?"

"Yes, all systems are online and looking good."

"So, are you going to fly her down, or am I?"

"I'll fly, you make sure everything else works."

"Ok. How do I bring up the weapons?"

"One sec," Said Datch and pressed a couple of invisible buttons that were hovering in mid-air.

The weapons systems lit up on Clax's side.

"There you go."

Clax put on his headset and the weapons started tracking with his head movements.

"Ok, ten minutes until we enter the star system and another two until we reach the moon."

"You're not planning to die again, are you?" asked Clax.

"No, and no one else is allowed to, either!"

"Ok, just asking. What happens if they find the Raven?"

"You get her the hell out of there. Head straight out of the system and to Tancanar."

"Then what?"

"Contact Don. We'll hide out in the caves until help gets to us."

"OK. Try not to get shot while on the planet, won't you?"

"I'll try. Ok time to get everyone up here."

Datch pressed the ships comms.

"We're just about to enter the Arcaneus system folks. Time to buckle up."

The rest of The Pack came into the cockpit and sat down. Half of them looked like they had just been to a fancy dress party in the dark and only had black makeup to put on.

Datch turned to everyone.

"Ok folks. This is where the fun begins!" He grinned.

An alarm indicated that they were entering hostile space. Datch and Clax started focusing on the controls. Turning the ship was easy normally because they were in normal space but the Raven was still in Interspace and the ship was very slow to respond. The Raven turned towards the third planet and headed towards the moon. Datch dropped down to interspace factor two and got ready to drop to normal space. As they approached, they could see one of the large Plantar starships. It was very big and looked very menacing with an array of gun ports and a flight deck with a large fighter compliment. Datch brought the Raven very close to the moon and dropped out of interspace. The Raven entered the moon's upper atmosphere and stopped.

"Clax, any sign of movement?" Asked Datch.

"No, nothing. I don't think they spotted us."

"So how long have we got to stay here for?" Asked Fred.

"About an hour, looking at the sensors. It's just starting to get dark over the capital now. I want to make sure it's dark before I take the Raven down. I'll need to drop out of interspace inside the lower atmosphere and hit the reverse thrust at the same time or there's going to be a very big hole in the planet."

They all looked at each other and then at Datch.

“I think I need the bathroom.” Said Peebop.

“Me to!” Added Tank, Jep and Hagger all at the same time.

What followed was a sudden exit of half the cockpit and the waste control system working overtime.

“Well at least they’re going now. How are we looking for Plantar ships.”

“Still nothing. Looks like they can’t see us.”

“Good, Let’s hope it stays like that!”

“Tactical gives them as having forty fighters per ship and it looks like another hundred or so on the planet.”

“Is their tech as old as we thought?”

“Yes, it looks like they are still using radio waves to scan for ships. Also, the fighters doing recon are only using short range scanners. However, the two large ships do have a sensor array that could track us if they get a lock on us.”

“Well, let’s hope they don’t!”

“I’ll second that!” Said Fred.

The rest came back from the toilet and sat down. They sat and waited until night’s dark shroud covered the city below and then it was time.

“Ok folks this is going to be rough so hang on!”

Datch primed the interspace drive and the Raven jumped to interspace.

The planet started to get very big very fast as it filled the whole view outside. Down below they could see the flickering lights of the city. Datch got ready to pull back hard on the controls. The interspace drive disengaged and they dropped to normal space. The atmosphere hit the Raven like a wall. Datch pulled the control hard back. The ship shook and screamed as it battled with the atmosphere outside and then the shaking stopped. The Raven came to a stop a few metres off the ground.

Datch looked for the ravine and slowly turned the ship towards it and then dropped the Raven in it at the top end before manoeuvring backwards under some half dead trees.

"Any sign of activity?" he said.

Clax did a few scans.

"No, nothing is moving. It still looks quiet."

Datch let out a sigh of relief and put the Raven on the ground. He waited a few moments before he shut down the engines.

"Err... Let's not do that again!" Said Jep.

"Yes, let's not!" Added Tish.

Hagger and Peebop decided they needed the bathroom again and everyone else started to get up.

"Clax, monitor our implants while we're gone, it should allow you to work out where we are."

"Ok, I'll watch them."

"I'll take a comms unit with us but only use it in an emergency. Only contact us if you really need to and if you need to get out of here don't hang around, ok?"

"Ok Datch, you take care out there."

"I will... Ok time to go I think, everything still clear?"

Clax looked at the sensors again.

"Yes. still clear."

"Cool!"

Datch got up and headed to the cargo bay. The part of The Pack that was carrying out the rescue attempt were there. They each had a rucksack with supplies just in case they got stuck. That is apart from Timbo who had a very large bag strapped to his back.

"Err… Timbo, you do know we're going in to caves don't you? That bag's a bit big."

Timbo turned to Datch.

"I've got stuff we might need." he said.

"O..K.. I just didn't want you getting stuck in there."

"I won't."

Datch looked at him and then felt sorry for any cave that might try to stop him.

"Right then. Everyone ready?"

"I was a lot more ready in space than I am here." Said Tish.

"Hey, it's a nice night to go for a stroll on an alien world." Said Dapo.

"I'd prefer a nice warm beach with a nice cold beer." Said Fred.

"Well, if we hurry, we'll still have time at the villa when we get back." Said Carina.

"OK Everyone, settle down!" Said Datch.

He walked over to the comms panel,

"Clax, Everything still good?"

"Yep. Looks like they are settling down for the night."

“Ok, we’re moving out. Gilla, lead the way.”

“See you when you get back.” Said Hagger.

“You will.” replied Datch.

The cargo bay doors opened and they walked down the ramp. The air was fresh, well, fresh ish after the ships air conditioning. A cool breeze blew across the ravine and carried a lot of strange smells and a slight toxic odour.

Gilla led them into the bushes and then started to head down the ravine towards the mine workings. They slowly picked their way across the waste land using the dead bushes and tumbled down structures as cover. They avoided the pools that bubbled with poisonous chemicals and gave off some very strong toxic smells. After a few minutes they got to the old buildings near the edge of the site. From here on, they would have to be careful.

It was Fred who spotted them. A row of poles in the field.

“Are you sure?” Asked Datch.

“Yes, it’s a detection grid.” He said looking at a portable scanner he was holding.

“So, what do we do?”

“They are a very old design and rely on local movement to trigger them.”

“Hmm... lets head for that hedge over there and very slowly work our way along it. Stay close to me.”

Datch opened his backpack and took out a disc.

“What’s that?” Asked Fred.

“It’s a souvenir!”

“From what?”

"Err… the Arachnoid." Datch grinned.

"You mean it's the scattering field generator from around its neck."

"Yes. and it still works."

"Why would you want that?"

"So, Alex can't scan me while I'm in the bathroom."

"The bathroom?"

"Yes."

"Ok, never mind."

"Anyway, it's come in handy. One sec while I turn it on."

Datch pressed a couple of buttons on the disc and a small light lit up on the front showing it was active.

"There. As long as everyone stays close it should stop any active sensors seeing us."

"Yes, but what about the passive ones?"

Datch thought about this for a moment.

"We'll just have to sneak past them." he said.

"Err. I'd just like to point out, the ones over there are passive sensors."

"Oh."

"Look, there is a ditch running along the edge of the hedge. If we stay very low in it, the sensors should not detect us."

"Ok. Everyone, follow Fred and make sure you do what he does."

They slowly moved over to the hedge. When they reached it, Fred entered the ditch first. It was mostly dry but had a lot of plants growing in it, however, it was quite deep so it gave them a lot of cover.

They picked their way through it, pushing the plants carefully out the way as they went making sure they were put back after. That way if a patrol came along it would look like an animal had gone through it.

They got close to the poles and Fred turned to the others and moved his hand down. The others looked at him and then copied him. He did it again. They looked blankly at him and did it again.

"Didn't anyone ever teach you hand signals?" He whispered.

They shook their heads.

"OK, we need to crawl along this bit, especially Timbo. The first pole is just up there." He pointed with his finger just up a head. "One at a time so we don't make any noise."

They all nodded.

Fred went down on his hands and knees and headed about twenty metres further down the ditch. He stopped and took a very careful peek at the top of the ditch. Then ducked down again and waved at them to come. Datch sent Carina first followed by Gilla and Tish. It was then Timbo's turn. They decided that the bag would be carried by Dapo as there was no way Timbo would get by with it. He crawled his way to Fred followed by the others and then it was Dapo's turn. He went to lift up the bag and couldn't.

"What the Jaxx has he got in here. I can't shift it." whispered Dapo.

Datch thought for a second.

"You pull, I'll push, but slowly, ok?"

Dapo nodded.

They started to move along the ditch ever so slowly. Edging the bag along and trying not to make any noise. It took a good fifteen minutes to get it to the others. Timbo grabbed the bag with one hand and put it on his back. Dapo looked at him and then at Datch who just shrugged his shoulders.

"Right folks, we need to get maybe another twenty metres and we should be well clear of the sensors." Fred said still keeping his voice down.

They carried on along the ditch and then Fred put his head up and looked back the way they had come.

"Ok, looks good the sensors are all facing the other way and the breeze is blowing towards us."

"Err… what's the breeze got to do with it?" Asked Tish.

"It carries sounds. So, if it is blowing towards them, it would carry any sounds we make to them, but because it's coming towards us, it stops them hearing us." Said Fred.

"Oh. I never knew that." she said.

"Wow that's amazing." Said Carina.

"Yes, pretty cool." Added Dapo.

The others were all looking at him. It was then that it dawned on him that he was undertaking a commando style raid with a load of ex college students, the only two positive things were, one, no one knew they were there and two, they had Timbo. He sighed.

"Come on." he said.

They carried on following the ditch and had nearly reached a small cluster of trees when they heard a noise.

“Down!” Said Fred.

Everyone ducked into the bottom of the ditch. An engine noise got louder and louder.

“Do you think they know we’re here?” Asked Datch as the noise got louder.

Then before Fred could answer a scout ship flew overhead going in the direction of the city.

Everyone was quiet until the noise faded away. Then Fred spoke.

“No, they were not looking for us. They would have come in slower if they were.”

All of a sudden, the scattering field around Datch’s neck beeped. He looked at it and pressed a flashing green button. Clax’s face appeared on it.

“Err.. Clax? What are you doing on my scattering field generator?”

“Oh, that’s what it does. Yes, are you guys alright?”

“We have just had the crap scared out of us but yes, I thought we were going to not use comms unless in an emergency in case they picked them up?”

“Ah well. I’m not sure how I’m talking to you but about thirty minutes ago a little light started flashing on the comms panel so I’ve just pressed it. It’s not using normal comms as far as I can tell.”

“Oh. That’s how he did it!” Said Datch.

“Datch, what do you mean?”

“The casino boss. I wondered how he could talk to the spider without him becoming lunch. Or to that matter getting found out.”

“The scattering field, the ships scattering field must be linking to this one.”

“One sec, let me check something.” Said Clax

Clax turned away from the screen for a few seconds before turning back.

“Wow, that’s so cool dude. Your scattering generator is connecting to this one using the same frequencies as the field.”

“And?”

“Well, we could talk all day and they would have no idea at all what was going on.”

Datch thought about it for a moment,

“Ok, that’s cool so we can talk to you. Do you know where that ship was going?” asked Fred.

“It was heading from one of the Plantar ships to the city. It was just levelling out when it flew over you. It’s just landed at a large building in the centre.”

“Ok. That’s cool. Can you give us a call if you happen to see anymore heading this way?”

“Sure. How far are you from the caves?”

“Gilla, how far?”

“About fifteen minutes I guess.”

“Thanks. Clax, I’ll call you just as we go inside, ok?”

“Ok. Talk soon. Raven out.”

They carried on along the ditch and then entered the wood at the end. Fred got out the small case from inside his bag and opened it. Inside was a tiny little drone. It was a small circular disc shaped object with little cylindrical thrusters around the outside. It had a vid on the front with a small scanning array above it and on the back were two small thrusters. The little drone flew along the path they needed to take, looking for anything out of place.

"It looks good folks."

They started to pick their way through undergrowth and other than a few scratches from brambles, they made it to the other side in one piece. In front of them was an open field with very little cover.

"So how do we do this?" Asked Carina.

"Hmm it's a big space. It will take a good five minutes to walk across it."

Datch looked at it.

"I can run it in about one and a half." he said.

"What if someone comes?"

"Err, we run like a rampant Jaxx to the caves."

"Ok, but we need to check the coast is clear first. I'll send the drone up again and you put a call into Clax."

He launched the little drone and it flew across the field at the same time Datch pressed a button on the disc and Clax appeared.

"You guys at the cave already?"

"No. we're just about to run across a very big empty field and want to know if the coast is clear?"

“Oh, ok. There is nothing on the scanners at the moment. The nearest movement is around one of the battleships. In orbit.”

“Battleships? When did we get battleships?” Asked Datch slightly worried.

“Oh, that’s what I’m calling the big ones in orbit. It sounds better than the big ships.”

“Ok then. So, we’re good to make a run for it?”

“Yes, but hurry up about it. It would only take a couple of minutes for one of the ships from the city to get to you.”

“Ok. Ping me if you see movement?”

“Ok. Clax out.”

“Fred, Are we good?”

“Yes!”

“Ok everyone, get ready, three, two, one. Run!”

They ran for the opposite side of the field. It seemed a lot bigger going across it, than it had looking from the edge of the wood. Their feet pounded the ground as they ran and every step got them closer to safety. They reached the far side and stood under a tree getting their breath back.

“I need to work out more.” Said Dapo panting.

“Me too!” Said Fred.

Timbo was leaning against a tree or it was leaning against him, either way he was looking around as if he had taken a light stroll.

“Timbo, do you ever get out of breath or break into a sweat?” Asked Fred.

“No. I don’t allow it.”

“Remind me to ask you to show me how you work out when we get back.” Said Fred.

“I will make a note to tell you.”

“Thanks.” Said Fred who then had a second thought and was all of a sudden slightly concerned about finding out.

“How far?” Asked Datch.

“Just up here.” Said Gilla.

They headed through a little group of trees and came to a half-collapsed building.

“This way.” Gilla said.

She led them into the rubble and stopped at a hole. It didn’t look very big but when they got close, it opened out a bit revealing a passage down into the darkness. Well, darker darkness. Datch reached inside his backpack and pulled out a head torch placing it on his head. He entered the hole and turned it on. The tunnel led down through piles of bricks and rubble from the building and into a narrow passage that led into the darkness beyond. Datch went a bit further down and the passageway opened up into a small cave. The others came in behind him and put their head torches on as well. With all the lights the cave was quite well illuminated.

“Ok, this way.” Said Gilla and headed to the far side of the cave.

There was another passage way that headed down behind a bolder. It was quite a small gap but everyone got through ok. They started to make their way into cave system. The passageway was damp and a strange luminous moss was growing on the walls which had the effect of making the place look very eery. Here and there were stalactites and stalagmites growing towards each other, casting strange shadows ahead of them, adding to it all was a constant sound of dripping water in the distance.

“Do these caves flood by any chance?” Asked Fred.

“Not the way we’re going. There’s an underground river that flows through them and takes the water away. You’ll see it in a bit as we have to cross it.”

“Err… I didn’t bring my trunks.” Said Dapo.

“Don’t worry, we climb over it.”

“Oh.”

They carried on their decent into the caves. The air was cold and smelt fresh with a slight breeze.

“Is that fresh air?” asked Carina.

“Sort of, the river flows in through a large cave about six kilometres from here and the air is dragged in with it.”

“Cool, the caves have their own air con.” Said Dapo.

“Yes, but don’t drink the water. It’s got a lot of city waste in it. Oh, and it smells.”

“What, you mean its full of rubbish?”

“No, not that sort of waste.”

It took a few moments for it to click.

“Oh, crap!” he said.

They came to the end of the tunnel and went through a hole into a large cavern. The sound of rushing water was quite loud now. Gilla put out her hand out to stop them going forwards. In front of them was a shear drop. Datch looked down. It was about a hundred metres at least.

“Wow, that’s a long way down.” He said and his voice echoed around the cavern.

“Cool, it’s an echo.” Said Dapo trying it out.

‘Echo, echo, echo…’

This was followed by all of them having a go.

“Ok.” Said Fred, “Now that’s out of your systems can we carry on.”

“Yes, let’s go. This way guys.” Said Gilla.

She led the way up a narrow path in the side of the rock face. It was only wide enough for one person at a time. Slowly but surely, they picked their way up the side of the cavern. Here and there a rock would drop and they would all freeze until it hit the water below. Then they would carry on up the path a bit further.

“I’m glad I can’t see down.” Said Carina.

“Me too.” Added Tish.

They got quite close to the roof of the cave. Gilla put up her hand and stopped.

“This is the hard bit. We’re about to cross over the river and the path will be a bit slippy so be very careful of your footing before putting your weight down. It’s a very long drop and no escape from the water at the bottom.”

“So, we fall, we die?”

“Yes.”

“One second then,” Said Datch, “Timbo, do you have any rope?”

“Yes Datch, medium or heavy duty?”

“Medium would be good.”

“How much?”

“I want to tie everyone together so if one of us slip, we can catch them and pull them back up.”

“That sounds like a good plan.” Said Fred.

“OK, pass it along.”

Along piece of rope came out of Timbo’s bag and was passed along the line until everyone was tied to it.

“Gilla, you move forward and we’ll follow one by one.”

“Ok.”

Gilla moved forwards until she was at the end of the rope then it was Datch’s turn followed by Carina. The party worked its way cross the roof of the cavern making sure that everyone in the party felt secure. It took about thirty minutes to get across to the other side and down again to where the path opened up into a flat area. They sat down to have a rest. Timbo fetched a floating light out of his bag that turned on. It lit up the whole cavern.

“Wow.” Said Carina looking around.

“Yes, double wow.” Added Tish.

The moisture made the rocks glisten in the light from the lamp and they could see the river rushing along far below them.

Datch got out the scattering field generator and pressed the button on the side.

“Clax? You there?”

Clax’s face appeared on the front of it.

“Yes, Datch I’m here, what’s up?”

“I just wanted to check in, we’re having a rest at the moment. Everything still ok up there?”

“Yes, nothing much going on. Just the odd patrol that flies around the city. But other than that, it’s quiet.”

"Gilla, how far do we have left to go?"

"Err, about the same again but the caves give way to the city tunnels in a bit and they are easier to move along."

"Did you hear that, Clax?"

"Yes Datch. That will put you arriving at around 3am city time I think."

"Ok, I'll call you when we have the next break."

"No probs, I'm going to swap with Peebop in a couple of minutes and have something to eat. I'll try to get a bit of sleep as well."

"Yes. you may need it. Datch out."

"Stay safe folks."

With that, the channel closed.

Carina handed Datch an energy bar to eat.

"Well, at least we are making good time. What are we going to do when we get there?" She asked.

"Get Gilla's mum and dad and head back why?"

"Well, what about the rest of the planet?"

"We can't fit them all in the Raven." Said Dapo.

"I know that, that's not what I meant."

Datch thought about it.

"Well, I hope when her dad gets to the IPSF they can sign a temporary treaty so they can rescue the planet."

"Sounds good to me." Said Fred.

They finished the food and all had a drink before setting off again down another tunnel. This one was a bit wider than the other one and seemed to be a lot easier to walk along. They could almost walk along in pairs it was that wide.

They arrived at an intersection and Gilla stopped and looked on the wall. About half way down was a small scratch on the wall.

“This way.” she said.

The party headed down the right passage and after a few minutes walking the passage came out into a brick lined tunnel. The walkway split into two now with the sewage flowing down a channel in the centre. Here and there would be a small bridge allowing you to swap sides.

“We’re under the city now so we need to be quiet.”

“Ok and let’s kill some of the lights just in case someone comes the other way.” Said Datch.

“Good call. That way they will only see a couple of lights.” Said Fred.

“Yes, and then Timbo can disable them.”

“You mean knock them out?” Asked Dapo.

“Err, yes.”

They moved along the tunnels stopping here and there looking for marks that Gilla had left when she escaped. They also left some symbols of their own on the walls which all pointed the wrong way. This was Fred’s idea so if they were followed, the people following would go the wrong way.

The odour in the tunnels was very strong now with the smell of human waste hanging in the air. They spotted at least three or four large rats running along up head of them.

After a few minutes they came to a large open area where a number of tunnels came together. Water was cascading down the centre with a number of other tunnels feeding the flow. Gilla looked around for a mark and found the one she was looking for.

“Up here.” she said and headed up another tunnel.

A few minutes later she turned into smaller tunnel and the rest followed her up to a brick wall.

“Err… This is a dead end.” Said Datch.

“Yes, the tunnel ends here.” she said.

Gilla went to the end of the tunnel and looked up. Above her was a metal grill and a wooden hatch.

“Here, we need to move this.” She said trying to move the grill. It wouldn’t move.

“They must have locked it.” She looked very down hearted.

“Timbo, can you let us in please?”

“Sure Datch.”

Timbo moved to the front and started to work on the grill. It took a few minutes as he had to do it quietly. The metal finally gave way and was moved to the side. Gilla put her head through the hatch. It was clear so they all climbed through it.

The other side of the hatch was a cellar, it was dirty and had a number of pipes running it through it. There were a number of cobwebs, a load of old boxes along with a wine rack. There was also a few broken garden tools and a number of garden seats in storage. Datch sat on one and Fred sat down next to him. Gilla was about to go up the stairs.

"Wait!" Said Datch, "There may be guards up there, if they see you, it will give us away."

She stopped and came back down. She wanted to see her mum and dad so much but Datch was right she needed to wait.

"So, what do we do?" she said.

"Send Fred's little toy in."

Fred got out the little drone and took it over to the stairs moving up to the door. There was a small gap at the bottom just big enough to fit it through. He placed the little craft just inside the hole so the sensors could see out and turned on the vid comm in his hand.

The drone's sensor array scanned the corridor and an image appeared on the display. It looked like daylight even though it was in darkness. Fred pushed the drone inside and it took to the air.

They watched as it flew down the corridor. It had a set of stairs running up one side and was quite wide with plush carpet on the floor. The other side had a coat stand with a number of coats hanging on it and a small cabinet with some papers on the top. There was no sign of any monitoring devices. The display would show any active devices that had power to them as it went along but there was nothing. It reached the front door and Fred made it fly to the window. Outside stood two Plantar guards and a small vehicle in the road with another officer inside it. Fred turned it around and took it into the room on the right.

It was a sitting room with big plush chairs and a large vid on the wall. Over in the corner was a small table and a communication unit. The drone detected a power signature coming from the unit.

"If we go in. No talking in the sitting room. Ok?"

Everyone nodded.

The drone moved to the next room. It was a study with an open desk and a lot of papers scattered about as if someone had been looking for something in a hurry. The drone circled the room before heading back to the hallway. It crossed over to the other side and went into the room. It was a dining room and had a large table in the centre with six chairs around it but was only laid out for two. The drone circled the room checking for bugs and then headed through the next door into the kitchen. The cooker was still warm along with the dish washer. There was a pile of laundry in the corner waiting to be ironed and some bread sitting on the side.

"I could just go for a couple of slices of that." Said Dapo who was craning over Datch's shoulder to see.

It was still looking good. The drone headed back to the main corridor and moved towards the stairs. There was a noise from outside and Fred spun the drone around and flew it back to the window. Two more guards were coming up to the door. They all held their breath. The two new guards said something to the others and they all laughed before swapping places and the old guards headed off down the street.

"It's just a guard change." Said Fred.

Everyone started to breathe again.

He turned the little drone and headed to the stairs. As it started to go up them Gilla turned to Fred.

"My room is the first on the left and my mum and dad's room is on the other side."

"Are there any spare rooms?"

"Yes, the two at the back, but one is my dad's office."

"Ok, we better check them first."

Fred flew the drone up to the first floor and turned to the back two rooms. The first was as Gilla had said an office. It also had a lot of papers thrown about. Then Fred flew the drone on to the second room. It had an extra bed in it but other than that, it was empty.

"How do you want to play this Gilla?"

"I don't know." she said. "I just want to see they are ok."

"Hmm... well we can't just go running in. The guards at the front door will see us. Is there any way we could get a message to your dad without alerting the guards to our presence?"

Gilla thought about it.

"Does the drone have audio?" she asked

"No, all it can do is beep."

"Can you get it to beep a number of notes?"

"Err... it will be a bit limited but yes if I know what notes to do."

Gilla started to sing a little melody and Fred pressed some buttons on the vid comm. When she was done, Fred pressed a few more keys and then the vid comm started to beep.

"How's that?"

"Yes. it will do. My dad used to sing that song to me when I was little to get me to go to sleep."

"Ok let's go to your parent's room and see if it will get his attention."

The little drone flew across the corridor and headed into her parent's bedroom. There in the bed were her mum and dad sleeping. Fred scanned the room for devices, it was clear. He then moved the drone in front of her dad and told it to start playing the tune. At first nothing happened and then her dad started to stir. Fred repeated the little tune and her dad opened his eyes. He looked and spotted the drone,

"Why you vile creatures." he said.

He jumped out of bed, picked up some papers and rolled them up ready to hit the drone. He was just about to take a swing at it when Fred repeated the tune. He stopped in mid swing and looked at it. Fred repeated the tune and he looked at the little device.

He lowered the roll of paper and looked at the little drone. Fred played the tune again.

"What's up?" Said her mum stirring.

"Err... Nothing, I just heard a noise and it made me jump. Stay there while I go and check it out."

Her mum sat up in bed. Fred played the little tune again and turned the drone around and started to head back to the stairs. It reached the top and Fred turned it around to make sure her dad was following. He was. Fred slowly piloted the drone back down the stairs and to the cellar door with her dad following it. He turned it around at the cellar door and played the little tune again.

Her dad opened the door and came in the cellar closing the door behind him and walked down the stairs seeing the light from Fred's Vid comm.

"Who are you?" he said turning the light on.

Gilla ran to him and gave him a big hug and then burst into tears.

"Oh, my gods, I thought you were dead." he said.

She gave him another big hug and he looked at her and then at the others.

"I'm not." she said.

"But they said the freighter had been destroyed."

"It was, but on the way back for you." Said Fred.

"They told me you had been killed." He said looking at Gilla with tears in his eyes.

"Well, we're here to get you and your wife out of here. We need you to sign the treaty before we can get the IPSF to save your planet." Said Datch.

"Oh."

"Oh. What?" Asked Fred.

"Well, it was about to be ratified when the Plantars invaded."

"It was never ratified?"

"No. We didn't get chance."

"So, what do we do to get it ratified?"

"Well, we need six of the council members to do it."

"Six?" asked Fred.

"Yes. Six. It has to be a majority vote."

"Oh Jaxx!"

"OK! how do we get six members to ratify it in a hurry?"

"I don't know. At the moment the Plantars only let us be together when they're there and then they watch our every move and double check every bit of paper."

Datch fetched out the scattering field generator and pressed the comms button.

The screen came on and Clax appeared.

"Hi Clax, we seem to have a problem."

"What sort of problem?"

"Well, the treaty was never ratified and everyone has now been put under house arrest."

"Oh, that's a problem. We can still rescue Gilla's mum and dad though?"

"I'm sorry but I'm not leaving until I know my planet is going to be safe." Said Gilla's dad.

"Hmm... What if we take the other members of the council with us as well?" Said Fred.

"There are ten plus myself."

"Oh. So how many did you say you needed to ratify the treaty?"

"Six. As I said it has to be a majority decision."

They were all quiet for a while and then Datch spoke.

"What if we take five more then and ratify it on the way."

"The way where?"

"We have a starship hidden not far from here. She is more than able to take seven more but someone's going to have to sleep in the rec room. The plan is to fly you to the starship Carpaycus and they will take you to the IPSF council to Sign the treaty. The Plantars will then be removed from your world."

"The Plantars will try to stop us leaving. They have two battleships in orbit."

"Ah yes, we flew past them on the way here. The ship we have is a little bit special."

"Special?"

"Yes, Special." Datch was grinning.

"I don't think it will work?"

"Why?"

"Well, as soon as any members of the council disappear the Plantars will lock down the planet."

"Well, you will all have to disappear at the same time then." Said Datch.

"But how?"

"The sewers!" Said Fred. "There must be other entrances?"

"Yes, they are all over the city, most of the houses have access to them. It's how a lot of the sewage is carried away."

"Yes, we noticed the sewage on the way here." added Dapo.

"Can you get the word to five of the other council members and tell them to meet us in the sewers?" asked Fred.

"I can but we may have to go and get them. Some of them won't even know how to get into them."

"Ok, make it tonight just as it gets dark. That way hopefully we can get back to the ship before daylight." Said Datch.

"I'll see what I can do."

"Clax. Are you guys ok there for twenty hours?"

"Yes, we should be. Looking at the tactical scans, their ships are avoiding this area like a plague. Their navigations system won't like the radiation and the scattering field will be making the old types of sensors go nuts. The Raven is well hidden anyway so until we move, they won't have any idea we're here."

"Ok, we'll hang out here until tonight and then head back."

"Ok folks, stay safe! Raven out."

"Err... Looks like you've got house guests. Well, cellar guests anyway."

"Can I see mum?" asked Gilla.

"Ok. But let me go and fetch her. If the guards see you, they will search the house."

He turned and put the light out before opening the door.

"Stay in the cellar and try to keep quiet." he whispered as he left closing the door behind him.

Two minutes later there was the sound of footsteps coming down the stairs and then turning and coming to the door. It opened and a woman stood in the doorway.

"Mum, come in and shut the door."

She did and Fred turned the light on.

"Mum!" Said Gilla and gave her mum a big hug.

Her mum had tears running down her face.

"I thought we had lost you. They said you had been killed." she said.

"I thought I'd never see you again."

The hugging continued for a few minutes and Gilla told her mum what had happened and how she had come back for them. Eventually, her mum reluctantly headed back to bed.

“So, what now?” Said Fred.

“Well, I think we should take it in turns to get some sleep.” Said Datch.

“This floor is a bit hard.” Added Carina.

“Timbo, you don’t happen to have a bed by any chance, do you?”

“Yes Datch.”

He reached in his bag again and pulled out three inflatable mattresses along with inflatable pillows.

“Timbo. You’re a star!” Said Carina.

“Thank you.” he said.

“Ok, who’s going first?”

“I’m ok at the moment.” Said Fred

“Me too.” Said Timbo

Dapo and Tish also said they were ok, so Datch, Carina and Gilla settled down for a nap while the others found various things to sit on and made themselves comfy. Timbo had also brought some playing cards with him and they sat playing a game called ‘Cross the Jaxx.’

# Time to Run

Lunch time arrived and everyone in the cellar had slept for at least five hours. They were now all sitting around Fred watching a movie on his vid. They heard voices outside and footsteps coming to the cellar down. They ducked down behind various boxes and items laying around.

The door opened and Gilla's mum could be heard saying 'I'm just putting this junk in the cellar.' The door shut and the light came on. She came walking down the steps.

"It's ok, you can come out. The guards are still outside."

They emerged from their hiding spots and came over to her.

"I've brought you some food. It's not much but I can't exactly send out for pizza."

She opened the bags and there were various sandwiches, some bits of cake along with a few chocolate bars thrown in for good measure. She had also put a number of bottles of soft drinks and a flask of coffee.

"This is great mum, thanks."

"You're welcome. Your dad has just gone out to tell the others the plan and organise their escape. I had better head back up to the sitting room before a guard starts to wonder why I'm taking so long. They are sunning their selves in the garden at the moment. As long as they see me through the window, they won't come in."

"Ok thanks err… what do I call you?" Asked Carina

"Catha, my names Catha and Gilla's dad is Tinfa."

"Ok Catha, Thanks for the food."

"No thank you. You brought Gilla home so I'm very grateful… Ok, I had better go or the guards will get suspicious. See you later."

She left the cellar and went back to the sitting room to wait for Tinfa. In the cellar there was a lot of munching noises and a few burps.

That evening, Tinfa came to the cellar under the pretence of getting some wine.

"We're all set, but we might need to break some of them out."

"What do you mean?" Asked Fred.

"Well, some of the grills to get into the sewers haven't been opened for years and have rusted shut."

"That's not a problem. We have a Timbo."

"A Timbo?"

Timbo stood up and up and up before the roof stopped him.

"Hello." he said.

Tinfa looked at him up and down.

"Hmm… I think a Timbo will work."

"I do." He said and grinned.

He sat back down again. If the roof could breathe, it would have let out a sigh of relief.

"Ok, I've told everyone to wait till dark and then turn the upstairs lights on as if we're going to bed to have, well you know."

"Ewe. Dad! Too much information."

Everyone just looked at her.

"Well, it's my dad."

There was a round of nodding and then they all looked at Tinfa.

"Ok, how long?"

"It's about three hours till darkness."

"Ok. We'll be waiting."

He left and went back into the house.

Datch got out the generator and pressed the comms button.

Clax appeared on the monitor.

"What's up Datch?"

"It's a go. We will be moving out in about three hours. We'll be collecting the other council members on the way so get the Raven prepared for launch in say ten hours. Also, it may be an idea to make sure the weapon systems are hot. I think it may get a bit busy on the way up when they realise the council members are missing."

"Ok, understood. See you in a few hours."

"Later dude."

Datch closed the link.

"Well folks the fun starts in a couple of hours. Let's try and chill for a bit."

The sat and tried to catch a few minutes of sleep.

Three hours later there was the sound of footsteps coming to the door. Datch and Fred sat up. The door started to open and then two figures appeared. It was Catha and Tinfa. They closed the door and turned the light on.

The others got up.

"Are we ready?"

Datch stood up.

"Yes, sorry we nodded off."

The rest of them got up and started to pick up their bags.

"You will have to lead the way." Said Fred.

"Ok."

"Make sure you pick everything up folks. We don't want to leave any clues."

They all headed to the grill and one after another entered the sewer. Tinfa led the way to the end of the tunnel.

"Ok, where first?"

"This way, to Janus."

They followed Tinfa along the main tunnel and then turned to the left entering a long tunnel. They hadn't noticed the smell so much on the way in as it had built up slowly. Now however the stench was very strong. Tish had put a nose clip on to stop it, but it didn't seem to be helping. They entered another tunnel and then another. Tinfa stopped and looked at a small tunnel leading off to the right.

"This way."

They moved up the tunnel and at the end was a grill at the top. It had a bit of white cloth tied to one of the grates.

"This is it." he said looking at the white cloth.

"Are you sure?"

"Yes, I told them all to put a white rag on the grate so that we could find them."

"Good idea." Said Dapo.

The gate was loose but seemed to be sticking on one side.

"Timbo."

Timbo came up and looked at it. Then he grabbed it and pushed. The bit of brick that was jamming it decided it was a good idea to move and happily stepped aside. The grate opened. Tinfa went up and opened the wooden door. There was a slight intake of breath and then Tinfa spoke.

"Janus?"

"Yes, we're here."

"Ok follow me."

Tinfa came back down with a man and a woman following.

"Hello!" He said as they entered the tunnel.

"This is Datch and The Pack."

"That's a great name for a commando group."

"Yes, it is, but we're a rock band."

"What?"

"Don't ask. It's a long story." Said Fred.

"We do have a really cool ship." added Tish.

"You do?"

"Yes." Said Datch.

"Are you sure about this Tinfa?"

"Yes, and to be totally honest, they're our only hope."

They all moved into the main tunnel and headed to the next tunnel and the next council member. This one was a little small but they got to the grate and with a good shove it opened. The council member came down with his wife and son.

"Datch, I'm starting to think we may need a bigger spacecraft." Said Fred.

"Why?" asked Datch who was standing in the main tunnel.

"Well, I'm not sure the rec room is going to be big enough."

The group came back to the main tunnel.

"Oh, I see what you mean."

They followed Tinfa to the next tunnel. This time there was a very large door made of iron bars blocking the way.

"Timbo."

Timbo looked at the door and took a few steps back and then started to run. There was a loud crash as Timbo met metal. The metal did not fare well and fell off its hinges. Tinfa opened the wooden trap door. A head appeared.

"Hi Tinfa."

The head looked at the crumped iron work.

"Err… I do have a key."

"Oh. sorry. If we get the planet back remind me to buy you a new gate."

They moved back into the main tunnel and headed down a long passage to another tunnel and intersection. Tinfa looked at the map in his pocket.

“Over this way.”

They crossed over the flow of sewage and headed up another tunnel.

“Here, I think.”

Tinfa went up another tunnel.

“Yes,” he said, “the white cloth is here.”

“Haper, you there?”

the wooden trapdoor opened.

“Yes, we’re here.”

Haper, his wife and two young children came down. He opened the gate and they walked into the tunnel. Fred looked at them.

“Datch, I think you may need to tell Clax that it’s going to be more than six.”

Datch looked at the small group of people in the tunnel and fished out the scattering field generator.

“Clax?”

“Hi Datch, everything ok?”

“Yes, so far, we have two more to pick up and then we’re heading back to the ship. Can you break out anything people can sit on?”

“Ok, but why?”

“Err… we have nine so far with three kids and we’ve got two more stops to go!”

“Ok. I’ll get Tank on it.”

Datch closed the comms and they carried on down the tunnel. They went past the large junction Datch had seen on the way in and then headed up the side tunnel. They arrived at the grate and opened it. Tinfa opened the wooden cover and put his head through. The cellar was empty.

“Somethings wrong.” he said.

He entered the cellar with Fred and Timbo in tow. Voices could be heard in the corridor outside. Fred looked through a hole in the door. He could see a guard with a man and a woman. The guard was blocking the way to the cellar.

“I think we need Timbo.”

“Timbo? there’s a guard out there who needs a nap. He sounds very tired to me.”

“Ok, I’ll help him get some sleep.”

The man and woman carried on arguing with the guard and the door behind him slowly opened. Then from the darkness a very large shape appeared. The man and woman stopped talking and then the guard realised they were looking at something behind him he spun around and found he was looking at someone’s chest. He started to look up and then everything went black. The guard fell to the floor.

“Thanks, Timbo. I’m sure he’ll enjoy the nap.” Said Tinfa looking around him.

“Laran, come on.”

Laran and his wife stepped over the sleeping guard and headed into the cellar.

“Err. What are we going to do with him?”

“We should tie him up in the cellar. It will take a while before he comes round. Hopefully we’ll be long gone by then.”

Timbo picked the guard up and took him to a chair in the cellar. They found some rope and used the White cloth as a gag. They stood back and looked at him. It would take him quite a while to get out of ropes and raise the alarm. Dapo insisted on putting a sack over his head as he had seen it done it in the movies. Fred let him to do it as the guard might think they were still there and it may put him off try anything for a while.

The party headed into the tunnels again and back to the main intersection.

“The last one is in the route to the caves. This way.” Said Tinfa.

“That’s good, the sooner we’re out of here, the better.” Said Fred.

“Yes, we need to get back to the ship before that guard can raise the alarm.”

“What sort of ship is it?” asked Laran.

“It’s a pirate ship.” Said Dapo.

“What your pirate’s?”

“No, we’re a rock band that has an ex-pirate ship.” added Carina.

“A rock band? I’m not sure this is safe Tinfa.”

“Hey we have a Timbo. Everything is good.” Added Datch.

They all turned and looked at Timbo. They had to agree that Timbo would stop most things including tornadoes, meteors and maybe even a moon falling on you.

“Look we all know that as soon as the Plantars don’t need us anymore, we’re dead. These folks are risking their lives for us. My daughter trusts them and therefore, so do I.” Said Tinfa

“Ok. Fine.” Said Laran.

They set off down the tunnel again with a large entourage following.

They reached the last tunnel and headed to the grate. This one needed the Timbo touch. The hatch opened and there was a woman holding a baby and two young children. Behind them was a young man with a beard.

“Datch, call Clax and ask him if he has any crayons.” Said Fred down the tunnel.

“You know, this was meant to be an easy rescue of Gilla’s mum and dad. Now we’re opening a kindergarten.” Said Tish.

“Well at least we’re not getting bored under a palm tree on a beach somewhere.” Said Carina.

“Yes, definitely a lot more fun. It’s like Welly Four all over again. Well, that is apart from us being in a sewer.” Added Dapo.

“It would be handy to have Tajiquay’s men here right now.” Said Datch.

“I’ll second that.” Said Fred overhearing what they were talking about.

The group now headed to the caves. It took thirty minutes to get to the cavern with the river in it and they stopped to work out how to get over the river with the kids. Timbo fetched out the floating light and sent it to the middle of the cavern where the crossing was. It was decided that everyone should be tied together again. Datch led the way with Carina and Fred behind. When they got to the other side, they tied the rope to a large bolder and went back to help the kids.

They were on the second trip when one of the younger children caught her foot on a wet patch and slipped. Datch grabbed the rope and she hung a metre down. She started screaming. Datch and Carina slowly pulled her back up to the path. She grabbed Carina and wouldn't let go. Carina picked her up and carried her to the other side. She finally calmed down when her mum made it across. After twenty minutes they made it into the other tunnel and started heading for the entrance in the fields.

The head of the Plantar invasion sat on the end of his bed. It was three in the morning but he couldn't settle. He had a nagging feeling something was wrong but didn't know what. He pressed the communicator next to his bed.

"Is everything ok?" He asked.

"Yes sir." Came the response.

"Any sign of other ships?"

"No sir. All screens are clear sir."

"What about the city?"

"A couple of our troopers had a fight earlier but it's very quiet now sir."

"OK. Let me know if anything changes."

"Yes sir."

He still had a nagging feeling something was not right and decided to have a drive around the city. He got dressed and headed out to his transport. The Guards saluted as he got in.

"Where to sir?" Said the driver.

"Hmm... I don't know, just take me on a tour around the council's homes."

The driver started the engine and headed down the road.

Datch and Fred were up ahead with Gilla, they had made it to the cave entrance and could see star light coming down the shaft leading to the surface.

"Nearly there now. Only a couple of fields to cross and we'll be at the mine." Said Fred.

"Yes, I'll be very glad to get to the Raven." Added Datch.

"Ok folks, forty-five minutes to the ship." He shouted down the tunnel.

Back in the city the commander looked at the house and called the guards from the front door.

"Morning sir." They said and saluted.

"How long has that light been on?"

"Well, err since they went to bed sir."

He got out of the vehicle and went to the door.

"Have they come out at all?"

"No sir. We think they were, well, you know and have fallen asleep with the light on."

"Wake them."

The commander's hairs were standing up on the back of his neck. Something was not right. The sentry banged on the door. Nothing happened.

"Again!"

He hammered on the door. Still nothing.

"Break the door down."

The sentry ran at the door and smashed it open. There was no noise from inside. The commander ran up the stairs to the bedroom. The light was on and music was playing but the bed was empty.

"Search the house!" He yelled.

The guards went from room to room. They were all empty.

"Command, contact the other guards on council duty. I want to know that they are in their homes. Also, put the city on alert."

Datch and the party had reached the small cops and were having a break to let the kids recover when Datch's backpack beeped. He fetched the generator out of the bag.

"Hi Clax, what's up?"

"Err, I think the city just went on alert. There is also a number of fighters that have been scrambled from one of the battleships."

"Ok. we'll hurry. Prep the Raven for take-off."

"Ok. ETA?"

"Err… fifteen mins."

"Ok. Clax out."

Datch turned to the others.

"OK folks, we need to move. Looks like they know you're missing. Everyone, grab a child and run for the ditch!"

The started to run towards the ditch.

“What about the sensors?” shouted Fred

“If we trip them, we trip them, it’s what a ten minute run to the Raven?”

“Yes, if we sprint.”

Datch looked at the others as they entered the ditch.

“OK fifteen.”

They ran through the plants and shrubs in the ditch pushing them to the side as they went. They passed the line of polls and the end one started beeping.

“We’ve tripped them. Get out of the ditch and run for the mine workings!” Shouted Fred.

Back in the city the commander’s comms beeped.

“Yes?”

“Sir, the fence in grid seven, seven, three just activated.”

“Ok send a fighter out there and send a shuttle to my position.”

Datch and the party reached the mine working and picked their way up the hill to the ravine. Down below a fighter came in lower scanning the field. Datch watched as it flew to the ditch and then back to the field.

“They’re coming folks! Move it!”

They ran up the ravine and there was the Raven with its rear door open.

“Guys, sort these folks out and fast. Make sure they have safety straps or ropes. This is going to be a rough take off! I’m heading to the cockpit.”

Datch sprinted up to the ship and straight up the ramp. Thirty seconds later he jumped into the pilot’s seat.

“Hi Datch!” Said Clax.

“Hi, get the weapons systems to full power there’s a fighter in the valley below.”

“I know, I’ve already locked on to it and the engines have been targeted.”

“Sorry, sort of panicking. First time and that.”

“You just fly. I’ll do the rest.”

Datch looked at Clax and put his headset on. He pressed the ships comms.

“Everyone on board and seated?”

“One second, just getting the last one seated now and then heading to the cockpit.” Said Fred.

“Ok.”

Datch brought the main thrusters online and the Raven started to move. The rest of The Pack took their seats. Then after a moment Fred came jumping up the stairs and took his seat.

“Clax as soon as we clear the ravine take that fighter’s engines out.”

“No problem.”

The Raven lifted out of the ravine and the fighter turned towards them. There was a sudden jolt as the weapons fired.

The fighter started spinning in the air and then crashed into the field in a large explosion.

“Wow, that was a kick.”

Datch pointed the nose up and pulled hard back on the throttle. The Raven accelerated up and Datch primed the interspace drive.

“There are two fighters heading towards us.”

Datch hit the interspace drive and the Raven vanished.

“I want that ship! At any cost. Do you understand!” shouted the planetary commander into his comms.

“Yes sir!” Said the captain of the battleship in orbit.

The Raven headed into space and turned towards Tancanar.

“Looks like we have company.” Shouted Clax

The large battleship turned towards their trajectory and started to move.

“How fast can they go?”

“Looking at the tactical, about the same as us.”

“Computer. Set course for Tancanar and engage, maximum interspace and don’t bother with the warnings.”

The ship adjusted its self and the stars started to flicker.

“They’re following.” Said Clax.

“Yes, but are they gaining?”

“No, but as soon as we drop out of interspace, they will be on top of us.”

“Ok. computer how long to Tancanar?”

“Thirty-eight hours twenty-seven minutes. Would you like an alarm before arrival?”

“Yes, one hour please.” Said Datch.

“Are we ok?” Said Carina.

“Yes, tactical is showing them very slightly slower.” Said Clax looking behind him.

“Ok. looks like we’re good for now. I need a beer.”

“I’ll watch things here. You go and chill.” Said Clax.

Datch got up and headed to the rec room.

When he walked thought the door. There was a group tied to the sofa and two people tied to chairs. He went over to the sofa and started untying them.

“Sorry folks, we didn’t want you hurting yourselves as we took off. Just to let you know we left the Arcaneus system two minutes ago and are on route to the Tancanar star system.”

“Are we safe?” asked Laran.

“Safe ish. The Plantars are in pursuit but can’t catch us. Hopefully my friends ship will be waiting when we get there.”

“How long?”

“Just under two days. So, just chill for now and sign the treaty. Then when my friends arrive it can be agreed and your planet freed.”

“You have friends with that sort of power?”

Gilla had followed Datch in.

"This is Datch and The Pack. They have saved worlds."

Datch went a little pink.

"Well, one world and a president." Said Dapo as he came through the door. "Oh, and a ship's crew and not to forget Bob."

Laran looked at Datch. Datch just grinned back and ask the computer for a beer.

Laran's wife turned to her husband and said something in his ear.

"Really!"

"Yes."

"Oh."

Laran went a bit pink.

"Ok, Grucks for the kids." Said Datch and turned to Laran.

"Laran, what would you like to drink?"

"Err…" he was unsure what to say.

"He'll have a beer. And I'll have a wine if you have any?" Said his wife.

"One beer and one wine coming up."

Datch got the drinks and then turned to Laran.

"I will save you and your planet." It wasn't a promise but more of a statement.

Laran looked at him. He was a young man but at that moment Laran knew Datch meant what he said.

"You really will save my planet, won't you?" Laran said as if needing affirmation.

"Yes."

Everyone started to get some food and drink. They started to relax a bit and the atmosphere started become a little less stressed.

# Escape!

The council members all met in the cargo bay to ratify the treaty. It was a little cramped as there was now a Creche for the youngsters in the corner and a number of mattresses in the middle of the floor. Also, there was a cartoon being played on the wall from one of the holo emitters. The council chamber had been constructed near the locker with space suits in. It consisted of a number of pink cushions and a picnic table. On the table was a pen and a small plastic hammer that had been borrowed from one of the children while they were watching the cartoon.

"It's not quite the citadel, is it?" Said Laran sitting down on one of the cushions.

"No. but at least it's not a prison cell." replied Tinfa.

"I hope this works?" Said Janus.

"It will. Once the treaty is signed by the IPSF they will act and free our world." Said Laran.

"Ok then, does anyone want to question the treaty?" asked Tinfa.

"No. I think we all know what we need to do." Said Haper.

"Do we all then agree?" Said Tinfa.

"Yes." they all said.

"Ok then. I hereby ratify the treaty."

Tinfa banged the toy hammer on the table, it squeaked and wobbled about. Then, one at a time they all stepped up to the picnic table and signed the document before returning to the cushions.

“You do realise we need to get it to the IPSF for them to sign as well.”

“Yes, I think these folks have got that bit in hand.” Added Tinfa.

“Ok. Any other business?” Said Laran.

“Yes, any chance of a shower?” asked Haper

“Ask Datch. Anything else?”

There was silence apart from the sound of laughing from the cartoon.

“Ok, if that’s all? I declare this meeting of the council closed.”

They all got up off of their cushions and headed back to the rec room looking for Datch and maybe a shower.

Datch was sitting in the pilot’s seat looking at the tactical plot when Clax walked in. He had been watching things while Clax had gone to get some sleep.

“Any change?” he said sitting down.

“No. They are still following but I think we are pulling ahead slightly.”

“Good, we’ll need all the space we can get when we come out of interspace.”

“Yes, I’m sort of hoping Don got my message.”

“We’ll if he’s not there we’ll just have to dive for the planet and hope the security services reach us first.”

“I know, it’s going to be rough.”

“Datch, just chill for now dude and go and get some sleep.”

“Ok.” he sighed, “I’ll go get my head down.”

He got up and headed for his room. When he arrived there, Carina was sleeping. He got undressed and climbed in next to her. She turned and put her arm over him and then carried on sleeping. It took Datch a while to fall asleep. The thoughts of the ship following them kept going through his mind and it worried him. Eventually he drifted off to sleep.

Nine hours later Carina woke him up. Datch opened his eyes and looked at her. She was dressed and had a coffee in her hands.

“Morning Lover, here, I brought you this.”

She handed him the coffee.

“Morning. Err. How long did I sleep for?”

“Nine hours.”

Datch started to get up and Carina stopped him.

“Don’t panic, everything is fine. Clax is sitting in the cockpit watching things and I think Tinfa is chatting with him.”

Datch relaxed a bit.

“How are you doing?” he said.

“I’m ok, just a bit worried about the ship following.”

“It will be fine.”

“Hey, Datch, don’t tell me not to worry. You were tossing and turning in your sleep. You’re worried!”

He looked at her weighing things up in his mind.

“Well, I am a bit. I hope Tancanar has a decent security force or we’re in a lot of trouble.”

“I thought Don was coming?”

“I was hoping he would but I haven’t had a message so I think he’s too far away.”

“Would he tell you?”

“Oh yes! He would have sent me a very loud message telling me not to be stupid.”

“Ok, so what’s the plan?”

“I don’t know, I’ve got some ideas but need to think about it a bit more and then run them past Clax.”

“I’m sure you’ll work it out. You always do.”

She gave him a big hug and a kiss.

After half an hour Datch got dressed and they headed for the cockpit.

“How long until we reach Tancanar?” Said Datch sitting down.

“I think about twelve hours.” Said Clax

“Where are the Plantars?”

“They have dropped back a bit but are still following. Looks like we’ll have maybe a minute or two at best when we get there and then they will be on top of us.”

“Ok, you go and get some sleep, I think you’ll need it. I’ll watch things.”

“Ok Datch, will do.”

Clax got up and headed to his room. Carina sat in the co-pilot’s seat.

“So, what’s the plan?” She asked.

“I need to check some things out first.”

He pulled up the tactical display and told the computer to show him Tancanar and their current entry vector.

Datch looked at it.

“Computer, change the vector to enter here.”

He pressed a few virtual buttons.

“New course laid in.” Said the computer.

“What did you do?” ask Carina

“I’ve adjusted our course to take us past one of the moons.”

“Why?”

“The Ravens built to land on planets and therefore can go by it without any problem but that battleship is built to stay in space. It will have to change course to avoid it because of its mass. The moons gravity will be too strong for a ship of that size to manoeuvre close to it.”

“Ok, but how does that help?”

“Well, I plan to turn behind the moon, by the time battleship can turn to follow us we’ll be in the outer atmosphere and then the security forces can deal with any fighters they launch.”

“Err, Won’t they try and shoot us down?”

“No, I’ll be talking to them.”

“Ok. You owe me a drink.”

“Why?”

"Because I helped with the plan."

"You did?"

"Yes."

"Which bit?"

"I brought you coffee."

"Oh. Ok." Said Datch and smiled.

They sat talking and every now and again a person would come and ask how things were going and then head back to the rest.

Eight hours later Clax came back and Carina went to start to get the others ready for what could be another bumpy ride.

"So, what's the plan?"

"How do you know I have a plan?"

"Well, the course has changed and the scattering field is off. Also, it looks like we're going to crash into a moon."

"Ok, I have a bit of a plan..." Datch explained to Clax what he was going to do and Clax nodded making a few comments along the way.

The one-hour warning went off and everyone stowed anything that could fly about. The creche was closed and people started to tie themselves down. Finally, The Pack assembled in the cockpit and sat down. Datch started to put his plan into action.

"Tancanar control, this is the Raven come in please!"

"Hello Raven this is Tancanar control."

“Tancanar Control, we are being pursued by a Plantar battleship and we have the ruling council of Arcaneus onboard. Please Help!”

“Raven, this is control, please say again.”

“I say again. We are being pursued by a Plantar battleship and have the ruling council of Arcaneus onboard. We are coming in on a vector of 226.2 by 107.2 please help!”

“Ok Raven. We are alerting the security services please stay on that vector and when you’re in the atmosphere head straight to the capital city space port. There will be a security detail waiting for you. How long before you drop out of interspace?”

“Seven minutes and twenty seconds. The Plantar ship is about thirty seconds behind us.”

“Copy that, Standby.”

Clax turned to Datch.

“You know the security forces may not have the fire power to take out a ship of that size.”

“Yes, but I bet the captain of the battleship doesn’t want to start an interstellar war either. The IPSF would wipe them out.”

“I hope you’re right.”

“Ok, two minutes. what’s the battleship doing?”

“Looks like it’s following us in.”

Datch pressed the ships comms button.

“Everyone, hang on. This is where it gets bumpy!”

“The battleship’s slowing.” Said Clax.

“Yes, I think they just spotted the moon.”

Datch got ready to drop out of interspace.

"Ok! Here we go!"

He pressed a button and the stars stopped flickering. Then proximity alarms started to sound. The moon was just to the right of them. Datch took the Raven down low, skirting just above the surface. The battleship dropped out of interspace and launched a fighter wing. As soon as the Raven was on the opposite side of the moon Datch pulled up and headed for the planet. The fighters spotted them and started to follow. Datch reinforced the shield and the Raven hit the outer atmosphere.

"Clax, see if you can give one of them a bloody nose."

"On it!"

There was a kick as the Raven's rear canons fired hitting one of the fighters, it lost one of its engines and then hit the atmosphere destroying it in the process. The fighter behind it fired hitting The Raven's rear shield. The Ship rocked with the explosion. Just then ten ships came up through the clouds firing at the fighters. They banked away and turned back towards the battleship. Datch pushed the engines and the ship rocked and rolled in the thicker atmosphere.

"Datch, slow down, SLOW Down!!"

Datch backed off the power and slowed down.

"We might not be out of this yet. I'm getting another large ship coming out of interspace."

"Oh crap. The other battleship?"

"I can't tell."

"Ok, spaceport in two minutes."

Datch hit the breaking thrusters and the Raven slowed to a more normal landing speed.

Up above the planet a large white starship came out of interspace and turned towards the battleship. The battleship fired its forward canons at the other ship and its shields lit up like a firework show.

The captain of the starship turned and looked at the screen.

"Well, that wasn't very nice. Disable their weapons, engines and main power systems."

The starship now opened fire with a huge volley of light and energy. It ripped through the battleship's shields and then explosion followed explosion as system after system was destroyed. Fire erupted from its engines and lights started to go out across the ship.

"Open a channel to that ship."

The captain of the battleship appeared on the main screen. Behind him, smoke could be seen rising from damaged consoles and people were running about.

"I am captain Don Ronediamar of the IPSF starship Carpaycus. Why have you just fired on me and more to the point why are you even in this star system?"

The captain looked at him as if weighing things up. He didn't have a lot of options. His ship was crippled and the fighters he sent out were now destroyed. If he tried to launch anymore fighters, he was likely to find himself floating in open space without a ship.

"We were in pursuit of escaped prisoners and mistook you for them."

"Hmm... so a ship like yours and you couldn't tell the difference between a small black spaceship and a galactic class starship?"

The other captain was starting to wish he had taken the day off and then decided a year would have been better.

“Err… No, I mean yes.”

“Hmm...” Don gave him a thoughtful look, “Captain, all my weapons systems are currently targeted on your ship. You are to surrender your ship to the local authorities. You and your crew will be taken to a holding area before being taken back to Plantar.”

“My government will not take kindly to this!”

“Your government will have a lot more to worry about now the treaty has been signed. Next time. Do not fire on my friends. I don’t like people take pot shots at them. Now, you have five minutes to address your crew and prepare them for being boarded. If you resist, you’ll find that the vacuum of space is very hard to breath in!”

“But, but.” The captain was lost for words.

“FIVE MINUTES!” Don shouted .

Down below on the planet Datch shut the engines off.

“What’s happening above?”

Clax turned to Datch with a grin on his face.

“Don’s here.”

“What about the battleship?”

“Let’s just say, I think they need to get a new one. It looks a bit on the dented side.”

“Oh.”

He hit the ships comms.

"OK folks, you can all get up. The battleship won't be causing you anymore trouble."

People started to get up and then the comms beeped.

Datch opened the channel. Don's face appeared.

"Datch, what the hell did you think you were doing?"

"Err..." This was worse than his dad telling him off. "Just saving a world?"

"Just saving a world! Bloody Jaxx Datch, do you think you are superman or something?"

"Err… No. I'm Datch." he said not knowing who superman was.

Don looked at him for a moment.

"Well next time you're planning to be a super Datch, talk to me first!"

Datch looked at the screen.

"Ok, does this mean I don't get ice-cream?"

Don looked at him and then started to smile.

"No, you don't get bloody ice-cream and I'll be coming down after I've sorted a few things out up here. You are going to buy me and Alex a few beers for this one."

"No Problem. Let me know when you're on your way."

"OK, and no more super Datch today. Carpaycus out."

"Err… I don't think he was very happy." Said Clax.

"He'll be fine." Said Datch hoping he was right.

Datch got up and headed to the cargo bay. The council members were there waiting. As Datch walked in they all clapped.

"Datch," Said Tinfa stepping forward, "on behalf of us all, thank you. You risked your lives for us and no matter what happens now it will not be forgotten."

He offered his hand to Datch. They shook hands and then one by one all the council members came up and did the same. Finally, Laran stepped forward and looked at Datch.

"I'm sorry for what I said earlier, I was wrong, you are true warriors."

He shook his hand. Datch cleared his throat.

"Thank you all, but we're not done until your planet is free."

"Yes, but with you here I know it will happen." Said Gilla.

"Ok… but at the moment I really need a beer."

He walked over and opened the bay doors. On the outside there were a lot of troopers all of which were pointing guns at them.

Datch froze to the spot.

"Err… hello?" he said.

The squad commander moved forwards.

"Drop your weapons!"

"Err… we don't have any."

The commander looked at him.

"Please identify yourself?"

"I'm Datch and this here is Tinfa the leader of the Arcaneus Council."

The commander stopped and looked at them and cocked his head to one side and waited. Then after a pause he said.

"I need to scan your implant sir."

Datch stepped forward and the commander scanned Datch's implant and then the commander put his head to one side and looked into space for a moment.

"Ok, the starship captain has vouched for you and the rest of your crew. Please step forward one at a time."

One after another The Pack stepped forward and were scanned. Then it was the turn of the Arcaneus council.

"I am the leader of Arcaneus. Prime minister Tinfa."

"Ok sir please let me scan you."

Tinfa stepped up and was scanned after which he cleared his throat.

"Commander, these people do not have implants apart from my wife and daughter. We are an evolving world. I will vouch for every one of them."

The commander stopped and looked into space for a second.

"Ok, all of you with implants please come here."

Gilla and her Mum stepped forward and were scanned.

"The ones without implants will have to follow me to immigration control. The rest of you are free to go but please do not attempt to leave the planet until we have interviewed you."

Datch turned to the commander.

“Err, Commander. You don’t happen to know a good bar around here, do you? I need to buy the captain and first commander of the Carpaycus a beer or two.”

The commander looked at him for a moment.

“There is one just outside the spaceport that is quite popular. It’s called The Night Sky.”

“Thank you. If you need us, we’ll be in there. Are we ok to leave the Raven here?”

“Yes, it will be fine there for now but can you move it within the next twenty hours.”

“No problem commander.”

“Datch. I’ll stay with the others, but is it ok if Gilla and Catha come with you?” Asked Tinfa.

“Sure, the more the merrier.”

“I’ll bring the others over when we’re done.”

“Commander, sorry to bother you again but which way is out?” asked Datch.

“Head over to that gate, the officer will want to scan you again. But will then direct you to the main concourse.”

“Thank you, sir.”

“You’re welcome.”

Datch turned to the others.

“Come on folks, Beer’s waiting.”

The Pack plus two headed to the gate and then into the concourse. Datch stopped on the way across and sent a message to Don telling him where they were going to be. He looked at the vid com and thought for a moment before sending another message asking him how long he was going to be and what drinks did he want.

They exited the spaceport onto the main throughfare leading to the city centre. It was nice and warm with the sun shining down. The streets were lined with boxes of flowers and every now and again they would walk by a café with people sitting outside enjoying a drink and some food in the fresh air. People were walking around sightseeing and shopping as well as a few who were heading to or from the spaceport. It was a slightly surreal scene for The Pack after what had just happened less than an hour ago in orbit. People were smiling and chatting totally unaware of it. Datch wondered if something like it had ever happened at home and then decided no. He was sure he would have heard about it if it had. They walked down towards the city centre and after a few minutes spotted the bar that the commander had recommended.

It was on the corner of a junction and the bar stretched at least fifty metres down each of the streets. It had seating outside as well as inside. Above the door was a large dark blue sign with stars and moons painted on it along with its name, 'The Night Sky'. Next to the door was a sign saying 'Please take a seat.' in ten different languages.

"Are we sitting in or out?" Asked Clax.

"We have just spent two days underground in a lot of very smelly caves and another two inside a spaceship running from aliens!" Said Tish staring at him.

"Point taken. Outside it is then."

Datch realised that it was also lunch time.

"I think we all could do with some food as well as the beers." he said.

"I'll go with that." Said Tank.

“Me too.” Added Carina.

This was followed by general agreement that food was needed. They found a number of tables and pushed them together before sitting down. A few moments later a waiter came out.

“Good afternoon. What can I get for you?”

“We would like a few drinks and some food please.” Said Tank.

“Certainly. Let me take your food order first. What would you like?”

“Do you do buckets of fried hacks wings and fries?” Asked Datch.

“We do fried chicken coated in seasoned breadcrumbs which is very similar and comes with fries. Would that be ok sir?”

“Sounds good to me, can we have three large buckets with fries and do you do pizzas?”

“Yes sir. We do the triple cheese, the meat feast and the tropical?”

“Tropical sounds nice, what’s on that?” Asked Carina.

“It has Pineapple, Mango, Mushrooms, Ham and a sprinkle of rum.”

“I’m up for that.” Said Rosey who liked the idea of pizza and alcohol combined in one.

“Ok, we’ll have two of them as well please.”

“Medium or Large.”

“Large please and tell them not to skimp on the rum.” Said Rosey.

"Certainly. Anything else?"

"No. I think that's it for food."

"Ok, Thank you. Now what would you like to drink?"

They went around the table and Gilla and her mum were not sure but Datch insisted and he also told the waiter to add a tip for himself. The waiter then headed inside to get the drinks.

While they were waiting for the drinks there was a lot of noise from inside and Fred turned around to see what was going on.

There was a group of people looking at the vid screen above the bar and there in the screen was the Raven entering the atmosphere with fighters chasing it. Behind in the distance the battleship could be seen turning in space and firing at a ship emerging from interspace. Fred watched as the Carpaycus returned fire.

"Well, it looks like we made the news!" Said Fred.

"We did?" Asked Peebop.

"Yes, and judging by the vid, the Plantars battleship was totally wrecked."

"Oh, wow."

Just then the waiter came back with their drinks and spotted Fred looking.

"It's pretty amazing sir, isn't it?"

"Yes."

"I can't believe it happened in our star system."

"I'm sure the people in the black ship are very nice people though." Added Tank.

"Yes, they were the High Council of Arcaneus according to the news channel."

"Oh, weren't they taken over by the Plantars?" asked Jep looking innocent.

"Yes, it was the Plantars battleship following behind that got taken out by the IPSF. Good job they were here. Anyway, if you want anything else just wave at the bar and I'll come over."

"Ok. Thank you." Said Fred.

An hour and a half later they sat feeling very full and looking at the remains of the food. Datches vid comm beeped. It was Don.

"Datch, Get two very large beers ready. We're on our way. ETA ten minutes."

"Ok, they will be on the table when you get here."

"See you in a few."

Fred looked over at Datch.

"How did he sound?"

"Err..." Datch paused, "a lot better now."

"Good."

"Waiter?" shouted Datch and waved at the bar.

The waiter came walking over.

"Yes sir, what can I get you?"

"Two very large beers please – the biggest you've got."

"Certainly sir."

The waiter went and fetched the beers while The Pack sat enjoying the sun watching people go by. It felt so good to be relaxed and sitting in the fresh air.

A shadow fell across Datch.

“Ensign Datch!” A voice boomed.

Datch nearly fell off his chair. All the passers-by looked at Datch. The Pack on the other hand burst out laughing. Datch looked up. It was Alex.

“Alex!”

Another shadow fell over Datch. It was Don.

“I have your beer.” Said Datch looking worried.

“You do. Good!”

Datch tried to work out if he was in trouble or a lot of trouble.

Don and Alex sat down and both took a very big gulp of beer. Datch sat watching them intently waiting for a telling off. He had another large gulp of beer before wiping the froth off his lips and putting the glass down.

“Ahh…” Said Don.

Datch was still watching him. He looked at Datch.

“If you’re waiting for me to shout at you, I’m not going to. I just want to know why?”

Datch looked Don straight in the eyes.

“Because no one else would!” he said.

Don looked Datch up and down.

“You are just like your dad. You can’t wait for anything.” He said and took another gulp of beer.

"Oh... and you're buying mine and Commander Isbar's beer all day."

Alex looked at him and smiled.

"Err... what happened to the Plantar ship?" asked Gilla realising it was safe to ask.

Don turned to her,

"Let's just say that we did a bit of..." He paused while thinking of the word, "Yes, remodelling to it and it won't be going home."

"What it's destroyed?"

"No. but it will be. It has been seized for violating IPSF space and firing on you and also more to point my ship."

"Did anyone get hurt?" Gilla was concerned.

"Not on our side. Let's just say it was a very short battle and the Plantar ship what is left of it, has been impounded. The crew are in custody waiting to be returned home, that is apart from the captain who will stand trial for opening fire in IPSF space."

"What happens now?" she asked.

"Datch buys us more beer!" he said.

He picked up the glass and downed the drink, Alex followed suit.

Datch put his hand up and the waiter came over.

"Two more very large beers please?" asked Datch.

Alex turned to Datch,

"Oh Datch, by the way, Qwots is not happy with you. We really had to hammer his engines to get here. He was moaning about them for the last seven hundred light years."

“Err… tell him sorry and thanks.”

The chat then turned to what had happened on Arcaneus and The Pack told the story.

The afternoon went by and the Arcaneus council members arrived with the rest of their families and a security detail. After a round of introductions, it turned out that the security detail was for their protection not anything else. More tables were then pushed together and now the party took up the whole of one side of the bar. People were now starting to look at them as they had armed officers standing in front of the bar and were watching everyone coming by.

Datch sat looking at them, “I take it these are here for your safety?”

“Yes. The president of the planet has assigned them to us until we get passage off world.” Said Tinfa.

“Oh cool. It’s a bit like one of our gigs.” Added Hagger.

“When do you think you’ll be leaving?” Asked Carina.

“Well, a copy of the treaty has been sent to IPSF central to be ratified by them. Once that is done, we will be summoned to the planet Olympus to sign the binding agreement.”

“Olympus. We have a few gigs there in three weeks. If you’re there I’ll get them to send you some VIP tickets.” Said Datch.

“So, where are you staying?” Asked Fred.

“I’m not sure yet. They are still trying to sort something out. It has been a busy day for them what with the battle and all that. I take it you stay on your ship.”

"Oh no, we have a private villa on one of the equatorial islands. You want to ask if there are any free. They are very nice." Said Clax.

"Talking of which, I think we had better be heading there soon. Anyone fancy a barbeque?" Said Datch.

"I could go with that." Said Fred.

"That's that then, party at ours."

While they sat finishing their drinks Tinfa called the government and found out there were two more villas free and after a bit of a discussion they were able to hire them. It was decided that everyone would get on board the Raven and head to the island for food and drinks. Datch put a call through to Peter at the villa saying they would be back in about an hour and could they sort out a large barbeque as they had a lot of guests coming.

Forty minutes later the Raven took to the sky. The take-off was a little slower than the last one. On board were The Pack, the council delegation and eight large body guards. They also they had a fighter escort consisting of four ships. This did mean however the flight plan was already cleared before take-off and therefore all Datch had to do was lift off, tell the computer to follow the pre-programmed flight plan and then land at the other end.

The island came into view just as the last few rays of sunlight were touching its shores. Datch landed the Raven softly on the landing pad at the side of the villa. The fighters did two circles around the area before landing in a field next to the villa. Datch came down the ramp followed by two of the body guards. Peter was waiting for him.

"Hi Peter."

"Hello sir. We weren't sure how many people we were catering for so we've gone with twenty-five. Is that, ok?"

“You had better add another twenty as we have the Arcaneus delegation along with their families and a number of security personnel. Sorry to have done this to you at short notice.”

“It’s fine sir. I’ll send out for extra supplies immediately.”

“Well, please accept a hundred credit tip each for you and the other staff as a thank you.”

“Thank you very much sir.”

“Oh, and can you get the Raven refuelled and if possible, a full systems check. It was a bit of a rough trip.”

“Certainly Sir, I’ll sort it out in the morning. I take it you will be having drinks by the pool?”

“Yes, sounds good.”

“Will that be all?”

“Yes, thanks Peter.”

“I shall go and get things started sir.”

With that he turned and headed into the villa.

The rest of the occupants of the Raven came out and Datch led the way over to the pool area. It was a beautiful evening and the sun was dropping below the horizon creating a stunning sunset. The air was warm with a slight sea breeze. Datch went and put some chillout music on the sound system and Peter found some extra chairs for the guests. Everyone relaxed.

Datch finally decided to sit next to Don and Alex. He turned to Don.

“Err… I’m really sorry about putting your ship in danger.” he said.

Don laughed.

"My ship was never in danger. The Plantars ships are no match for her. If anything, it gave my weapons officer a bit of target practice. Firing at drones is one thing but a ship that's firing on you is another."

"It's Qwots you need to say sorry to. I got him to max out his engines on the way here. He was not impressed."

"Yes, but we did get interspace thirty out of them. He'll be bragging about it for years." Added Alex.

"Wow thirty, that's fast!" Said Carina who had come over to check on her boyfriend.

"So, what happens now?" Asked Datch.

"Well, as soon as the IPSF ratify the treaty agreement and Tinfa over there signs it, a small fleet of IPSF ships will turn up at Arcaneus and the Plantars will be told to leave."

"And if they don't?"

"We'll be ferrying what's left of their crews home in cargo ships."

"I wouldn't like to be in the Plantars commander's shoes. It's not going to end well for him." Added Alex.

"I don't know, he'll likely blame the captain of the battleship for not getting the Raven."

Don paused and looked thoughtfully at Datch for a moment.

"Datch, I've got to ask. How did you get to the planet and back without being seen or shot down?"

"I used the scattering field generator the spider had to hide us from their ships sensors and sat in the moons atmosphere until it was dark. Then I engaged the interspace drive and did what the casino boss did and dropped out of interspace in the atmosphere."

"You do know that's only meant to work on the way up, don't you?" Asked Alex.

"That explains why the ground came rushing up towards us then." Said Clax who had just walked over.

"How close?" Asked Alex.

"Err, about fifty metres."

"Wow, that was close."

"Yes, very," Said Rosey sitting down, "Hagger had to change his underwear."

"He did?" Asked Datch.

"Yes, it took him an hour to calm down."

"Wow, he hid that well." Added Clax.

"Oh, and Tank broke wind." She added.

"Yes, but that was just nerves." Added Tank.

"I must say Datch, that's some fancy flying." Said Alex trying to change the subject before bathrooms came up.

"Thanks, I was sweating a bit."

"I take it you did the same on the way out."

"Sort of, we had a fighter on our tale to start with but Clax got rid of that, then we headed straight back here past the Plantar battleship, that's when they must have seen us and gave chase."

"Didn't they fire on you?"

“No, I think we went past too fast for them to even turn the weapons on.”

“I bet; we were already doing factor sixteen by that point.” Added Clax.

“Yeh, that little ship has a lot of go in it, that’s for sure.” Said Tank.

“I take it they were on your tail the whole way then?”

“Yes, we were slowly pulling ahead but not by much. I turned the scattering field off halfway back. I was hoping you would get here but had planned for evasive action. I headed very close to the moon. The battleship was too big and would have to go round.”

“That was good thinking.”

“And of course, you know the rest.”

“Well, next time wait for me.” Said Don, “You seem to have a habit of putting your neck out and hoping it won’t get chopped off.”

“Well, it works!”

“Err… you’ve died once already.” Added Alex.

“Oh, yes. Well, it works most of the time.” he corrected.

They laughed.

“So, where to next?”

“We have a couple of gigs in the Serpentis and then we head to Olympus. We have two more gigs there along with an embassy opening before turning for home and heading to Leepure and Hyacus. Then it’s a stopover at Welly Four for two gigs and a few days off at The Oasis Spa and Hotel.”

“Is that Faberfab and Tajiquay’s place?” asked Alex.

"Yes, and Dag's, He's in partnership with them. It's a very nice hotel and we always get the best rooms."

"Yes, and Jamby is generally in the bar." Added Carina.

"What the Monk."

"Yes, he uses the bar for contemplation and relaxation. So, he says."

"I bet!"

"Does he bless the wine or something?"

"Apparently, Bellatrixian ale is one of his favourites at the moment. We were asked to bring a barrel of the real thing for him."

The light from the sun disappeared and darkness came to the island. The lights came on around the pool area lighting up the grounds with soft pastel colours. The party finally finished just after midnight and people headed off to their villa's or spaceships and their beds.

The next day Datch opened his eyes and turned over, Carina wasn't there. He looked around the room but there was no sign of her. Then the sound of splashing could be heard outside. He got up and walked to the window. Outside The Pack were sitting around the pool. He put his shorts on and walked outside.

"Morning all." He said yawning.

Tank turned to him.

"Morning? Datch, it's mid-afternoon duded."

"You have been asleep for nearly fourteen hours." Added Fred.

Carina climbed out of the pool and came walking over.

“Afternoon lover.” She said giving him a very big and very wet hug.

“Err, you could have woken me up.”

“I tried to, but you were out for the count. So, I thought I’d let you sleep. Do you want something to eat?”

“I am a bit hungry.”

She took him over to a chair and sat him down.

“What do you want?”

“A Jeader roll would go down well.”

“You stay there and I’ll get it for you.”

He relaxed into the sun lounger while Carina fetched him his breakfast come mid-afternoon snack.

The afternoon was spent chilling by the pool and then in the evening they all took a walk to one of the local sea food restaurants.

The following day a team turned up at the villa to refuel and service the Raven. It took them most of the morning and they even cleaned the cockpit windows. Datch was called over to see the team leader when it was finished.

“Hello sir. It’s all done for you. One of the shield emitters was damaged so we have replaced it. The reactor fuel has been replaced and the main fuel tank filled. We have also recalibrated the navigation systems.”

“Thank you. How much do I owe you?”

“Four thousand three hundred and twenty-nine credits sir.”

He handed Datch a vid comm. Datch looked at it a pressed a couple buttons and waited for the unit to scan his implant. It beeped and Datch gave him it back.

“Here you go, I’ve added a hundred credit tip for you and your team.”

“Thank you, sir.”

The man smiled and headed to the maintenance shuttle that was sitting next to the Raven. Two minutes later it took off and headed into the distance. Datch walked back to the pool area.

“How is she?” Asked Clax.

“Good to go. One of the rear shield emitters took a beating so they replaced it.”

“That’s all?”

“They also recalibrated the navigation system, refuelled her and even cleaned the cockpit windows.”

“Wow! How much?”

“Just over four thousand credits.”

“That’s not bad.”

Fred came walking out the villa.

“Datch, Don called, he was wondering if you were around later as he said he wouldn’t mind a beer on the beach.”

“Everyone ok with an afternoon on the beach?”

Carina looked up from her sun lounger.

“Is it ok if me, Tish and Rosey head into the little village for a bit of shopping?”

“In that case what about heading to the beach in front of the village? There’s a bar right on the seafront.” Said Peebop.

“Sounds good to me.” Said Clax.

The others all nodded.

“I’ll give Don a call.” Said Datch.

Datch picked up his vid com and called Don before going inside to get a bag of towels and some sun lotion.

Thirty minutes later a shuttle touched down next to the Raven and Don came out this time with Fizz.

The Pack had spotted it coming into land and were waiting at the side of the landing pad, bags in hand. After a round of hellos, they headed down towards the village. It was a nice slow walk down a little lane that weaved left and right as it descended down the hill levelling out the slope as it went.

The village only had a handful of streets, all of which led off the main one that ran along the beach front. Most of the buildings were white or light blue in colour with little verandas and roof top gardens. The gardens had flowers and colourful fruits hanging from them. The main street had a number of bars and restaurants scattered along it with shops in between selling souvenirs, knickknacks and trinkets. Children were playing in the water next to a small jetty where the pleasure boats were moored up. There were a few people about but it wasn’t a busy type of village, more a sleepy one.

They found the bar which had some nice seats under a group of palm trees all of which were in easy reach of the sea. Tish, Carina and Rosey headed off for a wander around the shops. Fizz, Dapo and Fred along with Timbo and Tank headed into the water to cool off.

After they had acquired a round of drinks Datch sat down and turned to Don.

"I thought you would be heading off by now."

"No, we had to stay and sort out the Plantars making sure they didn't send another battleship. Their crew are being put on cargo ships and sent back to Plantar. It also looks like we'll be taking the Arcaneus delegation to Olympus in about two weeks time. We have been ordered to stay in orbit for now."

"Have they accepted the treaty then?"

"Yes, but the senate wants to clarify a few things before it's officially signed off."

"Oh cool. We might see you at Olympus then."

"You might. I think you'll like it there. Where are your gigs at?"

"We've got two, one in the capital Olympus Prime for two nights and another two nights in Olympus Ceti. Oh, and we have an embassy opening for Welly Four while we're in the capital. Although on the up side Welly Four is paying for our hotel rooms while we're there because we will be in our roles as ambassadors."

"Well both the cities are very beautiful places. Just be careful going in to the system. It's very busy in the space lanes with a huge number of ships going in and out all the time."

"I'm going to ask for auto navigation when we enter the system."

"Wise move, you can enjoy the ride in and you'll love the view."

Datch picked up his beer and took a gulp.

"I think I'm going for a swim to cool off." he said.

"I could do with a paddle myself."

They got up and headed down to the others at the water's edge.

The following week was spent either on the beach or around the pool. Don, Alex and Fizz made a few more visits and they bumped into various members of the Arcaneus delegation who insisted on them going around to their villas for a barbeque or two which led to a few late nights.

# Back On Tour

The following week arrived and it was time to leave. Datch sat down in the pilot's seat and started to go through the pre-flight checks. Clax came and sat next to him and started to do the same. It took about fifteen minutes to go through everything. It was a bit longer than normal as the Raven hadn't moved since they got back from Arcaneus and Datch wanted to make sure everything was ok. Finally, the rest of The Pack started to come in and sit down.

Datch turned to the others when everyone was sat down.

"Is everyone ready folks?"

They all nodded.

Datch brought the thrusters online and prepared to lift off.

"Diamar control. This is the Raven outward bound to Serpentis. Ready for lift off."

"Good morning, Raven. Please be advised traffic is light until orbit and then due to the ongoing security situation the flight corridors are very busy."

"Copy that Diamar control. Ready when you are."

"Raven you are cleared for launch please follow beacon 2788123 to orbit and transfer to Tancanar control for further instruction."

"Thanks, Diamar control. Locking on to beacon 2788123."

The Raven lifted off into the morning sky and headed up towards orbit. As the sky got darker, it also got busier. They joined a steady flow of ships leaving the planet. After they reached orbit, they had to detour past one of the space stations and then follow the other ships out into space. It took nearly an hour before they were in open space and clear to engage the interspace drive. This was due to the fact there was the remains of a battleship in the way.

"Computer set course for Serpentis interspace factor fifteen." Said Datch.

"Course laid in. Do you want the standard alarm?"

"Yes please. Engage Interspace."

The stars in the front of the ship winked out and then started to flicker.

"Ok, who's up for Solar Ball?" Said Datch getting up.

Serpentis was a warm planet with an average temperature of 30C and had an equatorial temperature of around 50C. They were performing a two-night concert in the northern hemisphere and the same in the southern. They had also got three talk shows to do, two of which had been booked on route when the galactic press had found out where they were going.

The Pack were in their dressing room cooling down. The stadium had been packed with fifty thousand people. It had been a very good gig with three encores and by the end of it everyone had green sparkles around their heads. They were all buzzing from the atmosphere and felt normal again. They had just got changed and sat down when there was a knock on the door.

"Yes?" Said Fred.

A security guard came in holding a letter. Fred looked at him.

"If that's a letter asking for help we're not here."

"I don't know." Said the guard and gave it to Fred.

Fred opened it.

"Oh, ok, thanks."

The guard left.

"So, who's it from?"

"It's from Gilla."

"What again?" Said Clax.

"Yes, it says thanks again for everything and they will be on Olympus when we are there. She wants to know if they can get tickets to the gig in the capital."

"Err… Yes." Said Datch, he paused and then asked. "She's not outside by any chance?"

"No. It was sent via the booking office in Olympus." Said Fred.

"Oh, that's good then. I'm all adventured out at the moment."

Everyone looked at him and burst out laughing. After they stopped Datch stood up.

"Ok, Let's go find a quiet bar."

They all thought that was a good idea so Datch stuck his head out the door.

"Timbo?"

"I'll get him for you sir." Said the security guard outside the door.

Five minutes later Timbo came walking in.

"Hi Timbo, we would like a quiet little bar somewhere to chill please."

"Ok Datch, give me a few minutes I just need to sort a couple of things out."

"Sure thing. No problem, dude."

The Pack were taken to a little bar on the out skirts of the city. It was a very sleepy bar and only had a hand full of people in it. That was until The Pack and their security entourage turned up. One of the security officers drank in there and had recommended it. The barman had shouted upstairs for help when they came in. Then when he realised who they were, he had insisted on getting a picture of himself with them in front of the bar and having them sign the white piece of wall next to it. He did however give them a round of drinks for doing it.

They stayed in the bar until the early hours and then headed back to the hotel. They had a chat show recording in the afternoon followed by another gig in the evening. Then a day off which was then followed with the remaining chat shows the day after.

Datch woke up. It was mid-morning and the sun was shining through the widow. He looked around. Carina was in the shower and humming to herself. Through the door he could see a tray sitting on the table with pancakes, pastries, fruit juice and coffee on it. He got up and headed into the other room and picked up a pancake. It had chocolate filling which squeezed out as he bit into it. He was just picking up a second one when the shower stopped and Carina walked out with a towel around her.

"Morning Lover." She said as she walked over to him.

"Morning babes." He said offering her a pancake.

She gave him a kiss and then took a bite out of his pancake.

"Oh, these are good!" she paused and inspected the pancake before taking the one he had offered her.

"So, what's the plan for today?" She asked and took a bite.

"Well, we need to be at the studio a three ish. So, if you want to have a walk around the city, we have plenty of time."

"Yes, I was thinking we could start looking for rings."

Datch looked at her with a puzzled look and then he realised what she meant.

"Rings?"

"Yes, well it's been four years now. What do you think?"

"You mean to be joined type of ring?" He said as if he was looking for confirmation.

She turned and looked straight at him.

"Yes."

Datch looked at her. He loved her very much and had been thinking about it himself lately. But he hadn't found the right time to ask her. It was a big thing after all.

"Yes, it sounds good to me." he said with a very big grin.

She dropped her towel and led him back into the bedroom.

The Pack were all sitting in the hotel bar when Datch and Carina came down. They walked across the bar with big smiles on their faces. A waiter spotted them coming and walked over to the table ready to take their order.

"Morning all." They said sitting down.

The others all looked at them and then at each other. Fred had to ask.

“Err, what’s going on?”

“We have an announcement to make.” Said Carina and paused.

“And?” Said Rosey.

“We are going to be joined.” Said Datch.

“Well congratulations!” Said Fred standing up.

He gave Carine a kiss then shook Datch’s hand before giving them both a hug.

The others all joined in.

“I wondered how long it would be before it happened.” Said Jep.

“Well, it’s been on the cards for a while.” Said Tank who had a tear in his eye.

“Do you have a date yet?”

“Err, no we don’t even have rings.” Said Datch.

“Well, first things first.” Said Clax, “Waiter can we have twelve glasses of your best sparkling wine!”

Fred turned to the happy couple.

“Have you told your parents yet?”

“Err, we’re over a thousand light years away and we only decided this morning.”

“Well, send them a vid call. We’re in the public eye and it will get out sooner or later.” Said Fred.

“OK. Carina, Lets go over here while the drinks come out.”

Datch and Carina went over to one of the windows that was overlooking the lake outside. Datch set his vid com up so they could stand together using the window as a backdrop.

Datch called up his dad's vid com first. It was going to take four days for the message to get there.

"Hi mum, hi dad we have some great news for you." They paused and then smiled at each other, "We have decided to be joined. And no, we don't have a date yet but we are going shopping for rings later. Love you lots. Datch and Carina."

Carina then did the same with her parents.

They finished the calls and headed back to the table. The waiter had brought over the glasses filled with bubbling wine.

"Ok all," Said Fred raising his glass, "Please raise a glass to the happy couple."

They all lifted their glasses and took a sip.

"Congratulations. We look forward to the invites."

Then they all sat down.

"We need to sort out a date and a venue but want to do that with our parents." Said Carina.

"Yes, we've got some planning to do."

They drank the wine and then had another round to make sure it was done properly.

They followed it with a light lunch before heading out to the shops on the way to the studio, Rosey and Tish were very excited and wanted to help Carina and Datch look for rings but Fred told them it was a very personal thing and they should be allowed to do it on their own.

The Pack minus Datch and Carina headed to the touristy bit while the happy couple to be, headed to the jewellery quarter.

“So, what type of ring are you thinking about?” Asked Datch.

“What about two Iridium bands?”

“Hmm, Ok, that sounds good, let’s see what they have got.”

They looked in a couple of windows. One had iridium bands but they didn’t look very good. They moved a bit further along and then at the sixth shop down Carina spotted something.

“Look.” she said pointing to a shelve halfway up the shops window.

There was a small tray with a number of shiny white metallic rings with different patterns and symbols on.

“Shall we have a look?”

“Yes.”

They went in.

The inside of the shop was lined with glass display cases from floor to ceiling. At the back of the store stood a counter with a woman standing behind it. She watched them as they came in. The centre of the room had a large oval display case and, in its centre, a revolving display with brightly lit gems. Datch looked at them.

“Fire Jewels.” he said.

“Yes, they look very nice.” Said Carina.

The woman coughed quietly.

“May I help you?” She asked.

“Yes, we are planning to get joined soon and we’re looking for joining bands.” Said Carina.

“Did you have anything in mind?”

“Yes, we’re looking for something in iridium?”

“What sort of price range were you looking for?”

“Well, we haven’t thought about the cost, it doesn’t matter really. If possible, please could you show us a selection.”

“You do know iridium bands are very expensive?”

“Yes, credits are not a problem.” Said Datch looking at her and smiling.

“Ok if you would like to follow me.”

She led them over towards the counter at the rear.

“These here are iridium; we can have them etched with whatever design you wish at an extra cost.”

They looked closely at the white shiny rings.

“I don’t know?” Said Carina, “They look nice but they are not quite what I was hoping for.”

“What was it that mam wanted?”

“I’m not sure to be honest. Something special?”

The shop assistant looked at her and thought for a moment.

“Why don’t you come over to the counter. I have a vid that can show you the full range we do.”

They went over and the assistant brought up a display on the vid. It had a large number of rings of different shapes and sizes. They looked at this one and that one but it was hard to choose. After about fifteen minutes the shop assistance turned to them.

"Would it be easier if I uploaded the catalogue to your implants and you could take it away with you. That way you could take your time to discuss it? It is a big decision after all. Then, when you have narrowed it down, we can try to get your selection in for you to look at."

"That sounds like a good idea." Said Carina.

"Ok." Added Datch.

"If you would like to both stand here and accept the file when you see the box in your mind."

They did and were pleased to see the full range of rings in their heads. They thanked the assistant for all of her help and headed back outside.

"She was very helpful. I wonder if they deliver?" asked Carina.

"I doubt it, we live over a thousand light years away. Maybe we can find something on Olympus. In the mean time we can look at the catalogue and work out which ones we like."

"Sounds like a plan. Let's head back to the others."

They headed to the touristy area to find the others. It took about fifteen minutes to find them. They were all sitting outside a café having a coffee.

"So, how did you get on?" Asked Rosey as they walked up.

"We're still looking! But we now have a catalogue." Said Carina sitting down.

"Can I see?" Asked Rosey.

“It’s in our implants.”

“That’s handy.” Said Fred.

“It sure beats looking things up on the vid com.” added Tank.

“Ok Rosey, hit accept.”

Rosey sat looking into space for a while before turning back to Carina.

“This is great. It’s all indexed and then the rings appear in your head and spin around.”

“That sounds cool, I wonder if they do that for bikes?” Added Peebop.

They all had another cup of coffee before heading to the studio.

The studio was a large glass fronted building with ‘Serpentis interstellar Broadcasting Services’ in big letters above the doors. They walked through the doors and headed over to reception. After a few introductions they were escorted to a waiting room while the host was informed of their arrival.

The room had some plush sofas and a bar that had large selection of coffees, beers and spirits. There was also a selection of food on a long table which mostly consisted of sandwiches and various pastries with a couple of bowls of fruit thrown in for good measure.

They all went for another round of coffees.

Datch and Carina sat looking into space.

“Are you two, ok?” Asked Hagger.

“Yes, why?” Said Carina.

"You're very quiet."

"We're looking at the catalogue." Said Carina.

"Oh."

"42?" Said Datch

"42 what?" Asked Rosey.

"No, I don't like the pattern."

"Ok."

"42 what?"

"It's a ring." Said Carina.

"Oh."

"What about 56?"

"Hmm, not sure about the shape."

"Ok."

"Err… are you two going to be doing that a lot?" Asked Tank.

"We've got four hundred pages to get through."

"Really?"

"Yes."

"Oh wow." added Peebop.

They sat there watching Datch and Carina having a discussion about things only they could see. Rosey was also staring into space trying to see the rings that Datch and Carina were looking at.

Five minutes later a production assistant came to fetch them to the studio.

The studio was quite small and the set consisted of a number of sofas and a very big coffee table.

"71?"

"Hmm... Let's short list it."

They were taken over to the show's host and introduced. They had their makeup and hair sorted and then waited around the back of the set. The host went on the stage and after walking from one side to the other for the vids he turned to the front.

"Ladies and Gentlemen, it gives me great pleasure to introduce my next guests. Please put your hands together for The Pack."

There was a round of canned applause and The Pack walk onto the stage.

"So, Datch, The whole galaxy wants to know what happened with Arcaneus?"

"Well, we met the daughter of the president of Arcaneus after one of our gigs and she asked for our help." he said.

And then one by one they took it in turns to explain what went on.

The interview lasted around fifty minutes by the time they had gone over this and that along with different camera angles being needed and a quick makeup adjustment half way through. The broadcast length was only going to be ten minutes but the studio needed to edit things. Datch figured that they needed to make things last so long to keep the editing staff in a job. After all, it can't be that hard to use a vid, you just point it and press go.

The interview finally finished and after the host thanked them, they headed out into the sunshine.

"So, we stopping at a bar on the way?" Asked Peebop.

"No, let's head back to the hotel. We've got the last gig in a few hours." Said Datch.

They took a slow walk back to the hotel and chilled in the bar.

The gig went well as did the remaining interviews and then it was time to head to Olympus.

The next morning, they had breakfast before heading to the Raven. After a quick check to make sure everything was onboard Datch brought the engines online and they headed into orbit. They had to wait to join the long line of ships all on route to Olympus. After a few minutes Datch left orbit following other vessels in what looked like an interstellar conveyer belt made up of ships.

He set the course and engaged the interspace drive.

Datch sat looking at the navigational display. He counted twelve more ships within five light minutes of their position. He had never seen this may ships so close in interspace. The flight corridors were restricted to interspace fourteen for safety reasons due to the high volumes of traffic heading to Olympus. Datch turned to Clax.

"Wow, its busy out here."

"Wait till we get near the Olympus system. If you think this is busy, you're in for a shock."

"Computer how long till we reach the Olympus system?"

"Two days six hours and forty-seven minutes." The computer replied.

"Well, I think it's time for a beer."

“Sounds good. Computer set alarm for one hour before arrival.”

“Unable to comply. Olympus requires contact two light years outside their defence perimeter.”

“Ok computer, set the alarm for fifteen minutes before then.”

“Alarm confirmed.”

Clax got up first and stopped to wait for Datch who was still mesmerised by the display.

“Err Datch?”

Datch pulled himself away from the display and looked up.

“Oh, sorry.”

He got up and they headed to the rec room.

Two days later the ships alarm sounded. Datch was just eating breakfast with Carina when it went off. He finished his mouth full and headed up to the cockpit. Clax was sitting in the co-pilot’s seat waiting for him.

He sat down and put on his headset.

“Wow. Look at all the ships.”

The navigational display was showing seventy-nine ships in the local vicinity.

“Yes, it’s getting busy out there. Better contact Olympus control.”

Datch opened the comms channel.

"Olympus control this is the Starship Raven heading to Olympus Prime, Private landing area three requesting entry to the system."

There was a short pause.

"Raven – This is Olympus control please transfer ID's and purpose of visit."

Datch pressed a couple of virtual buttons and the system beeped.

"Olympus Control – Data sent."

"Thank you, Raven. Please stand by."

A few moments later the comms burst into life again.

"Raven, Your ID's are confirmed. Please note auto navigation is mandatory on approach to Olympus Prime."

"Olympus Control, we request auto navigation as soon as possible please, at what point are we able to lock on to beacon?"

"Raven, beacon is available now."

"Olympus Control, please can we have auto navigation?"

"Raven, lock on to beacon 754.OP981.732"

"Thanks Olympus Control locking on to beacon."

Datch instructed the computer to follow the beacon.

"Olympus Control, we are now locked on, Raven is yours."

"Raven, Welcome to Olympus enjoy the ride."

"Thanks Olympus Control, Raven out."

Datch looked up and realised the star in the middle of the window was in fact a ship. He looked around and spotted three more.

“There are ships everywhere.” he said.

“Yes, this is one hell of a busy place.” Said Clax.

Datch hit the ships comms.

“Guys, I think you should get up here. The traffic is getting really busy, We’re already on auto pilot heading for Olympus Prime.”

The rest of The Pack started to come up the stairs and one by one sat down.

More ships stared to appear in front of them and then the computer announced they were entering the Olympus system. The ships were now all around them and getting closer. There was a huge cargo ship to the right side of them that was almost as big as the Carpaycus. On the other side a star liner and for the first time the Raven seemed very small.

The Raven flew on passing the outer planets and as they entered the inner star system they dropped to interspace factor three. Outside the window they were greeted with an amazing site. To the right of them was an enormous ship.

The ship was so big the Carpaycus could have landed in one of its landing bays and disappeared. It must have been bigger than three moons of Bellatrix five put together. Along the side of it were five sets of three interspace engines each of which must have been ten times the size of the Carpaycus. The hull was lined with docking ports, each of which had large cargo ships entering and leaving them. The Ravens sensors were showing it had the gravitational mass of a small planet.

“Wow, that’s one hell of a ship.” Said Datch in awe of it.

“That is a trans galactic transport ship.”

“You mean one of the ships that go between Galaxies?”

“Yes. They go to Andromeda from here.”

“Wow. That’s incredible.” Said Carina who had got up for a better look.

They watched as a freighter in front of them left their stream of ships and headed towards the enormous ship.

“How do they even power a ship that size?” Asked Dapo who was now craning over the top of Clax’s seat for a better look.

“Each of the interspace units have their own singularity to start with.”

“You mean that ship has...” He stopped while he counted them. “Err, twenty-seven black holes powering it?”

“It’s thirty-two in total. There is also a couple inside supplying power to the rest of the ship.”

“Wow.”

The Raven flew on adjusting its flight path as it went. It took five minutes before they cleared the trans galactic transport ship. They headed towards the inner most planets and towards Olympus prime. All around them were ships. They included a lot of IPSF starships some of which were a lot bigger than the Carpaycus along with cargo ships, liners and service ships. The IPSF ships were grouped together in groups of ten all looking like they could take down a star system without even thinking about it. Datch spotted the Carpaycus in one the groups and it looked very small next to some of the other ships.

The Raven then dropped out of interspace and in front of them was Olympus Prime.

Olympus Prime was a bright blue world. It shone like a bright blue gem sitting in space. Surrounding it were a large number of space stations all of which were in themselves shining like stars. They orbited the planet making it look like it had a ring of diamonds around it. The air was crystal clear and down below the continents could be seen surrounded by crystal blue waters.

In front of the Raven was a long line of ships descending to the surface like some sort of planetary conveyer belt. They felt the ship slowdown as it started to enter the atmosphere. The atmosphere was glowing with the continuous line of ships entering it at the same point. The Raven entered the lower atmosphere and turned into another line of ships. The ships were now more spaced out and then the comms beeped.

"Raven - This is Olympus Prime control, Landing area in three minutes. Please be advised thrusters will be at your control on arrival."

"Olympus Prime control – This is the Raven, ready and thanks for the ride."

"Your welcome Raven, enjoy your stay. Control out."

The Raven turned heading towards a large city. It was full of huge glass towers reaching into the sky. Each was connected to its neighbour with a glass transport tube and they spread out across the city like a silken spider's web. In between them were large open parks with lakes and fountains. Then the main stadium came into sight.

"Looks like the gig venue over there." Said Clax.

"Wow that's a big stadium." Said Datch.

"They said it was a two hundred-thousand-seater." Said Fred.

"I hope we fill it or it will seem very big." Added Datch.

“It’s sold out for both nights.” Said Fred.

“Cool.” Said Carina.

They flew on past a huge building built of white marble and edged with gold and silver. It was ringed with large white towers capped with gold and two massive particle cannons sat on either side of the building.

“Wow! Look at that place.” Said Datch.

“That place is the Senate. The seat of power for the IPSF.”

“Can we see it?” Asked Carina who was currently craning her neck over the top of Datch’s seat so she could see out the window better.

“They do tours when they are not in session. So, we may get lucky.” Said Clax.

“Cool.”

Then up ahead appeared a large landing area full of very expensive looking ships. The Raven slowed and came to a stop hovering two hundred meters in the air above the entrance.

“Raven – Olympus Prime control – You are clear to navigate. Have a good stay.”

“Thanks Olympus prime control. Raven out.”

Datch took control and contacted the landing area to find out where to land. They were on pad seventy-three. Datch positioned the Raven over to it and brought her in for a soft landing. He shut down the systems and stood up.

“Well folks, I think we should head to the hotel and then go for a walk and find a little bar somewhere.”

“That sounds good to me.” Said Peebop.

The others all nodded in agreement before getting up. They collected their bags before heading to the cargo bay and the bright new world outside.

At the bottom of the ramp, they were greeted by two attendants wearing blue uniforms.

“Good morning, ladies and gentlemen. Welcome to Olympus Prime. There is a private shuttle service over there to take you anywhere in the city and we also offer a full range of services for your ship while you are here.”

“Thank you. The Raven just needs refuelling, everything else is good thanks. We also have booking at the Grand Palace hotel.” Said Datch.

“Very good choice of hotel sir. I will inform the shuttle teams to expect you. Your ship will also be refuelled within the hour. Is there anything else sir?”

“Yes, this is Timbo our Road crew manager. He will need to transport some items to the stadium the day after tomorrow. Could you sort out a shuttle for him.”

“Certainly sir. Consider it done.”

“Thanks again, give yourself a twenty-credit tip.”

“Thank you, sir. Have a great stay.”

They headed over to the shuttle area and boarded a shuttle to take them to the hotel. This time they were flying low through the city passing building after building and each was a shining tower of glass and steel.

The shuttle slowed down as it approached the hotel. It looked very impressive with white marble steps leading down from the landing pad to a large entrance hall with huge glass doors. The building looked like it had been carved out of white marble which ran around in a circle behind the entrance hall.

They walked in and over to the reception desk.

“Good afternoon, sir. How can I help you?” Said a very posh looking receptionist.

“We are The Pack and you should have nine suites for us? They may be under Welly Four.”

The receptionist pressed some buttons on a vid com built into the desk.

“Could I please scan your ID?”

Datch nodded and the receptionist pressed another button. After a moment the vid com beeped.

“Ah yes. Nine suites. They are in the green zone on the third floor. Please can I ask you to step up in room order so I can scan each of you for the door access system.”

Carina stepped forward and stood next to Datch.

“I’m with him.” she said.

“Ok, you are both in suite G302.”

One after another the process continued until they were all booked in.

“Ok sir.” Said the receptionist turning back to Datch. “That’s all done for you. I hope you enjoy you your stay with us and if you require anything please do not hesitate to ask. Please wait while I get the porters to take you to your suites.”

A number of android porters came out of a doorway next to the reception desk and picked up The Pack’s bags.

“Please follow me.” Said the lead android in a very Bellatrixian sounding voice.

Datch suspected that it would be able to say it in a very alien sounding voice as well if it wanted to.

They followed the porters out of the opposite side of the reception area and into a large circular area with pools and gardens in the middle along with a number of small bars and two open air restaurants. The hotel encircled the area with high marble walls with coloured arches which match the colours of the zones and crystal glass windows which glistened like diamonds in the sun light. The porters led them through a garden area full of lush palms and ferns. They arrived at a doorway with a green marble arch over it and went in.

"This is very posh." Said Clax.

"You're not kidding. It makes the Excelsior in Traxsent look like a cheap motel." added Peebop.

"It's certainly very impressive." Said Fred.

They arrived at their suites and went in to freshen up. The porters unpacked their clothes and then put them away before heading back to wherever androids go between jobs. Datch had arranged to meet the others outside near the pool in about thirty minutes.

An hour later they were walking down the streets of Olympus Prime taking in the sights. To say the city was grand was a major understatement. The streets were lined with white and cream buildings and the pavements were so clean you could eat off them. The city temperature was a constant twenty-eight degrees Celsius. Here and there as they walked along the street environmental controllers could be seen built into the buildings and above them shield generators to keep the cooler air in.

They found a bar with a large grassy area at the front that had a number of long tables. Each table had a number of umbrellas put along its length.

"This city is amazing." Said Carina sitting down.

"Yes, it sure is." Added Rosey.

An android came out from the main bar and headed over to them.

“Good afternoon, what can I get you?”

Datch looked at it. It was speaking Bellatrixian.

“We’ll have beers all around please, oh and some nibbles.”

“Nibbles sir?”

“Yes, crisps and nuts in small bowls.”

“Certainly sir. What type of ‘nibbles’ would you like?”

The android’s chest lit up displaying a list of crisps and various bar snacks. Datch found most of their normal nibbles and went with a selection. It was then time for the beer. The bar had a very extensive selection. They spent a few moments looking through them before selecting what they wanted.

“Is that everything sir?”

“Yes, thank you.”

The android turned and headed back inside.

“I know the bots at the hotel knew we were Bellatrixian but how did that one know we came from Bellatrix?” Asked Datch.

“The androids here are able to do a low-level scan of your implant so they can ascertain the persons language. It’s meant to make you feel more comfortable with them. You’ll find all the bots here do it and trust me there are a lot of them.” Said Fred.

“Wow.” Said Datch.

The beers came out first followed by the nibbles.

"So, what's the plan?" Asked Peebop.

"Hmm… Well, we have two days before the gigs at the stadium and then a day before the embassy opening and that's followed by two more gigs in Olympus Ceti. So, the plan is a bit of sightseeing tomorrow and then a chill out day before we start work." Said Datch.

"Sounds good, what do we want to see first?" Asked Fred.

"The Senate!" Said Carina with a grin.

"Ok, I'll check my vid comm for tours."

"Can we go shopping to?" asked Tish.

"Yes, there is a big mall over near the Senate." Added Clax.

Fred looked up from his vid com.

"There are tours in the morning only. The senate is in session the day after tomorrow. So, they close at lunch for security scans." Said Fred.

"Ok, when is the latest?"

"Err… nine in the morning but this world is on a twenty-hour clock so it is just before 11. Remember ten is midday."

"Ok, book us in for that." Said Datch.

Fred pressed some buttons on the vid comm and it beeped.

"Ok all done."

They sat enjoying their drinks watching as people and aliens went walking past.

"Four hundred and nine." Said Carina.

"Err… I don't like the edging." Said Datch.

"Ok."

"How far are you into the catalogue?" Asked Tank.

"Err… page one hundred and seventy-eight." Said Carina

"Oh, and how many more?"

"We're just under half way." Said Datch.

At that moment a strange looking bubble came past with two aliens inside it walking down the street.

"Wow, look at that." Said Rosey.

"They are from Gahore. They are methane breathers and therefore travel around in the bubble so they can explore the planet." Said Clax.

"Oh wow. That must be strange seeing everything through a bubble. I wonder what they do if they need the bathroom?" Asked Hagger.

"Ewe, did you have to say that?" Asked Tish.

"To answer your question. Their bodies do not work the same as ours and therefore they don't need bathrooms."

"Oh, cool." Said Rosey.

They had another round of drinks before heading off in the direction of the new embassy. They figured as Welly Four were paying for their hotel they had better go and say hi before they turned up for the opening.

The city was spotless with beautiful statues and sculptures dotted here and there. They arrived at the part of the city where the embassies were. They all looked very impressive with large white marble columns and ornate entrances. They turned the corner and up ahead was the Welly Four embassy.

The embassy was at least twice the size of the one on Bellatrix and was a hive of activity with lots of colourful banners and bunting going up. As they reached the front and turned towards the door, a man came running down the steps waving his arms and saying 'Sorry, we're not open yet!'. He got to the bottom of the steps and stopped. He looked hard at them for a second and then went bright red.

"So very sorry dudes. I didn't recognise you, Music Warriors. Please accept my humblest apologies."

He bowed to them.

"That's ok dude," Said Datch, "Is Widfab around?"

"Yes, he is in the main office sorting things out. Would you like for me to fetch him for you?"

"Is it ok if we just head inside to see him?"

"Yes, most certainly Music Warriors. Please follow me."

He bowed again and then led the way up the steps and into the embassy.

Inside was a scene of organised chaos. The room was very large with a reception desk along one side and a bar along the other. In the centre, tables were being put out along with a lot more bunting and balloons. Datch looked up. There in the middle of the ceiling was a green gem.

"Guys, Look up."

They did.

"Well, this is going to be one happy city." Said Clax.

"That's for sure." Added Tank.

They followed the aid up a flight of stairs and down a corridor to a set of large doors. The aid stopped and knocked.

“Come!” Came a voice.

The doors opened into a large office, the walls were bright and colourful, the carpet was a nice light green colour with a thick pile. In front of the windows was a large desk with three vid screens and sitting behind it in a big chair was Widfab.

“Sir, the Music Warriors are here to see you!”

“What! Err, get some beers or something!”

He jumped up and came running around the desk.

“Hi dudes and dudets. Sorry, you should have called.”

“Hi Widfab, we were just out for a walk and thought we would call in to touch base with you.” Said Datch.

Widfab came over and shook everyone’s hand.

“I’m very pleased to see you again. How are you doing?”

“We’re good. Yourself?”

“I’m very good thanks. Sorry, I couldn’t help you the other week, I hope everything worked out ok on Arcaneus?”

“Well, it’s still a bit fluid, but looks like it should work out ok.”

“Good, Good.”

“I see you have another gem here.” Said Fred.

“Yes, we thought we should, this being the capital of Olympus and the centre of IPSF.”

A number of people came in carrying glasses of beer.

“Ah, the drinks.” Widfab.

They started handing them out to The Pack. Each time the servant would give a large bow.

"Err, why is everyone bowing at us?"

Widfab went a little pink and looked a little awkward.

"Come on Widfab, spill the beans." Said Datch looking at him.

"Well, you're all sort of going to be made into demigods. Sort of just below gods and goddesses. The monks all voted for it after a very good party."

"They did?" Asked Jep.

"Yes."

"How much beer did they have to drink?" Asked Fred.

"Err, quite a lot but they had sobered up when they voted."

"And they still went through with it?"

"Yes. We had a big meeting about it and decided that after you saved our planet and brought life back to our world you deserved it. Father Jamby has been very thorough with his religious texts concerning you and they make a very good case for it."

"So, let me get this right. A lot of really drunk monks decided at a party to make us all gods after reading a religious text written by a monk who spends most of his time in the bar?" Asked Clax.

"Demigods," corrected Widfab, "and err. Yes dude."

"Oh, so, when is this going to happen?" Asked Datch.

"When you get to Welly Four. We are going to announce it to the galaxy when you get there and do the ceremony thing followed by a really good party afterwards."

"Well, I'm always ready for a really good party." Said Hagger.

"Err, we don't have to do sacrifices or anything, do we?" Asked Carina.

"We plan to sacrifice a lot of kababs, fried hacks, some Jaxx steaks, oh and a lot of beer." Said Widfab with a grin.

"Hmm, I can sacrifice a few beers." Said Tank.

There was a general agreement that the party was a very good idea and they were happy to be gods as long as they didn't have to do any god like things other than sacrificing a few beers and a steak or two.

"Ok, so what's the plan for the opening?"

"Well, I'll do the speech thing and then we'll have the food. Afterwards, I will unveil the gem and then introduce you and you can do your thing. Then, when you dudes have finished, we can all party."

"Sounds like a plan. How long a set do you want us to do?"

"Would seven songs be, ok?"

"Yes, I think we can do that."

"Great. We have another band coming in after you to keep the party going till midnight."

"Cool, we like a good mingle." Said Rosey.

"Yes, and we're gods now as well." Added Hagger.

"Not yet Hagger. Not till we get to Welly." Said Tank.

"And it's demigods." Corrected Dapo.

"What time do you want us here?" asked Datch trying to get away from the whole god thing.

"Would sixteen hundred be, ok?"

"Isn't that a bit early?" Asked Tish.

"No, we're on a twenty-hour clock remember, so it's just after nineteen hundred." Said Carina.

"Oh."

"Yes. That's fine Widfab. Timbo will come with a crew and set up in the afternoon." Added Datch.

"Ah Timbo. I thought you were one short but didn't like to say anything."

"Yes, he's gone off for a meeting with the stadium people at the moment. But I'll get him to give you a call and sort out the fine details with you."

"That's great, Thanks."

They finished off their beers and said their goodbyes before heading outside into the sunshine.

The next morning after breakfast, they headed to the Senate. They arrived outside just as the tour group was assembling ready to go in.

The tour guide started by explaining about the outside of the Senate and why Olympus was chosen for its location. The whole planet had been terraformed for the sole purpose of the IPSF. That way, the seat of power was in neutral space and no race would have a home advantage. The Senate had been enlarged fifteen times to make room for new races joining and now could hold over forty thousand delegates.

Afterwards they followed the guide in through two very large doors.

Inside they found themselves in a very long hallway lined with marble pillars. On each side doors led off to hundreds of side rooms which the guide said were used for private debates and meetings. He also explained how the IPSF came about and the interstellar wars that had happened before its existence. They arrived at another set of doors with very ornate carvings and the symbol of the IPSF carved in the marble above the door. The guide explained that inside was the senate assembly room and then he opened the door.

Inside was a very large amphitheatre which was set out in sections, some of which had clear enclosures with different atmosphere inside. In the centre was a platform with screens all around it which would display the subjects under debate but at the moment were displaying tranquil scenes from around the planet. This was the heart of the federation and all of the big decisions were made here. It was the place where the fate of worlds were decided and where allegiances were formed. It was the most powerful place in the galaxy. This was the place that governed the galaxy.

The guide explained about how the senate operated and how the leaders of the great civilisations across the galaxy would come and debate various issues. He added that they were coming together tomorrow to debate bringing a new race into the federations. The guide then let them stand on the podium and look out over the entire senate. Datch felt like he was on stage when he was looking out across the senate. It was a pretty amazing thing to be standing there and he could imagine what it was like when the senate was in session with the leaders of so many worlds standing in front of you.

Afterwards they followed the guide out and into the gift shop where you could buy various things including placemats for your dinner table with various pictures from the senate and the city outside. Datch picked up a set for his mum and dad and Carina told him to get two sets as she was sure her mum and dad would like them too. They went for ones with pictures of Olympus and the outside of the Senate on instead of picture from inside the senate as they didn't like the idea of eating with all the senators staring up at them.

They were just coming out of the senate when someone shouted ‘Datch’.

Datch looked around and Tinfa was waving at him. The Pack walked over to him.

“Hi Tinfa, how are you?”

“I’m good thanks. How are you folks?”

“We’re good. How’s it going with the Senate?”

“Very well, we’ve answered all the questions and they seem happy with everything.”

“So, when does it get the stamp of approval?” Asked Fred.

“We think it will be in five days time. We are scheduled to go before the senate then. They have a few things to sort out before we become members.”

“Cool. That’s the day after the embassy gig. You’ll have to let us know what happens.” Said Datch.

“I’m sure it will all go ok. They have already given us an office and four members of staff.”

“Cool.”

“Oh, thanks for the tickets to the concert, Gilla is really looking forward to it.”

“No problem. I think they are quite good tickets. I’ll ask the security to bring you back to our dressing room after for a drink.”

“That’s great, I’m sure she will like that.”

“Do you know when the IPSF will kick the Plantars off your planet?” Asked Hagger.

“I think that’s what the Senate are working out. They have told us that the Plantars have been told to leave but we don’t know what the answer was. Knowing them, I suspect it was no.”

“That’s not going to work in their favour, that’s for sure.” Said Clax.

“We have been talking and want to reward you for your help. Would you be able to come to Arcaneus for a couple of days after we get it back?”

“Err, I’m not sure. We have to be in Leepure in a week’s time followed by Hyacus a week later and then two weeks after that Welly Four.”

“What if I could sort you transport out?”

“I didn’t think you had any ships as such?”

“We don’t have any now but the IPSF have said they are planning to assign a tactical group to our star system for a few years until we can get our defences sorted out. Part of the treaty is that we build six large starships. Four to protect our planet and two to be part of the IPSF fleet. So, it means we’ll have ships at our disposal.”

“OK, Well, if you can sort it out so we don’t miss our gigs, we would be honored to come.” Said Fred.

“Yes, we don’t want to miss becoming gods.” Added Dapo.

“Gods?” Tinfa looked at Dapo.

“It’s a long story. We’ll tell you at some point.” Said Datch.

“Ok, I’ll look forward to it. Well, I had better let you folks get on. I’ll see what we can do with the transport and will let you know when it will be.”

“Ok. Tinfa, say hi to the others for us.”

“I Will. See you all later.”

With that he headed off around the side of the Senate to find his office and The Pack went towards the centre of the city in search of a bar that did food.

# Party Night

It was the night of the embassy opening. The Pack's gigs had gone well and they were now glowing as normal. They had worked out that after the gems had been activated it took around a week before they stopped glowing. Which was fine during daylight but at night they looked like walking street lights. They had a small meal before leaving the hotel and heading to the embassy. The early evening air was a nice warm 26C and the sun was just starting to drop in the sky. Another hour and it would be dark.

The Pack arrived at the embassy just as the press were setting up. The security forces had set up a cordon and were checking IDs as beings went past them. The Pack walked up to the check point and were let in. They headed to the steps and an aid came running down the steps and then bowed to them.

"Welcome Music Warriors. Please, follow me."

They followed him inside and found Timbo sitting in a chair directing a small group of people setting up the stage and PA system. He had a look of frustration on his face. They walked over to him and the group of workers all bowed.

"Hi Timbo, what's up?" Said Datch.

"Err, all is good but these people keep bowing at me and won't let me do anything. They just keep telling me to sit down."

"Err, If I was you, I would just expect them to do it all. We'll explain later. Is everything else, ok?"

"Yes, Datch. It's just about all set up now. Just a few minor adjustments."

"Cool, we're just going to find Widfab. We'll see you in a bit."

"OK, Datch."

"Oh, and Timbo, just chill."

"OK."

They headed off to find Widfab. He was behind the bar checking the staff were up to speed on the various drinks and any odd rituals that the invited races had. He even checked the kababs were ok and the pizza oven was working.

"Hi Widfab!" Said Datch as they walked up.

"Ah, Music Warriors. You're here."

A number of the bar staff turned towards them and bowed. Datch looked at them for a moment.

"Err, Widfab. Any chance you can stop people bowing?"

"Don't you like it?" he looked a little worried.

"Not when we want a beer. It just doesn't seem right." Added Carina.

"There is a god of beer on one of the other planets." He said hoping for some sort of middle ground.

"Yes, but we're not there."

He looked at them for a moment. Datch felt he needed a bit more.

"Would it help if we gave you a religious commandment or something?"

"Err, well I suppose it maybe, ok?"

Datch thought for a second.

"Ok, I hereby command that no bowing should be carried out when serving beer to any religious deity unless so requested."

"Ok, I'll tell them." He said looking a lot happier.

"Cool, that's great. So where do you want us?" Asked Datch.

"Your table is over there but if you want a quiet beer before it all starts, there's an office over there where you can chill out for now."

"That sounds good. Can we have a round of beers and no bowing please?"

"Sure, no problem, dudes."

Widfab showed them to the office that was at the back of the stage before going off to brief the staff on the not bowing when doing the whole beer thing.

They sat in the office having a drink and getting ready for the set. It was a strange office as it had nice comfy chairs and a large vid screen showing scenes from around Welly Four. It also had a number of colourful ferns that were glowing gently and a desert scene painted on the wall depicting the monastery with the gem on the monolith. There was even a tinted glass window that looked out into the main room. It was now starting to fill up with dignitaries and leaders from around the galaxy along with a number of representatives from the IPSF fleet.

"647?" Asked Carina.

"OK, add it to the list. What about 684?" Said Datch.

"Err, OK, add that too."

"How many have you got listed so far?" Asked Rosey.

"So far, 37 with another 12 maybes." Said Carina.

“Wow. I never thought choosing a ring would be so hard.” Said Tish.

“Well, it’s not just any ring, it’s the ring. It’s got to be right.”

“Yes.” Said Datch in agreement.

“Err folks, are we going to head out? The room’s starting to look a bit full now.” Said Fred before they ended up in a big ring debate.

Datch looked at him for a second.

“Oh yes, the gig.” He said as he departed ring land and re-joined reality.

Datch turned to the others.

“Ok, let’s get our game faces on. The set list for anyone who’s forgot is, Rocking the City, Star Lovers, Wilde Wind, Planet Rock, Music Warriors, Green Gems and Hot city nights with the encore being Supernova and Shoot for the Stars.”

“And don’t forget we have to be ambassadors tonight, so smile and pay attention. We are going to be spiritual leads of Welly Four soon.” Added Fred.

“You mean gods.” Said Rosey.

“We’re not going to be gods. Demigods are not gods.” Said Fred.

“What are they then?” Asked Hagger.

“They are below gods. If you like, the boss of a company is a god and the demigod would be like one of his mangers. The mangers look after things for the boss. Look it up.”

“So, we’re going to be god like mangers?” asked Hagger.

Fred looked at them and gave up.

"Yes, if you like. Either way we have to look the part, OK?"

There was a round of nodding.

"Right and just remember no one knows about the demigod thing so don't talk about it."

"Yes. No talking about it!" Added Datch just to make sure.

They finished their drinks and headed out to their table. The room was full of aliens and humans all of which were representing their worlds. Over the years since the return of the light to Welly Four it had become a very active member of the IPSF and they brought a new vibrant energy to the Senate. Because of this every major power was here and that meant the normal celebrities didn't get a look in. There were a small number of reporters and vid crews at the back but even their numbers had been limited. As The Pack went to sit down Timbo came over and joined them.

They sat looking around at the room when four waiters came over, bowed and deposited a round of drinks on the table. The room filled up and it wasn't long before everyone was seated. A few moments later the lights dimmed. A line of lights lit up the stairs going towards Widfab's office. Music started to play a sort of rock type anthem and people stood up.

"What is this?" asked Dapo.

"It's Welly's anthem." Said Fred.

They all stood up.

"Cool. At least it's not a boring one." Said Rosey.

"I suspect they got the idea from us." Said Tank.

"Very likely." Added Fred looking at Datch.

A spotlight illuminated the top of the staircase and Widfab appeared dressed in a long green and golden flowing robe.

He stepped down the stairs in time to the beat of the anthem and as he did fireworks went off behind him with every step. Above everyone the gem was pulsating to the rhythm. He reached the bottom of the stairs and then half walked and half danced to the podium on the stage.

"Wow, what an entrance! I wonder where he learnt to do that?" Said Tish.

They all turned and looked at Datch.

"What?"

"Nothing." Said Fred and turned back to look at Widfab.

"Ladies, Gentlemen, fellow humanoids, quadra morphs and fellow aliens. It is my greatest pleasure to welcome you to our new embassy in the beating heart of the federation..."

"He's getting very good at these speeches that's for sure."

"I extend the hand of friendship from the Welly star system across the galaxy to every world. Please let me..."

"Datch have you been giving private lessons?" Asked Clax.

Datch stared at him.

"I'll take that as no." added Clax.

"Now please accept our hospitality this evening and enjoy the entertainment. My staff are all on hand so if you require anything please do not hesitate to ask. But before the night's entertainment let's eat!"

There was a large round of applause and as it quietened down, he clapped his hands and an army of waiters came into the room carrying trays of food.

A group of four waiters headed for The Pack's table carrying a number of buckets of fried hacks, Weega fries and a couple of pizzas. They placed them on the table and then all bowed before heading back across the room. A lot of the other tables had gone for the four-course set meal from Welly Four. But The Pack had got to perform and only wanted a lite meal. Anyway, Widfab had said they were doing kababs later on. Seventy-five minutes later the food was finally finished and Widfab took to the stage again. He looked over at The Pack and nodded.

“Looks like we’re up folks.” Said Datch.

They all took a last drink and put their headsets on.

Widfab cleared his throat and tapped a little bell. The room fell quiet.

“Ladies, Gentlemen, fellow humanoids, quadra morphs and fellow aliens. I hope you have all enjoyed the food. We have brought a gift for you. Above your heads is a gem from Welly Four. The gems on Welly Four bring happiness and joy to our world and we hope this one will do the same here.”

There was a round of applause and he waited until it quietened down before continuing.

“I now have the very great pleasure to introduce you to the people that brought my planet out of darkness and into the light. Without them my world would still be a very dark and boring place. Please welcome on to the stage ‘The Music Warriors!’”

The Pack ran on stage and Datch went to stand at the front. There was a subtle beep in Datch’s ear telling him the mic was live.

“Thank you. Minister Prime. Hello Olympus. Are you ready to Party?”

The staff all cheered and some of the guests.

“I can’t here you. Are you ready to party?” He shouted.

At this point most of the room got the idea and cheered.

“Ok let’s do this!”

Datch grabbed his guitar and Tish hit the drums. In the ceiling the large gem started to glow, pulsing to the beat. They got to the first chorus and their gems energised and shot beams of light up to the gem in the ceiling. Rocking the city blasted out across the room and then the large gem started to get brighter and brighter releasing rings of energy out across the room. The Welly Four member of the party started to glow brightly along with The Pack.

The first song finished and it was time for ‘Star Lovers’. Datch and Carina started to dance around each other while singing and looking into each other’s eyes. The gem in the ceiling was now getting incredibly bright and as the song progressed The Pack slowly turned into columns of light. It came to the part of the song where Datch and Carina came together and kissed. As they did the large gem exploded with light sending a wave of energy across the city. Everyone in the room now had sparkles around their heads and very big smiles on their faces.

As people got up and started dancing. The energy in the room became electric. Everyone started to sing along, song after song and then the encores which had ‘We Can't Get High Enough’ added for good measure. Finally, they headed off the stage to huge applause and cheers. It took a minute for Widfab to snap out of his trance and then he stepped onto the stage.

“Thank you, Music Warriors. You are truly fantastic people and Welly Four is forever in your debt. I would like to say that they have not only saved our world but are in the process of saving another, Arcaneus, so if any of you folks can help, I’m sure it will be very welcome and thank you. OK! on with the Party! The Kabab and pizza counter is now open if you are feeling hungry and it’s time for the next band, put your hands together for ‘Loaded Star’.”

The next band took to the stage and had a mix of contemporary pop and a few rock numbers thrown in.

The Pack went and sat back at their table and downed a large beer each pretty much in one go. A group of waiters came over with more beers and also carrying a selection of large kababs with various sauces on. All of them had big grins on their faces and sparkles around their heads. In fact, everyone in the building had sparkles around their heads.

As the evening progressed people came and chatted to The Pack. They wanted to know all about Welly Four and also a number asked about Arcaneus. Some of the guests asked for autographs and wanted photos with them. Some people would see the Kababs ask what they were like and then ask if they could try a bit. The result of which was that shortly after they would go and get one of their own. The Pack must have got through two kababs each and only eaten one.

The evening finally came to the end and people started to head off home. The Pack, Widfab, a number of staff along with a few of the guests headed to a bar around the corner to chill out. It turned out that some of the group were members of the Senate. Also, the bar had a games unit with solar ball on it. Needless to say, the following two hours were fun and at two in the morning everyone decided it was time for bed and therefore headed off to their respective hotels.

The next morning The Pack did a bit more sight-seeing and brought a few souvenirs before getting ready to fly south. Around lunch time, Timbo called Datch to let him know that the gear was all in the Raven's cargo bay and they could leave when ready.

The flight was again automated and Datch was glad due to the amount of traffic in the sky. Everywhere you looked there were ships and shuttles going from A to B. It would have been a nightmare to try and navigate it. They arrived at the hotel in Olympus Ceti and after sticking their bags in their rooms they went to sit in the bar and have a beer. They were just finishing off their drinks before heading out to explore Ceti city when Datch's vid com started to play a little tune. He pulled it out of his pocket. It was Tinfa calling. He pressed the answer button.

"Hi Tinfa, how's it going?"

"Great Datch. How are you guys doing? I watched the embassy opening on the vid yesterday."

"What did you think?"

"It was different but in a good way and you sure made everyone happy. Gilla is still sparkling."

"Cool. How's it going with the senate?"

"That's what I was calling for. I wanted to let you know Arcaneus is now part of the IPSF and I wanted to thank you again for all your help."

"You're welcome."

"We now have a seat in the senate. The official vote passed easily. There also seemed to be a lot of people and aliens with sparkles coming off their heads."

"What, aliens as well. I didn't know it worked on them. Well, at least they will be happy for a while."

"Also, I wanted to invite you to our home coming if that's what you would call it. If I've worked it out right, it should be two days after your concerts in Hyacus."

"We would love to, but it's a long way to come. It would be about six days travel just to get there and we have to be in Welly Four two weeks later."

"It's all been taken care of if you want to come. We have arranged for a starship to it pick you up and then take yourselves and the Raven to Arcaneus. Then afterwards it will drop you off at Welly Four on time. If that's ok?"

Datch looked at the others.

"What do you think folks. Do you fancy a quick trip to Arcaneus on route to Welly Four?"

There was a consensus of opinion that it would be good as long as they got back to Welly Four on time and didn't have to crawl through any caves this time.

"Ok, we'll come."

"That's great, I'll make the arrangements for the ship to rendezvous with you. I'll contact you with the details as soon as I know."

"We will look forward to it."

With that he finished the call.

They took another drink of beer.

"Well, this is turning out to be a very busy tour." Said Fred looking Datch.

"Yes, it is a bit. I think we'll need a holiday when we get home just to recover."

"We do seem to be having a lot of parties." Said Carina.

"Yes, and a lot of excitement." Added Dapo.

"I'm not sure crawling around caves, being shot at and chased across a hundred and thirty light years of space can be classed as 'excitement'. It scared the Willys out of me." Said Peebop.

"Well, I liked it." Said Hagger.

"You had to change your underwear at one point."

"Yes, but it was still fun and just to put the record straight it was twice." He said with a grin.

"Ok, lets finish our drinks and head out before Hagger gets into the graphic details and we all feel ill." Said Fred.

"Good Plan." Added Datch.

"822?" Said Carina.

"OK." Said Datch

"How many pages have you got left?" Asked Tank.

"Err, 27."

"Thank heavens for that." Said Jep.

"So, how many have you got on your list?"

"48." Said Datch.

"Then we have to go through them again." Added Carina.

"So, do you think you'll have decided before we get home?" asked Clax.

"Err, we're not sure but we're going to try. My mum and dad are already making a list of friends they want to invite to the joining. I think they are very excited about it." Said Carina.

"My dad's talking about a really big do with all the family again." Added Datch.

"Err, don't you get a say?" asked Rosey.

"Yes, we're having a meeting at the ranch when we get back with both our parents." Said Carina.

"Yes, that way we can chill in the bar when we have it." Said Datch.

"Have you decided who you want for your ceremony manager?" Asked Fred.

"Well, we want one of you guys to do it but we're not sure who's getting the short straw."

"We would all be very honoured. What about man and maid of honour?"

"We have done a lot of thinking about this and would have liked all of you to do it but we can only have one. It's been a hard choice but would you like to do it Rosey?" Asked Carina.

"Yes. I would love too."

Datch turned to Fred.

"Fred would you be mine?"

"Why thank you, I would love too, but why me?"

"Well, you helped get me and Carina together at the start and you always look after us."

"Thank you, I'll do my best."

"I suppose we had better get another beer?" Said Dapo.

"Let's find a nice bar in the city somewhere."

"Let's ask the staff. Waiter?" Said Fred.

The waiter came over.

"Yes sir, how can I help?"

"Can you recommend a good lively bar to chill out in?"

"Yes sir. If you go out the hotel doors and turn right, follow the road into the centre of town and then, when you see the statue of the planets turn right and just down the road is a bar called 'Paradise'. It has a nice lively atmosphere and I'm sure you'll enjoy it."

"We'll give it a go. Thank you."

"You're welcome, sir."

With that they finished their drinks and headed out into the city.

# The Return

The Pack were sitting outside a small coffee shop in the capital city of the planet Hyacus three. They had finished their final gig in the star system the night before and were chilling out and having pancakes for breakfast. They were just on their second coffee when Datch's vid com beeped. He fetched it of his pocket and looked at it. It was a message from Tinfa. Datch sat and read it.

"Guys, that was Tinfa, He's entering the star system in three hours and wants us in orbit ready for transport."

"Ok, well that gives us plenty of time."

"I thought the news said they weren't taking the planet back for a couple of days yet?"

"I Don't know. Maybe they did it earlier or the Plantars gave in. They were majorly out gunned so they didn't have much of a choice really."

"Well, another coffee then and we'll head back to the hotel."

"I'll let Timbo know to get a move on."

Datch sent Timbo a message and then ordered more coffee.

After lunch they headed to the Raven and got ready for the trip. Tank put a large teddy bear he had been given in his room next to the one he already had and headed up to the cockpit. Datch sat in the pilot's seat going through the pre-flight checks with Clax sitting next to him. After five minutes he turned to the others.

"OK, folks. Everybody ready?"

There was a round of nodding.

"Ok, here we go."

He turned back to the front.

"Hyacus control, this is Raven requesting departure to orbital vector 345.23 by 233.9."

"Good afternoon, Raven, Clear to launch in two minutes. Follow beacon 12 to orbit then you will be free to navigate on your vector."

"Thank you, Hyacus Control, locking in to beacon."

Datch brought the thrusters online and the Raven started to rise into the air. He held at fifty metres and locked onto the beacon. A few moments later the ship turned on its own axis and then pointed its nose skywards. The engines roared and the Raven shot forward into the sky. The land became a blur as the ship climbed up through the clouds accelerating as it went. The sky started to turn to black and below them the planet turned into a bright blue and white sphere spinning in space.

"Raven, this is Hyacus Control. Beacon will release in 2 minutes."

"Thank you, Hyacus Control, Raven out."

Datch put his hands on the controls and waited.

"Raven, this is Hyacus Control the ship is yours. Have a safe journey."

Datch brought the ship around onto the new vector and headed into space. After a couple of minutes, a bright light could be seen in the distance and the comms burst into life.

“Raven this is the Carpaycus please lock on to beacon IP2371 for automated landing.”

“Affirmative Carpaycus, locking on to beacon.”

Datch pressed a few buttons and then went back to the comms.

“Carpaycus this is the Raven, Beacon locked on, you have control.”

“Thank you, Raven. Two minutes to landing bay.”

The Raven accelerated towards the bright light and it slowly became bigger and as it did a starship appeared.

“You could have told have told us it was the Carpaycus.” Said Fred.

“I didn’t know. Tinfa just said a ship was meeting us.”

Fred started to laugh.

“Looks like Don just got you back at your own game.”

Datch laughed as well.

“Yes, I suppose he has.”

The Raven started to bank towards the Carpaycus. The Raven slowed and in front of the ship flashing beacons lit the way into the landing bay. The ship slowed matching speed with the Carpaycus. Finally, the Raven lined up with the landing bay and entered the ship. It touched down and then the comms beeped.

“Welcome to the Carpaycus Raven please shut your systems down and a welcome party will greet you shortly.”

“Thank you Carpaycus, will do.”

Datch shut the engines down and there was a clunk as the pad's clamps locked on. He got up and looked at the others.

"Come on folks let's grab a beer."

They got up and headed to the cargo bay and the exit ramp. They started to come down the ramp and there was Tinfa waiting for them along with Don and Alex.

"Welcome aboard!" Said Don stepping forward with a big grin on his face.

"Hi Don." Said Datch.

He shook Don's hand and then went to Tinfa and Alex. After everyone had been officially greeted Datch turned to Don.

"So, where's the party at?" He asked.

"We thought you may want a beer when you got here so we have a reception arranged in the reception suite. Please follow me." Said Alex.

"We have also given you ambassador's quarters as technically you are Welly Four ambassadors." He added as he turned to face a corridor entrance.

"Only part time ones." Said Peebop.

"We're rock stars the rest of the time." added Dapo.

"And that's when we're not saving planets." Added Hagger not to be out done.

"Ok, either way please follow me." he said.

They headed down the corridor to the pod. Behind them a crew set about making sure the Raven was strapped down and secure.

They arrived at the pod and once inside Don hit his comms.

“Helm, set course to rendezvous with fleet and Engage Interspace drive factor twenty.”

“Course Laid in, engaging Interspace drive.” Came the reply.

The lights in the pod dimmed and then after a burp from Tank and Timbo, came back up again.

“So how big is the fleet?” asked Datch

“Ten ships. Including two planetary destroyers along with a number of ship similar to the Carpaycus. We wanted to make a point to the Plantars not to mess with us.”

“Are we going to blow up a planet?” Asked Hagger.

“No. Just frighten one.” Said Alex.

Just then the pod came to a stop and the door opened. Alex led the way up the corridor to a large set of doors. He stopped and waited for the doors to open. He stepped inside and then in a loud voice said to the people gathered inside.

“Ladies and Gentlemen please may I present the Welly Four ambassadors known as the Music Warriors.”

Datch followed Tinfa through the door. It was a large room with its own buffet and bar which had a number of the crew manning it to ensure everyone was being kept happy. Inside the room were all of the people they had rescued from Arcaneus except the children. Also, a number of ambassadors from other worlds and sitting in the corner with a small group of people, who were all sparkling, was Widfab.

The occupants came across and greeted them and the Arcaneus council thanked them for all that they had done.

After a while Datch and Carina wandered over to Widfab and his group.

"Hi Widfab."

"Hi dudes."

A number of the party got up and bowed to them.

"I thought you would be on Welly Four by now?" Asked Datch.

"Well, we had some bits to sort out on Olympus first and then I heard about this little trip and figured we would join the party. After all, they are going to Welly afterwards."

"Sounds like a plan." Added Datch.

"So, when did they take Arcaneus back?"

"Oh, they haven't yet. We're meeting the fleet on the way. It all sounds like it going to get a bit exciting."

"Err, isn't it going to be dangerous?" Asked Carina somewhat concerned.

"Oh no. The fleet has more than enough fire power to deal with the Plantars. It's being led by one of the carrier ships and with two destroyers, the only thing in danger will be the Plantar's underwear."

"Wow a carrier as well. The IPSF are not messing about, are they?" Said Clax walking up.

"No dude. They want to send a very strong message to the Plantars. Hopefully they will see us coming and make a run for it."

"And if they don't?"

"They are to be escorted back to their home world."

"Yes, but what if they shoot at us?"

"They will be walking home without space suits! It has all been decided at the Senate."

"Wow, I never realised the IPSF had so much power."

"The IPSF has been going for thousands of years. It has thirty-two thousand members spread across several million worlds. We all live together in peace and freedom because of it."

"What happens to worlds like the Plantars?"

"If a species is deemed to be too aggressive or of danger to other worlds they are first confined to their own star system and if they leave it and try to take other worlds then their ships will be destroyed and they are no longer allowed to have any more."

"What happens if they don't stop?"

"Well as a very last resort, and I mean the very last resort. They along with their solar system will be eliminated."

"You mean destroyed?"

"Err, yes."

"Has that ever happened?"

"Yes, a few times. There were originally four arachnoid races in this galaxy. There is now only one. The IPSF will not let its members be threatened or violated by any other races. We all enjoy the freedom to travel the stars and the security that the federation brings. In return we all support it with ships and supplies."

"Are we going to destroy the Plantars planet?" asked Carina.

"No. As I said they will be escorted home either with ships or without. And that bit is up to them. They will also be told that it is no longer allowed for any of their warship to leave their space. The Senate has informed them of this already and told them to leave Arcaneus."

"Oh well, I hope they got the idea and left."

"I'm sure they have and if not, they soon will. Anyway, getting on to more fun things. We have sorted out the pleasure moon at last and it looks great. If you get a chance while you're with us you should go and check it out."

"Yes, we'll try. It sounds quite fun from what I've seen on the vids."

"I hope so. We've set up a number of different zones for music and dancing to cover all the different types. Also, we've given it an atmosphere so you don't need space suites anymore."

"That sounds really cool."

"We've even added a low gravity water park."

"Awesome!" Said Dapo walking up behind them.

"Yes, we're very pleased how it turned out ourselves."

"Are we going?" Asked Dapo.

"We'll try and fit it in." Said Datch.

Just at that point Janus came walking up behind them.

"Hello all" he said.

"Hi Janus." Said Datch.

"I haven't had a chance to speak with you since the rescue. I wanted to thank you on behalf of myself and my wife for all your help."

"You're welcome."

"It was quite fun really." Added Dapo.

They chatted a bit more and then Datch headed over to Don who was standing next to Tinfa.

"Hi again, sorry to break into the conversation but I was just wondering Don, what time do we meet the fleet?"

"It should be at seven hundred hours give or take a few minutes, why?"

"I've never seen any of the other ships close up. We were too far away from them at Olympus."

"Yes, they keep us away from the shipping lanes. You'll just have to get up early tomorrow. It should be a sight to see."

"Cool. Any chance I can see it from the stellar auditorium?"

"Now you're asking Datch."

Don looked at him and thought for a moment.

"Hmm, I suppose so, as long as you're not in there too long. I'll get Fizz to fetch you at what, six seventy-five?"

"That would be so cool. Thanks a lot. I'll go and tell Carina."

Don laughed as Datch turned and headed back over to Carina.

"Stellar auditorium?" Said Tinfa

"Yes. I'll show you later if you like."

The next morning Datch's alarm went off at six twenty-five. He stopped it, turned to Carina and gave her a peck on the shoulder. She stirred and turned to look at him. He was grinning.

"What time is it?" She asked.

"Six twenty-five."

"What in the morning?"

"Yes. But in real time it's around seven thirty ish."

Then she remembered what he had told her and started to move.

"Come on then, we don't want to miss it." she said getting up.

They headed for the shower while the food dispenser made them a couple of strong coffees and some toast. Fifty minutes later they were sitting on the sofa looking out at the stars when the door pinged.

"Enter." Said Datch.

The door opened and Fizz walked in.

"Good morning ambassadors."

"Fizz. It's us!"

"I've been told to use your titles for this trip."

"Ok, well just do it when other people are about, OK?"

"Ok. Are you ready to go to the Stellar auditorium?"

"Yes, we just need to finish our coffees."

They finished their drinks and then headed to the pod.

"You're going to be amazed." Said Datch.

"I'm looking forward to it." Said Carina.

"Err. Just to let you know there will be a number of others in there with you." Said Fizz.

"There will?" Asked Datch.

"Yes. After you asked the captain about it a number of other guests asked if they could come."

"It is really great in there. How many?"

"Well, most of them. Only the bikers are staying in bed."

"I hope we can turn the lights out."

"I'm sure that is the plan. Rendezvous with the fleet is in fifteen minutes."

The pod slowed down and came to a stop. They stepped out and walked up the corridor to a large set of doors with 'Stellar Auditorium' in big letters on them. The doors opened and inside was a large round room like a big amphitheatre with seats laid out in a large circle around the edge. The celling was an enormous dark dome. There was a large group of people in the centre and they all turned to look as they walked in.

"Morning." Said Tinfa walking forward.

"Hi Tinfa. Wow, that's a lot of people."

"Yes, we were told this place is amazing."

"It is when the dome is open."

"We were told to wait for you to do it. Apparently, the ship listens to you."

Datch laughed.

"Yes, it does know me."

Datch cleared his voice.

"Ok folks. I know this sounds really silly at seven ish in the morning but everyone lay on their backs and look at the celling."

There were a few titters.

"No, I mean it!"

They looked at him and people started to lay down. It took a couple of minutes but soon everyone was laying down and when everyone was settled Datch spoke.

"Computer, this is ensign Datch. Activate the dome."

The celling vanished and there were a number of large gasps as the star light flooded in. The feeling was like floating in space. For a few minutes they forgot they were on board a starship. They felt like they were floating amongst the stars.

"This is amazing." Whispered Carina.

"Told you." Said Datch.

They all lay there for a few minutes watching space go by, silenced by the beauty of the stars. Then one by one ships started to appear getting closer. The carrier ship was a huge long ship that looked like a flying brick and was brisling with weapon systems. It had two sets of interspace engines on each side and they were glowing with energy. Dotted along its side were landing bays and next to each one was a cluster of launch tunnels ready to dispatch fighter wings. The Carpaycus was tiny by comparison. Then two destroyers came into view. They were also large ships with two huge cannons that made up the whole of the front third of the ship. Datch realised that the guns were the planet destroyer's main weapon and could destroy not just worlds but whole stars. Then a number of other ships about the same size as the Carpaycus appeared. Each of them looking like insects against the carrier.

The Carpaycus started to match speed with the carrier and slowly came up alongside it. The carrier took up the whole of one side of the dome obscuring the stars.

After a few minutes Fizz spoke.

“Ladies, Gentlemen and Ambassadors, sorry to break things up but we need to leave as the ship will be going on tactical alert shortly. Computer, close Dome and increase lighting to fifty percent.”

The celling turned black and the lights came on. The group sat up blinking in the light.

“That was amazing.” Said Carina getting up.

“I told you it was cool.”

“I’ve never seen the stars so clear. It was like being part of the sky.”

“Yes, and when the ships came, it was incredible.”

Fizz cleared her throat again.

“If you could all head back to your quarters as soon as possible please.”

People started to move out of the room. Tinfa came over to Datch and Carina as they stood up.

“Datch, I’ve been thinking. How would you feel about taking us down to the planet? It would be nice to go back the way we left.”

Datch stopped and thought for a moment.

“Err, what if they shoot at us?” asked Carina.

“They won’t let us go until it’s safe and anyway, I’ll ask for a fighter wing escort.”

“Well, if it’s going to be safe, we’ll do it.”

“Ok, let me talk to the captain.”

“If he gives you the ok, let me know. I’ll need to prep the Raven.”

“Ok.”

They headed to the door and back to their quarters.

The sight out of Datch’s window was a little less impressive now as all they could see was the side of the carrier. Datch sat looking at it for a few minutes.

“That’s a very big ship.” he said.

“Yes, it is, but it does block the stars out.”

“Yes, just a bit.”

Datch looked at the view. He could see about four stars at the top of the window if he pressed his head against it and looked up.

“Are you really going to take the Raven down to the planet?”

“Well, if we’re allowed. If it’s not safe they won’t let us go. Anyway, we haven’t seen the planet yet. We spent last time crawling along in ditches in the dark and walking through caves or sitting in the cellar of a house.”

“Yes. No Caves.”

“Ok babes.” He laughed.

They got another coffee and then checked their vid comms.

An hour later the comm’s beeped and Datch went over to answer it. It was Don.

“Hi Datch.”

“Hi Don, what’s up?”

“We have been asked by the Arcaneus council if you can take them planet side. I have talked to fleet command and they have agreed to it if you are willing to do it. You will be under orders during the flight so you will need to do as you're told. Do you want to do it?"

"Yes, it will be cool."

"I know it might be cool but you cannot do your normal thing. You must do as instructed. I can't emphasise that enough."

"Ok Don. I promise."

Don looked at him through the monitor as if trying to gauge what he was thinking.

"Are you sure you can follow orders."

"Yes sir!"

"Ok then, be in the ready room at nine fifty hours and bring Clax as well. It would also look good if you put your uniform on."

"Yes, sir."

"Ok, see you in an hour."

The channel closed.

He walked back to Carina.

"That was Don. We are going to take the Arcaneus council to the surface in the Raven."

"I take it that's after the Plantars leave?"

"Err, I think so. I've got to go to the ready room with Clax in about an hour."

"Does he know?"

"Not yet, I'd better give him a call and tell him."

Datch went back over to the comms unit and asked it to connect to him to Clax.

Clax's face appeared on the console.

"Morning Datch, how's it going dude?"

"I'm good dude, How's it with you?"

"Great thanks. So, what's up?"

"We have been asked to fly the Council down to Arcaneus when it's safe. Don wants me and you in the ready room in an hour to be briefed."

"We have?"

"Yes, and I said we would."

"Oh. Ok. I'll be there. I think I need a few strong coffees first though!"

"OK dude, see you there."

The channel closed and Datch went back to Carina. They sat talking about the fleet outside and the upcoming trip.

An hour later Datch was on his way to the ready room. Fizz had brought him his uniform and Carina had made sure he looked the part. He arrived outside and Clax stood waiting for him.

"Hey Datch. Wow, you're in uniform."

"Yes, Don said it would be better if I was."

"Well, I'm sure he knows best."

"Ok, Let's go in."

They walked up to the door and it opened.

Inside Don, Alex and a number of other officers were sitting at a large table. In the centre of the table was a large holo screen displaying a number of other captains and commanders. Don turned to Datch as they entered.

“Ah ensign Thome. Please come here and sit down with your co-pilot.”

“Yes, sir.”

Datch went over with Clax and they sat down. Don turned to the images on the holo screens.

“Sir. This to Ensign Thome and his co-pilot Clax.”

The centre image increased in size showing a man in a commander’s uniform.

“Good morning ensign Thome. I am Fleet commander Jaycob.”

“Good morning, Sir.” Said Datch who was now so far out of his comfort zone he would need a map to find his way back.

“I knew your dad. How is he?”

“Very well, thank you sir.”

“Well, let’s get on with business. I am told you have some good flight skills?”

“Err. I’m not bad sir. My dad taught me sir.”

“Well, if your anything like your dad, I’m sure you will be fine and judging by what captain Ronediamar has told me, you know how to handle your ship.”

“Thank you, sir.”

“Good. To bring you up to speed. The Plantars are refusing to go and our long-range tactical plots show four

Plantar battleships in orbit. Weapon wise they do not represent a threat to the fleet but small ships could be destroyed. Therefore, all smaller ships will stay next to the carrier until the threat has been neutralised this will include the Raven. Ensign Thome you will have a fighter wing with you at all times. Follow the wing commander's instructions at all times."

"Yes Sir."

"We'll drop out of interspace one light year from the Arcaneus system. The fighter wings, troop carriers will launch along with the Raven and form up alongside the carrier. We will then jump to Interspace five to enter the system. Ensign Thome, you will not need to use you interspace drive. You will be inside the carrier's field. However, make sure your shields are at full power."

Datch nodded. "Yes sir."

"On entry to the system we are going to head straight to the planet. We will position ourselves directly in front of the Plantar battleships. Any aggression by them will be met with maximum force understood?"

"Yes sir." Said Don and the other captains.

"Ok. Get your ships prepared. We group up in fifty minutes."

With that the channel closed and one by one the other ships disconnected. Don stood up.

"Ok, you heard him let's get the ship ready. Datch a word with you and Clax."

The rest of the officers left and then the lights started flashing yellow.

"Datch. I know this has sort of been thrown on you. You sure you're ok with this?"

Don had his serious face on.

“Yes. I’m good sir.”

“You know you will be carrying the future of that planet in your ship.”

“Yes. I’ve already done it once.”

Don had to agree. They had rescued the council in the first place and they did have a bit of a track record.

“Don’t worry Don. I’ll look after him.” Said Clax.

“OK. But make sure you follow orders. Now go prep the Raven.”

“Yes sir.” Said Datch.

They got up and headed to the door.

“Oh, and you guys be careful out there.” Don said as they reached the door.

“We will.”

They left the room and headed to the landing bay.

The Raven sat there with pipes and power conduits connected to its auxiliary ports. There was a number of crew members around the ship checking out all the systems and making sure everything was correct. Datch and Clax headed over to her.

The crew members saluted as they walked up.

“How’s she looking?” Asked Datch.

“All systems ok sir. We have also tweaked the shielding a bit and they should give you another twenty tera watts of protection.”

“Wow. Thanks. Are we ok to do the pre-flight checks after the briefing?”

“Yes sir. We’ll disconnect the ports 5 minutes before launch.”

“Thanks.”

They walked over to the briefing room were the wing commander briefed them on the plan via the vid link. Afterwards they headed back to the Raven. A crew member stopped them before they went in.

“Sir, I have something for you and your co-pilot.”

She turned and went over to a rack in the corner and came back carrying two small plasma pistols.

She gave them to them.

“Err. What are these for?” asked Datch.

“Just in case sir.”

“Oh.” Said Clax.

They took the weapons and walked inside the Raven and headed up to the cockpit. Datch put his gun next to his seat and sat down.

“Datch?”

“Yes?”

“You good with everything?”

“Yes. I’m a little nervous to be honest and being given the gun has not helped.”

“Don’t worry I’ve got your back. Just do what you do.”

“Ok.” He paused and looked at the gun and then after the moment contemplation turn to Clax.

“I’ve never shot anything before.”

“Don’t worry, if they go to shoot you, you’ll soon work out how to and very fast.” Clax said with a smile.

“Have you ever shot anyone?”

“No, not a person but I went hunting a few times on alien worlds. Trust me, when something threatens your life, you will shoot it.”

Datch looked back to the gun for a moment before turning to the controls.

“Ok, let’s do the pre-flight.”

They set about carrying out checks and did them all twice just to be sure. Afterwards Clax got up and headed to the cargo bay to wait for the council members.

Datch connected to the comms and asked to talk to Carina.

“Hi babes. Sorry I didn’t get back to you I’m in the Raven. I’ve been a bit busy.”

“That’s ok. Are you alright?”

“Yes, but we have guns.”

“I’m sure you won’t need them.”

“I know. When you coming down?”

“I have been told to come to the loading bay in about fifteen minutes with the delegation.”

“Ok. See you in a bit.”

The comms closed.

Datch sat on his own and looked out of the cockpit. The landing bay was a hive of activity but he was lost with his thoughts then he had an idea.

He tapped the comms panel.

Alex appeared on the comms.

“Yes Datch?”

“I’ve been thinking. What if I put the scattering field on when we head to the planet? The Plantars will only see the fighter wing?”

“Hmm, that’s not a bad idea. Let me speak to the captain.”

The comms closed.

Datch sat with his thoughts for a few more minutes before the comms beeped.

“Hi Datch. You have clearance for the scattering field when the go for planet fall is cleared. The wing commander will give you clearance for activation.”

“Thanks Alex. Sorry, sir.”

“Ok, you have a good trip and keep your head down.”

A few moments later the lights in the bay started to flash. The Ravens ships comms bust into life and Clax’s voice came in Datches head set.

“Datch, start to power up the systems. The council members are here with Carina and Fred.”

“Ok, bringing them online.”

Outside the crews disconnected the auxiliary port and Datch brought all the systems online. Everything was looking good. A couple of minutes later Carina walked up the stairs.

“Hi Lover.” She put her arms around him.

"Hi babes."

Then she spotted the gun.

"Err, what's that?"

"That's the gun I was talking about. We have been given them just in case."

"Is it that risky?"

"It shouldn't be but the wing commander said they may try to assassinate the council members and to be prepared for anything."

"Don't we have troopers with us?"

"Yes, there are going to be twenty in the cargo hold. A number of troopships are going to land in front of us and secure the area before we are allowed to touch down."

"This is a bit scary."

"It will be fine babes. I'm here."

He gave her a kiss.

"Datch. it's time to get ready." Said Clax sitting down.

"Thanks, Clax. Sorry babes got to focus now."

Carina sat down behind him and Fred came and sat opposite Carina. The rest of The Pack were going down in a troopship as it had been felt that it would be safer for them along with the council's families. Also, and more to the point, it meant everyone got a seat.

Tinfa and the rest of the council filled in behind and started sitting down.

The comms crackled into life.

"Raven, this is fighter command. Wing Theta Gamma will be launching in three minutes. You'll will launch in four minutes and rendezvous with them on the right side of the carrier. Theta Gamma's channel is Two Four Two Seven."

"Copy that fighter command switching to dual band now."

Outside the lights dimmed and changed to a red colour.

"What's going on?" Asked Canina.

"We just dropped out of interspace ready to link up. The ship is at condition 'red' meaning battle stations." Said Fred.

"Are you ready for this Datch?" Asked Clax.

"No, but that's never stopped me before."

"Raven, prepare for launch."

Datch brought the thruster's online and there was a loud clunk as the docking clamps disengaged. The Raven lifted a metre off the deck and they waited for the launch command.

"Raven, Launch."

Datch flew the Raven out through the landing bay exit and into space. There were no planets, just stars and ships. He started to climb up above the Carpaycus following a flight plan on his tactical plot. As they reached the top of the ship the carrier came into view. It looked big before but now it took up the whole sky.

Datch started to head along the side of it. Every five hundred metres was a fighter wing each of them consisted of forty fighters all armed to the teeth.

"That's a lot of ships." Said Carina.

"Raven this is Theta Gamma, we see you. Join formation in the centre position."

“Copy that Theta Gamma, on vectored approach.”

Up ahead was a fighter wing sitting in space just in front of one of the interspace drive units. The drive unit must have been nearly the size of the Carpaycus. The fighter wing had made a gap in the centre for the Raven to slot into. Datch brought the ship in nice and slowly and turned to face forwards before dropping onto the hole.

“Nicely done Raven. Have you ever been in interspace without your engines before?”

“Negative.”

“Well, you’re in for a real show.” There was a slightly worrying tone to the voice.

“We’ll try and enjoy it, sir.”

“Fighter wing get ready one minute to interspace. Weapons Hot.”

“Clax.”

“Already on them.”

The Ravens cannons powered up.

The main comms started to count down to interspace. It reached zero. The stars at the front of the ship started to bend into a tunnel and then all the stars started to bend around them. Then a hole opened at the front of the carrier and the stars exploded forming a tube of light around the carrier.

“Wow!” Said Datch as the cockpit was flooded with light.

“You can say that again!” Added Clax.

“Wow.”

“You still with us Raven?” Came a voice over the comms

“Yes Sir. Just going Wow, Sir.”

“Well, just enjoy the ride, five minutes till show time.”

Datch watched as the stars folded over and over on themselves. Light itself was bent in some very strange ways. It felt like the fleet was falling through an endless plug hole of light.

# Battle Stations

Arcaneus was under martial law. No one was allowed to leave their homes and the Plantars had fortified the main square. Up above them four Plantar battleships sat in orbit each with a fighter escort. The fleet command was sitting in his chair on the bridge of his ship. On the screen was the Plantar planetary commander.

“Don’t worry. This is a small world. If they come at all they will only send a couple of ships. I’m sure they will leave us alone when they see we’re ready to fight for it.”

“I don’t share your optimism commander. But I hope you’re right. The deadline to withdraw was yesterday so if they’re coming it will be soon.”

“We’re ready for them don’t worry. A couple of shots from our forward cannons and they will turn tail and run.”

“Hmm... Well, keep an eye on your sensor arrays. And if you see anything let me know.”

“Sir!” came a voice.

“Yes. What is it? I’m on a call to the planet.”

“The sensors. They are showing a massive body heading towards the planet.”

“Massive. How massive?”

“Forty kilometres across sir.”

“Check your sensors again, a ship can’t be that big.”

“It’s nearly on top of us.”

“What’s going on?” asked the Planetary commander.

Outside the battleship, the stars started to vanish and space started to warp into a large black hole. Out of its centre the carrier emerged flanked with the fleet. They were right in front of the battleships.

"Oh… Crap sssssssssssssssssssssssssss." And the channel cut off.

"Battle stations, bring up the shields and fast." The captain of the battleship yelled as he started to panic.

The two destroyers targeted the front two battleships.

"Launch the fighters, Target the large ship in the centre with the forward cannons and fire." He shouted.

The battleship fired its forward cannons, the blast hit the carriers front shield and lit up the sky with a flash of light as the shields channelled the energy into an energy sink. Lightening flashed over the front of the carrier like it was inside a faraday cage. Fighters launched from the side of the Battleship.

One of the destroyers now fired its forward cannon at the battleship. The blast ripped through the ship's shields like they didn't exist and hit the hull. There was a massive explosion of expanding light and energy. The battleship exploded into trillions of particles as if someone had detonated a huge nuclear bomb inside it. Nothing was left of it a part from an expanding cloud of super-heated dust and gas.

The second battleship now fired at the destroyer lighting up its shields. The second destroyer fired its forward cannon at the battleship. It also exploded and became nothing more than an expanding cloud of dust and gas. The two destroyers started to turn to face the other two battleships lining up their forward cannons. The fighters from the first ship now attacked the carrier. Four fighter wings now engaged them flying straight at them. Blast after blast of plasma hit the carriers shields but had no effect. Then the fleet's fighters reached the fighters. Datch watch as all of the Plantar fighters were destroyed one after another.

The fleet commander hailed the two remaining battleships.

“To the remaining Plantar battleships. Drop your shields and deactivate your weapons or you will be destroyed!”

The two remaining battleships came to a stop. They lowered their shields and closed their weapons ports.

“I am Fleet Commander Jaycob. You will prepare to be boarded by our teams. Inform your crew that they will be expected to comply with any commands given. After we have secured the planet any remaining troops on the surface will be transported to your ships and you will be escorted back to your home star system. Note! Any deviation from these instructions will result in the loss of your ships and your lives!”

The captain of one of the remaining ships opened a comms channel.

“Fleet commander Jaycob. I am captain Herder; we have stood down. Do we have your assurance that we will be fairly treated?”

“As long as your crew complies with our requests. As stated, you and your crew will be looked after. Please go to your rear landing bay where a transport ship will be landing shortly. Yourself and the other captain will be brought on board the carrier for your official surrender and dinner later.”

“Thank you, commander. I’ll brief my crew.”

“Also, we have allowed your comms to function again. To stop any more bloodshed, it might be an idea to contact the commander on the planet and inform him of what has happened and that he and his men will be fairly treated if they also comply."

"I will try commander."

"Thank you, captain. I will give you ten minutes. Jaycob out."

Datch sat looking at the expanding gas cloud that was all that remained of the battleship. Small particles were hitting the carrier's shields making flashes of light as they were vaporised.

"They don't hang about do they?" He said without taking his eyes away from the view.

"No. They mean business. It's to show the Plantars not to mess with them." Said Clax.

"Yes. I can't believe it only took one shot. There's nothing left of it. Just dust."

The comms burst into life.

"First wave fighter wings get ready for planet fall."

"Looks like they are getting ready to invade." Said Datch.

"Yes. won't take long judging by what just happened." added Clax.

"Did we just kill all those Plantars?" Asked Carina still in shock.

"We didn't kill them as such. They were vaporised. They wouldn't have known what hit them. They would have just stopped existing." Said Clax.

They watched as the fighter wings near the front of the carrier started to form up in waves ready for planet fall.

Back on the battleship the captain manged to connect to the commander below.

"Captain where is the fleet commander?"

"He's gone along with his ship and one of the other battleships."

"What! I take it we're still in the fight though?"

"No sir. We have surrendered. I have been asked to talk to you in order to stop any more bloodshed."

"Didn't you try and stop them?"

"The fleet commander and the second ship got one shot off each. The blasts just hit their shields and bounced off. Then two of their ships opened fire. Just one shot each and the battleships were vapourised. There is nothing left not even debris just dust. I urge you to stand down or I fear you will all die."

"We can't let them take the planet."

"Commander, with all due respect. You don't have a choice. It's over."

"We'll see about that!" he said and closed the channel.

The captain sighed and left the bridge for the landing bay.

Down on the planet the commander turned to the fighter commander next to him.

"They don't get to the surface do you understand!"

"Yes sir!"

Up above the planet two more ships started to move into position. They had a large circular centre filled with cannons pointing down. One positioned itself in orbit above the capital city and waited. The second positioned itself over the next largest city. The fighters were now in large groups waiting for the go for planet fall.

The fighter commander on the ground ordered his fighter groups to launch.

The ship above watched and waited.

Down below the fighters got ready to take off.

Then the ship in orbit shot out beams of light targeting each of the fighters on the ground and then fired. The scene below erupted in fire as all the fighters were destroyed before they could even launch. Ground crews ran for their lives as the fires spread to the fuel tanks causing them to exploded destroying all of the support infrastructure.

After the orbital cannon platforms finished firing the fighter wings started to dive towards the surface.

There were massive explosions outside the Plantars offices. The commander got up to look just as the fighter commander came running back into the office shaking his head.

“All gone, all gone…” he was in a state of shock.

“Pull yourself together man. What do you mean all gone!”

“The fighters, there all gone. Nothing left. They didn’t even launch.” The man was shaking.

The commander got to the window and looked out. He was greeted by a sight of devastation. The fighters outside were all in flames and the buildings nearby were also burning.

“What all of them?”

“Yes, all gone.”

“What about the southern base?”

"Gone! All gone."

"Do we have any fighters left?"

The fighter leader managed to pull himself together.

"Err yes sir. Six that were on patrol."

Then out of the window the sky was full of fighters. The commander watched as they dived towards the surface.

"Tell them to eject!"

"Why?" Said the fighter commander coming to look out the window.

"Oh..." he said and ran out the room.

The commander pulled a gun out of this drawer and placed it on his desk.

Next to the carrier Datch was watching troopships getting ready to head down to the surface.

"Won't be long now. I haven't seen any Plantar fighters come from the planet?"

"No, me neither and there is nothing showing on tactical either, only our ships. Anyway, get ready we're up next." Said Clax.

They watched as the troopships dived towards the surface. Then another troopship came a long side the Raven and dropped in next to it.

On the surface the commander looked back to the window and could see the troopships coming down. He sighed and picked up his comms.

"Central, put me on planetary comms."

"Yes, Sir." Came the response.

"This is your commander speaking. We have no option but to surrender. We have lost the planet. Do not resist the IPSF forces. Save yourselves. There is no point dying for nothing. Thank you for your devotion and support. Commander out."

He closed the channel and looked at the gun.

Outside the troopships landed and troopers ran out with their guns ready. Plantar forces placed their guns on the ground in front of them and stood with their hands on their heads. The troops fanned out across the city scanning for Plantar life signs as they went. They were making sure there was no pockets of resistance before signalling to the ships above.

In the Raven the comms burst into life.

"Theta Gamma time to go. Planet is secure."

"Here we go folks!" Said Datch.

The Raven and the troopship moved forwards with the fighters.

"Raven, keep pace with us please and turn on the little black box I was told about."

"Affirmative Sir." Said Datch.

He turned the scattering field on and locked the tracking system on to the ship in front of them so the Raven would follow it towards the planet.

The tactical map showed hundreds of ships all of which were showing as green. Datch carefully matched height and direction as they started to enter the atmosphere. Plasma trails started to appear on the shields as they traversed the upper atmosphere before dropping down into the high clouds and getting ever closer towards the surface. Then the clouds cleared and down below fires could be seen burning in small groups. As they got closer to the ground, they could see the fighters on the ground in flames. Troopships were spread out across the capital with fires burning nearby them. The fighters started to fan out.

"Raven, hold position."

Datch brought the Raven to a stop hovering in mid-air.

Six fighters stopped with them while a troopship dropped down and landed outside the citadel.

"Some one's been busy down here." Said Clax.

"Do you think anyone is left?"

"Yes. That's why the troopers have gone in first."

Datch watched as the troops ran out of the ship and formed a perimeter setting up a number of very tall poles.

"What are the poles for?"

"It's a shield grid. It stops anyone shooting at us." Said Clax.

"Oh. That's good to know." Said Fred.

A few moments later there was a flash of energy from the poles as they energised.

"Raven you are cleared to land."

"Copy that."

Datch brought the Raven down in the centre of the area and landed with the smallest of bumps. He shut down the engines and turned off the scattering field before turning to the rest of them.

"Well folks. Welcome home."

He got up and went to walk out of the cockpit. Clax stopped him.

“Don’t forget that.” He said pointing to the gun.

Datch looked at it.

“Oh… yes.” he said with a sigh.

He picked it up and headed down to the cargo bay followed by Clax, Carina, Fred and the council members. Twenty troopers stood in the bay ready to disembark all dressed in dark grey combat gear with small lighter grey squares in random places on the body armour.

Datch walked over to the door and looked at the lead trooper. The trooper nodded and Datch pressed the door release. The door opened and the ramp extended down to the ground. The troopers ran down the ramp stopping in two lines and facing outwards. The lead trooper looked around before turning to Datch and nodding again.

Datch turned to the rest of them.

“Tinfa, gentlemen please let me escort you to your rightful place.”

They walked down the ramp and started to cross the plaza. They got about half way across when a shot ran out from the building opposite. Everyone hit the ground and ten troopers went running into the building kicking the door down on the way. They went running from room to room checking for Plantar snipers. There were a few shouts as plantar soldiers panicked and hit the ground. The ground floor offices were cleared and they started to move up stairs kicking doors open and checking every room, every cupboard, every alcove unit till they reach the commander’s office and opened the door.

The commander’s body lay slumped across his desk with a pool of blood dripping onto the floor. The side of his head had a large hole in it where the shot had torn through his skull. A large blood splatter covered one wall. On the floor near to where his blooded hand was hanging down was a small pistol which still had smoke coming from its barrel.

"Wow. He didn't want to live." Said a trooper as he looked at the corpse.

He pressed his comms.

"Command, we have found the Plantar commander. He won't be doing any more commanding. Looks like he took his own life."

Back out on the plaza the lead trooper beckon at the others to stand up.

"It's Ok folks. All clear."

"What was the shot?" Asked Tinfa.

"The Plantar Commander just killed himself."

"Holly crap." Said Fred getting up.

"It was his only way out, sir. The Plantars don't look on failure very well. He would have spent the rest of his life in prison no doubt."

"Oh." Said Carina.

She went a bit pale. It was ok when they were helping them to escape. Now she had seen the loss of thousands of lives and the burning fighters still with bodies in them. Now, finally the sound of the shot. She tried to focus on Datch but couldn't seem to do it, then everything turned black and she fainted.

The next thing she knew was Datch calling her name.

"Carina, Carina, are you ok?"

“Err… what happened?” she said coming round.

Her head was swimming. She opened her eyes and there was Datch kneeling over her holding her hand and looking very concerned.

“You collapsed. Are you ok?”

“Yes, I think so.” She said starting to move.

Datch helped her up.

“The medic said you fainted.”

“Yes, it was after that gunshot. My head started to spin and everything went black.”

“How are you now?”

“I’m ok, I think?”

“Look, head back into the Raven and lay down for a few minutes. I’ll come back when the council members are sorted out.”

“Ok. I think I will.”

She headed back to the Raven with one of the troopers helping her up the ramp. Datch ran to catch up with the others. They were just about to go inside the citadel. Fred spotted him running up behind.

“Is Carina, ok?”

“Yes, she just fainted. She’s gone back inside the Raven for a lay down.”

“Good. It’s been very stressful for all of us.”

There was a shout from across the plaza.

They turned around and there were two men waving at them. The lead trooper looked across at them.

“Yes sir, I’ll ask them.” He said into his comms.

He turned to Tinfa.

“Sir. There are two people claiming to be council members over there. Can you identify them.”

Tinfa looked across the plaza.

“Yes, It’s Tages and Glosh. They are council members. You can let them through.”

The trooper spoke into his comms.

The men were let through the security cordon and they came running across the plaza to meet them.

“Oh my god. We’re so glad to see you.” Tages said panting as he arrived at the group.

“Yes, we thought you were dead.” Added Glosh as he caught up.

“They told us you had been killed. They said it happened while you were trying to leave the planet. Then a few minutes a go the guards from outside the house ran away throwing their guns down as they went.”

“The Plantars are not in control anymore.”

“Who are these people?”

“They are the IPSF and so are we now.” Said Tinfa.

“When did that happen?” Asked Glosh.

“In our cargo hold about four weeks ago.” Said Fred grinning.

“Yes. Look let’s go inside just in case a rogue Plantar decides to take a shot at us. I’ll explain in there.” Said Tinfa.

They went through the doors. A number of troopers were inside making sure it was safe. The main assembly room had been ransacked and papers had been thrown all over the floor.

“Wow, what a mess. What were they looking for?”

“The treaty. I hid it in my cellar until these kind folks came to our rescue.”

“They did?”

“Our planet is free again thanks to these three folks and their friends. We owe them a great debt of gratitude. Let me introduce them. This is Datch, Fred and Clax.”

There was a round of hellos and then Tinfa went on to explain what had happened. How they had escaped from the planet and had been taken across the stars to the Senate at Olympus. He then told them about the fleet above them and the surrender of the Plantars along with the death of their commander.

“So, what happens now?” Asked Glosh.

“We need to make a public address. I hope the planetary address system is still working.”

They walked into the room at the rear of the building. It was a small room with a large desk at one end and a small vid station at the other. Datch stood looking at the controls.

“Datch, do you know how to use it?” Asked Tinfa.

“I don’t but I’m sure between me, Clax and Fred, we can work it out.”

“That would be great thanks.”

The council members went around the back of the desk and sat down with Tinfa in the centre.

"Ok, when you're ready Datch."

They stood looking at the panel. The Datch pressed a couple of buttons and the Clax pressed some.

"Hmm... It's not working."

Fred reached over and pressed a green button and a red light came on.

"There you go!"

"Thanks, I think we're live." Said Datch.

Tinfa stood up and Datch changed the camera angle and ended up pointing at Janus.

"Oops, One second."

He moved a lever and pressed some more buttons and the camera moved back to Tinfa. Well, the top of his head anyway. Datch fiddled with another lever and the camera panned down and stopped looking straight at Tinfa.

"Sorry about that, I'm new at this. I think we're good now!"

Tinfa raised an eyebrow then cleared his throat.

"Fellow citizens of Arcaneus, I am addressing you today as a member of a free world. We are once again free to live our own lives. Our friends from the Inter Planetary Space Federation have come to our rescue. Myself along with five other members of the council escaped this world thanks to some very new and very good friends. We were able to agree on a treaty with the Inter Planetary Space Federation and because of this the Plantars have been defeated. We are now free of their slavery and their commander is dead after taking his own life.

Please wait before coming out onto the street to celebrate as we are still securing the city. We will broadcast again shortly to let you know when it is safe to do so. Do not fear the IPSF troopers, they are our very good friends. Can I ask that all council members come to the citadel along with the ministerial staff! Also, can I ask the cleaning staff also attend as the Plantars seem to have been a little untidy. Oh, and a camera operator. Thank you everyone. Please stand by."

Fred pressed the green button and the red light went off.

"Well, I think that went ok." Said Clax.

"Yes, that is apart from the head thing." Added Fred.

"Err... yes, sorry about that. The vids at home just do their own thing. You just tell them what to look at and they do it." Said Datch.

"It's ok Datch, we got the message across. That's what matters." Said Janus.

"Tinfa, I'm going to head back to the Raven if that's ok. I want to make sure Carina is alright."

"Ok Datch you do what you need to do. We need to sort out a few things here anyway. We're very grateful for all you folks have done. Go and look after your wife."

"Thanks, she's not joined to me yet but will be soon if all goes to plan."

With that Datch, Clax and Fred headed back to the Raven.

Outside, the local fire patrol was putting out some of the fires and were being assisted by the troopers. The IPSF systems were very effective at fighting fires as well as starting them and a number of them were already out. The defence shield was being moved further back opening up the plaza. Check points had been set up on the entrances for security purposes. Two more troopships had landed and a group of Plantar soldiers were being marched into the back of one of them ready for transport off the planet. The IPSF troops were busy setting up a command centre in the ex-Planter offices and a large amount of equipment was being ferried into the building. It was next door to the citadel and the troopers had already placed two arial cannons outside it.

Datch watched as they brought out a black bag which was sagging in the middle. He realised with horror that it was the body of the Plantar commander. They took the body bag over to the troopship and placed it respectfully in the back.

The three of them arrived at the back of the Raven. Two troopers were standing guard at the bottom of the ramp and stood to attention as they walked up. Datch saluted back before going inside.

"Guys, you go get a beer, I'll check on Carina."

"Ok." Said Fred.

Clax and Fred headed to the rec room to get a drink while Datch walked down the corridor to his and Carina's room.

When he arrived, she was laying on the bed and sat up as he walked in.

"Hi babes, how you doing?" he said as he walked over to her and sat on the end of the bed looking very concerned.

"I'm ok now. I think it just got to be too much for me."

"I was worried about you."

"It's ok. I feel better now. I just needed to lay down. What's going on out there?"

"It's calming down now. The plaza is being cleared and the Plantar forces are being taken to the battleships above ready for transport back to their home world. Other than that, it's quiet."

"Can we go outside?"

"Yes, if you feel up to it?"

"I think so."

She got up and they headed to the cargo bay. They stood at the top of the ramp looking around. Datch turned her.

"You sure you're ok babes?"

"Yes. I'm ok."

"Let's take it easy and if you start to feel faint again, tell me, ok?"

"Ok."

They walked down the ramp stopping at the bottom in between the troopers.

There were only a couple of fires still burning and they were being delt with. The plaza was now clear except for the troopships and the Raven. The shield barrier was now along the very edge of the plaza and the checkpoints now had makeshift huts along with energy barriers that would de-energise to let people through. The troopers were now fanning out across the city making sure the streets were safe and free of Plantar soldiers. There was a steady stream of Plantar soldiers coming through the gate and being loaded on to the troopships for transport. All of them looked very dejected.

They watched as a troopship lifted off and headed into the sky on its way to the battleships. At the same time two more troopships came down to land in the plaza. The first one opened its rear door and a ramp dropped to the ground. Troopers came running out and lined up outside the IPSF command centre ready for orders. Then small groups of them headed off into the city. The second ship touched down and its rear door opened. This time armoured vehicles rolled out on to the plaza before heading off down one of the side streets.

“Wow. They are very busy. Do you think there is any more fighting going on?”

“I don’t know, but apparently the commander ordered his soldiers to surrender just before he shot himself.”

“That’s terrible. Why didn’t he surrender too?”

“The trooper said they would have thrown him in prison when he got home. So, I suppose he didn’t have much choice really.”

“That’s horrible.”

“The Plantars are apparently. If you’re feeling ok, shall we walk over to the citadel?”

“Yes. I’m feeling a lot better now.”

They started to walk over to the citadel when a shout came from the second ship. Datch turned round.

Running out of the back of it was Dapo with Tish in tow and behind them Datch spotted the rest of The Pack walking down the ramp followed by the families of the council members.

Tish and Dapo came over to them and stood panting trying to get their breaths back.

“Are you ok? We heard something happened to Carina?” Asked Tish when she could talk.

“Yes, we’re good, I just fainted, that’s all.”

“We heard they destroyed two battleships. We didn’t see any wreckage though.”

“There wasn’t any. They weren’t just destroyed they were vaporised.” Said Datch.

“What? Totally?” Asked Tish.

“Yes. Nothing was left but an expanding cloud of dust.”

“Can we change the subject please?” Said Carina.

“Sure babes.” Said Datch and looked at the others.

“Yes. no probs,” said Tish realising that it was upsetting her.

Just then the others caught up to them.

“Hi dudes.” Said Datch as they walked up.

There was a round of greetings and Tish telling everyone to not mention the battle till later as Carina was feeling a bit ill.

“Let’s head over to the citadel.” Said Datch pointing to it.

They started chatting and slowly walked over to the citadel. The families of the council members with a number of troopers caught them up on the way.

They arrived at the doors and went in.

Inside, the place was starting to look a little better. Most of the papers had been picked up and the chairs and tables had been put back in their places. Tinfa was directing things and there was a small army of people putting the place back together.

A number of troopers were standing guard at the door and saluted as they walked past. Datch saluted back. He was hoping he could get out of his uniform soon. This was partly because he was having to salute everyone but mostly because it was starting to itch in places it wasn’t polite to scratch in public.

They set about helping the council get the place straight and after an hour the place was looking good.

They were just sitting down when the IPSF fleet commander came in and walked over to Tinfa.

"I've just come to tell you that we have finished removing the Plantar forces from the planet. There are no more Plantar life signs on your planet. We will be escorting the battleships home in a short while. One destroyer will remain in orbit with five of the other ships. There is a number of supply ships in bound as well and should arrive in a few hours. The spaceport will also be operational again within six hours. The planet is yours again sir. If you require anything else, please don't hesitate to ask the commander in the IPSF offices."

"Thank you, Sir. On behalf of myself and my people, thank you. Can you also please thank your crews for us. We owe you and your fleet a very large debt of gratitude. We are going to try and organise a party tomorrow to celebrate. Tell the taskforce they are all very welcome to join us."

"Your welcome sir. I shall pass it on to the captains and commanders."

He saluted and headed out the door.

"They do things very quickly don't they?" Said Peebop.

"Yes. It's a very efficient organisation." Said Fred.

"I think it's time to do another broadcast." Said Tinfa

Datch went to get up.

"Err… no disrespect Datch, but I think we'll use a trained camera man this time."

"Ok. no probs dude." He sat back in the chair.

Tinfa and the other council members headed into the back room again, this time with a small man wearing glasses who looked like he knew what he was doing.

"Err. Trained camera man?" Asked Jep turning to look at Datch.

"Yes. Let's not go there." Said Clax.

"Yes, let's not." Added Datch who had gone a little red.

"Let's just hope no one recorded it." Added Fred.

Jep made a mental note to ask about it later after everyone had downed a few drinks. He had decided to try and write a book about The Pack's adventures. He figured it must be worth a few beers if nothing else.

Gilla came over to them.

"We're going to head home and check everything is ok. If you want you could come with us and I'll show you round some of the city afterwards."

"You don't happen to know any good hotels, do you?"

"Yes, there's a couple on route."

"If you find one you like tell them the council are paying the bill." Said one of the council aids who was standing nearby.

"Great. Thank you." Said Fred.

"You're welcome, sir. We would still be slaves if it wasn't for you."

The Pack got up and followed Gilla and her mum to the door. Four troopers also followed them.

Datch turned to the others.

"I'm going to get changed on the way folks. It will only take a couple of minutes."

"Are you allowed to?" Asked Gilla.

"Yes, I'm not actually part of IPSF. I sort of got given the rank of acting ensign thing on a trip. And to be honest, my arms starting to ache from all the saluting and I have an itch in a place I don't want to mention."

“Sounds like a plan dude.” Said Clax.

One of the troopers raised an eyebrow.

They headed across the plaza and Datch went running up the ramp into the Raven while the others waited outside looking around. The fires were all out now and the wreckage was being removed with military precision. The plaza was starting to look like any other city plaza now apart from the Raven and Two Troopship sitting on it. There were a number of statues on large stone plinths and an ornamental fountain in front of the citadel which was now working again. They watched as troopers started removing the shield. Now the Plantars were gone there was no need for it. The check points were also being moved to outside of the IPSF headquarters.

They were just watching a group of troopers moving parts of the shield into the back of one of the ships when Datch came trotting down the ramp. He was now looking normal.

The troopers at the bottom of the ramp looked at him.

“The uniform was only temporary.” He said and smiled.

They saluted.

“Err. Could you please not… Oh, never mind.” He saluted back.

They headed across the plaza. People were starting to come out into the streets. They all had big smiles on their faces and some were carrying baskets with food and drink in them.

Someone spotted Gilla and started cheering. This then caused everyone else to start cheering. People then started coming over to them.

Gilla pointed out that it was The Pack that rescued the council and brought about their freedom in an attempt to stop herself from being mobbed. With that the crowd picked The Pack up along with her and her mum and started carrying them through the streets.

"Err. What do we do?" Shouted Hagger.

"Go with the flow." Shouted Tank looking down to make sure the people underneath him were not about to collapse.

A number of people had tried to pick up Timbo but after several failed attempts, gave up and just went with patting him instead. They were carried through the streets that is apart from Timbo who just followed along with the crowd.

The crowd was cheering as they went from street to street and more and more people flooded out of their homes to join the crowd, they had no idea where they were going and Gilla shouted.

"We need to get to Dragma Street!"

The crowd slowed down while the instructions filtered down to the front and then it took a right turn down past a park and a large statue.

"Gilla, do you think this is safe?"

"Yes, I'm sure, they're just really grateful and happy, that's all. This is Dallamore park by the way." Said Gilla pointing to a green area.

"Oh good, nice park by the way. I wonder if we'll get a beer out of this?" Asked Peebop.

"Don't know but I'll need a bathroom soon." Said Carina.

The crowd started to slowdown and a man shout at Gilla,

"Which house?"

"The light blue one over there."

The crowd move over to it.

"Looks like our stop."

"What do we do?" Said Fred.

"Tell them where to go."

She was then lost in the crowd with her mum as they got taken to their home.

"But we don't know the city." Said Fred.

Then Clax had an idea,

"Anyone know a really great hotel?" He shouted.

There was a cheer from the crowd and they were carried off down the street. Then back around the park and up a street on the opposite side.

"Err. Do you think we're going to a hotel?" Shouted Carina.

"Don't know? But I think I'm going to need a beer after this!" Shouted Peebop.

The crowd turned and headed up another street. In front of them was a grand hotel with large vehicle parking area in front of it. The entrance had a large ornate front made of wooden carvings surrounding a set of four large doors. It had its name in gold letters above the doors. 'The Golden Crowns'. The crowd stopped at the doors and a number of people went running inside. The Pack were lowered to the ground.

"Thanks all!" Shouted Tank.

There was a huge roar from the crowd and they were taken into the hotel by about thirty people.

A man in a very posh suit came running over looking a bit flustered.

“Please come, please come.” he said beckoning at them to follow him.

They followed him across the hotel foyer.

“Err...” Said Datch trying to make sure everyone one was there, “We just want some rooms?”

“Certainly sir. We have six large suites on the first floor, would they be, ok?”

“Yes, do they have showers and on-suites?”

“Certainly sir. Please come this way.”

“Thanks. Your government is paying for this by the way. They told us to tell you to send the bill to them.” Said Datch.

“No Problem, sir. I will contact them directly.”

“I would wait a couple of hours if I was you. They’re still sorting things out at the citadel.”

“Wise idea sir. I’ll wait till later.”

The crowd stood outside cheering and laughing. They had also found some tables from somewhere and were setting out food and bottles of wine. The Pack headed into the bar and went to sit at the very back.

They were relieved to get away from the crowd. Being hero is ok but it can be a bit intense.

“Would you like any drinks?” asked the man.

“Err, yes please. A round of beers if you have it.” Said Tank.

A round of drinks were brought out and the staff retreated to the bar.

They all picked up the glasses and took a gulp.

“Ahh… That’s better.” Said Clax taking a really big gulp and half emptying the glass.

“You can say that again.” Said Peebop.

“Ahh… That’s better.” Said Hagger.

Everyone turned to look at him.

“Really?” Said Carina.

“Err what… it is.”

Everyone burst out laughing. The waiter came over bringing two bowls of complimentary food which turned out to be assorted crisps.

“Is there anything else I can get you?” He asked.

“Yes, I don’t suppose you have food menus. I’m sort of thinking steak?” Said Datch.

“I will fetch them for you sir and yes we do have steak.”

They ordered the food and then realised they had a small problem.

“How are we going to get our stuff?” Said Carina.

“That’s a very good point. It’s a long way back to the plaza and being carried is cool but it’s not very comfortable.” Added Tish.

“I had to walk!” Said Timbo.

Datch looked across the bar. The bar was filling up with people from outside and the street seemed to be getting more packed with people as word got around.

“Maybe we could call for help?” Said Dapo.

“We would need an army to get through that lot.” Added Clax.

“We have Timbo.” Said Datch.

“I’m not sure Datch. There is a lot of them and I wouldn’t want to hurt anyone.” He said staring at the door.

“Yes, that would not look good. ‘City riot started by invading rock band’. Defiantly not good!” Added Rosey.

“I don’t think even Timbo could cope with that lot.” Said Tank.

“So, how do we get to the Raven?” Asked Carina.

They sat looking at their beers.

“What if we asked them for a taxi?” Said Rosey

“That might work.” Said Hagger.

“Yeh, and if they pick that up, at least we’ll be comfy inside.” Said Tank.

“I’m not sure they would pick that up.” Said Clax.

“Hmm… if they did, a lot of people could get hurt doing it.” Added Fred.

At that point a number of waiters came out of a door next to the bar carrying a large number of steak dinners along with three plates of gammon and chips.

“Please enjoy the food. Do you require anything else?”

“Err… yes, can we have another round of drinks please?” asked Fred.

They had got about half way though their food when Datch’s Vid comm beeped he looked down at it.

“It’s Don.” he said.

He picked it up and answered it.

"Hi Don. How's it going?"

"Hi Datch, we've been trying to find you. Where are you?"

"We're sort of stuck in a hotel bar?"

"Why did I think a bar would be involved. What do you mean stuck?"

"We were carried here by a very excited crowd who are now standing outside having a party and waiting for us to put our heads out the door at which point they all cheer a lot."

"So, what are you doing now?"

"Err, having a steak dinner."

"Ok, What's the name of the bar?"

"It's the Golden Crowns Hotel and we're hiding in the bar. Why did you want us?"

"The fighter group you came down with wanted to go for a drink with you and also we need you to move the Raven to the spaceport soon."

"Oh. Well, get them to come here, we need rescuing."

"I never thought I would ever hear you say that you needed rescuing from a bar."

"Well, we need to get our stuff from the Raven if nothing else."

"OK Datch, we'll come to you. Tell the staff there are about forty people coming and to start pouring the beers."

"Thanks Don."

With that the channel closed.

“What’s going on?” Asked Fred.

“We have an army coming to rescue us. Oh, and they want some beers as well.” Said Datch grinning.

“Waiter!”

The head waiter came running over.

“Yes sir, can I help you?”

“Err... How many staff do you have on?”

“About four behind the bar sir. Why?”

“In a few minutes there are going to be about forty to fifty people coming through that door all of which will want a beer or two and maybe food as well.”

The head waiter looked across at the bar area. There was already six or more people from outside drinking at it.

“Oh... Thank you sir for the information. Please excuse me. I need to make some calls.”

“No problem. but can we have another round of drinks please before the bar gets over run.”

“Certainly sir.”

The head waiter went running back to the bar and started shouting at people before going into the back.

“I think you just put him into a blind panic.” Said Fred.

“Just a lot.” Added Tank.

“Well, it has solved the problem with our stuff.” Said Carina.

“I hope we get the beers before they turn up?” Said Peebop.

"Well, if Don was on the Carpaycus then it's at least twenty minutes to get down here." Said Fred.

"I'm not sure he was. He didn't look like he was on board the ship."

"They do have to get through them first." Said Tank looking at the crowd.

"Good point."

A number of staff came running out the back and started moving tables about to make more space. The head waiter came back out and started helping behind the bar before coming back over with more drinks.

They were just starting their next round of drinks when there was a roar of engines outside and people started to scatter. Then a shadow appeared in the street and a wind blew through the doors as a troopship touched down in the street outside the front of the hotel. People stood looking at the ship as the doors opened at the back. A group of men came walking out all with big smiles on their faces and waved at everyone. At the front was a captain, he turned and looked at the hotel.

"This is the place." He shouted.

He headed for the doors with the rest of the men following along behind. Then someone realised they were the IPSF crews and came running over and shook his hand. What happened next was a tidal wave of people descended on them shaking their hands and patting their backs. It took about five minutes before Don manged to get into the hotel. He came walking over to The Pack.

"Hi folks. How you doing?" he said.

"We're good. I take it you have been introduced to the crowd?" Said Fred.

"Yes, they are a little lively out there, aren't they? I see why you're a bit stuck."

"On the bright side, the steaks are nice here." Said Clax.

"Yes, and the beer is cold too." Added Datch.

He waved at the waiter and he came walking over. Just at that point, four other men managed to get through the doors and came walking over. Datch recognised the lead man as the fighter wing commander. He went to salute but the man held out his hand. Don turned to him and Datch.

"I'm sure you know each other but this is wing commander Tiker. Commander, this is Datch."

They shook hands and Tiker then introduced him to the other men with him and Datch introduced The Pack. Then as others slowly made it inside, they were introduced as well. Some of them knew The Pack from vids and news clips and were pleased to meet them in person. This also ended up with a number of pictures being taken with them along with a few autographs. The bar was soon swamped with people and after an hour Datch finally made it back to Don.

"It may be a while before we can get back to the Raven." Said Datch.

"Yes, I'll call in a drop ship when we're ready to go, they can drop you off at the ship before taking us back to orbit."

"We've got a suite of rooms here so I'm hoping it's a bit quieter outside later."

"The spaceport is only about ten minutes taxi ride back to here. So, you should be ok getting back."

There was another roar of engines from outside and a shuttle landed in parking area outside the doors. Once again people ran for cover as it touched down. The door opened and three security officers came down followed by a number of other folks.

"Looks like words getting around about our little gathering." Said Tank.

"Why?" Asked Datch taking a sip of beer.

"Datch!!" A voice shouted across the room.

Datch nearly spat all his beer out. He looked around and there was Widfab waving his arms in the air.

"Hi Widfab." He said wiping the beer off the table.

Widfab came striding over.

"We heard you were having a party and decided to come and help drink the beer."

"Well, it's sort of a drinking session as we don't have any music. Oh, and if you're hungry the steak is pretty good."

"We Welly folks always come prepared."

He turned and yelled across the room.

"Get the gear!"

A number of people went running out to the shuttle.

Datch sighed and waved at the head waiter to come over. He came running across looking very flustered.

"Err, I think we have a music system coming in. Is it ok?"

The man looked around at the crowded room and the speed at which credits were going behind the bar and started to grin.

"We're making a lot of credits. You do what you like!"

He retreated back to the bar.

Datch tapped the wing commander on his shoulder and he turned around.

“Any chance a few of your men could clear an area over there. We’ve got entertainment coming in.”

“Sure, no problem, that sounds good.”

He shouted over the room at a group of men standing in a semi-circular bay. They looked at where he was pointing and started to clear an area near the windows. Also, a small group of them went to help bring the gear in.

“So, what we got?” Asked Datch.

“Karaoke of course and also a portable kabab unit in case we get hungry later.” Said Widfab.

“Wow, you do come prepared don’t you.” Said the Wing commander.

“The Welly people do like a good party.” Said Don.

“You were such a quiet race until what was it called?”

“The end of darkness.” Said Widfab.

“I would love to meet the people who ended it.” The wing commander added.

Don and Widfab both turned and looked at Datch.

Datch felt a little uncomfortable and sighed. He knew where this was going.

“You can.” Said Don.

It then dawned on the wing commander that they were both looking at Datch.

“You, did it?”

"Err… well, not on my own. The rest of The Pack was there too, we sort of did it together."

"Yes, but why?"

"We thought the gem was some sort of lost treasure until we realised what it meant to the people of Welly Four. Well, you know the rest."

"Bloody hell, do you make a habit of saving planets? No, never mind, don't answer that. Hey chaps." He shouted across the bar, "These folks are the saviours of Welly Four as well!"

This started another round of people coming and shaking their hands and some more pictures this time with Widfab in the shot as well. It didn't take long to get the karaoke set up and then The Pack were talked into doing one of their songs on stage.

"Anyone got their gems on?" Asked Jep.

"Err… unfortunately, yes." Said Carina.

"Yep." Said Fred, Dapo, Trish, Rosey and Tank.

"Oh. Me to." Said Datch.

"Well, if the party wasn't happening enough to start with, it's going to be rocking now." Said Clax.

The Pack took to the stage, well the area that had been cleared in the bay windows which they were calling the stage. They did Supernova and as the song blasted out across the room, more and more people started to sparkle. Afterwards, over half the bar was sparkling and The Pack were glowing quiet brightly. Then just to make sure everyone was really happy. They did another three songs before heading back to the table where Don was sitting with their beers.

The party was now in full swing and some of the locals were now coming inside to join in and also to see the aliens who were now glowing. The street party also seemed to be in full swing outside with a number of street entertainers that had turned up from somewhere and were joining in and also a catering truck had showed up and started selling burgers. There was now a steady stream of people fetching drinks from the hotel's bars. The manager had opened up the front of house bar and that was also now fully staffed. More barrels of beer arrived to cater for the increase in demand and some of the fighter pilots went to help get the delivery inside.

The emergency kabab machine was brought in and started up. It upset the hotel chef to start with who came out and started shouting, however, he calmed down after being given one to try. Widfab went and explained how to make them and about its operation and then there was a bit of negotiation. As a result of which, Widfab entered into the first inter stellar trade contract with Arcaneus for said machine and the patent to make them on the planet. Also, the chef went off to start cooking burgers that also now seemed to be in very high demand.

An hour later Tinfa turned up with his wife and Gilla. He also had a number of security officers with him. After ten minutes of fighting their way through the crowd they finally made it inside.

"Wow, it's busy in here." He said walking up to Datch.

"Hi Tinfa, hi Catha, hi Gilla." he said.

"Quite a party you've got going. Did you know your glowing by the way?"

"Yes, we are glowing a bit. We sort of got stuck here and the party just sort of happened."

"Gilla said you got carried away by a crowd and then I heard a party was taking place in the street outside a hotel and guessed you were here. We thought we better come and check if you were ok."

"Yes, we're good but can I leave the Raven in the plaza till tomorrow as I don't seem to be able to get to it also, I've had a couple of beers and wouldn't want to knock the top off a building while I was trying to move it."

"No problem as long as you move it by mid-morning. We need the plaza so we can start setting up for our freedom party. We have decided to give you and The Pack bravery awards and the freedom of the planet for rescuing us and helping save our world."

"Wow, we're very honored. Thank you."

"You're all very welcome. So, what's the food?"

"We have kababs and burgers." Said a voice behind him.

He turned to the person behind him.

"Oh. Minister Prime, sorry, I didn't see you there."

"It's just Widfab. This is a proper party dude."

"Ok Widfab, but how did you find your way here?"

"I brought our shuttle down after I found out that Datch was having a party. You just missed the Music Warriors on stage. They were really cool dude."

"Oh, I wish we had gotten here earlier."

"I'm sure they will be back up on stage in a bit." Said Widfab looking at Datch.

"Yes, we'll do a couple more songs but we need our stuff at some point."

Then Datch had an idea.

"Widfab, is there any chance I can borrow the shuttle to take us to get our things from the Raven?"

"Sure, just tell the pilot I said it was Ok and he'll take you."

"Cool, I'll go and find the others. Thanks dude."

"Party on!"

Datch went and found the rest of The Pack and it was decided that they didn't all need to go. Five minutes later Datch, Dapo, Clax and Tank headed outside to lots of cheering, handshakes, hugs and people trying to help them into the air again. Finally, after a minute or so they managed to get to the shuttle in one piece. Datch turned in the shuttles doorway to face the crowd and shouted as loud as he could.

"We'll be back in a few minutes as we just need to get some of our stuff. We'll be doing a couple more songs then as well. Please stand clear of the shuttle! I don't want anyone to get hurt!"

The shuttle fired up its engines and everyone took a few steps backwards which was fine apart for those standing in front of the ornamental pond in the centre of the parking area. They suddenly found out much to their horror that they were now standing in half a metre of water.

The shuttle took off heading the short distance to the plaza. It was only a few streets away and after a minute, it came in for a landing at the back of the Raven.

The four of them walked out into the evening air. It was a lot quieter here now but there was still a lot of troopers busy moving equipment into the new IPSF offices. They headed inside the Raven to collect their bags. They also collected a bottle of Old Man's Boots for Hagger and Rosey as they said the local spirits needed a little work. After getting their things they stood outside cooling down for a couple of minutes before heading back onboard the shuttle.

The two-minute flight took five because they had to wait for everyone to get out the way in the carpark so the pilot could land without squashing anyone. Finally, they touched down and opened the door. The crowd realised who they were and started cheering again.

"Err… we need to take our stuff in there!" Shouted Datch pointing at the hotel.

A number of the crowd came forward to help with the bags and they were able to get back inside after a lot of patting and handshaking again.

"Wow, that was hard work." Said Tank.

"Yea, let's get the bags into our rooms. Don't forget the hangover pills. I think we're going to need them." Said Clax.

Datch shouted to the rest of The Pack to come over and they all went to put their bags in their rooms. Five minutes later they came back down and the party was continuing with a trio of troopers currently on the karaoke singing 'come on baby light my fire', they weren't half bad either.

Half an hour later it was The Pack's turn again and they headed back onto the stage area and this time they all had their gems on. They started singing and the bar lit up with sparkles. Even the bar staff had started to sparkle.

The Pack ended up doing another five songs before finally sitting down to eat a kabab each. The whole bar was full of people sparkling with little green flashes of light that circled their heads. This now also included quite a few people outside the hotel as well.

The Pack started to mingle and they partied on until the early hours. Tinfa told the hotel to send The Packs bill to the council. The hotel manager spent most of the night walking around with a big grin on his face and sparkles around his head. Apparently the Plantars had not been good for business but the IPSF on the other hand were very good indeed. The hotel was rammed until well after midnight and the street party outside was about the same. Finally, people started to head off to bed and so did The Pack, it had been a very long day.

# Freedom

Next morning when Datch woke up he found the bed was empty and singing could be heard coming from the bathroom. He got up and went to the window. It looked out across the city. It wasn't a big city as cities went, but the buildings were made of a pink sandy coloured stone and had nice stone carvings on their roof lines. The sun was shining and the birds were tweeting. It could have been a city back home but for the fact the sky had a light blue tint not a green one. He stretched his arms out and yawned. The shower stopped and so did the singing. Carina came walking out of the bathroom with a towel round her.

"Morning." she said.

"Morning babes."

Datch headed off to have his shower. She got dressed and sorted out their bags. After a few minutes Datch came back out and started to get dressed.

"So, what's the plan?" Asked Carina.

"Well, I need to move the Raven to the spaceport and also ask Tinfa what time he wants us. He did tell me last night but I can't remember what he said."

"Was that before or after the whole group dancing thing?"

"Err... After I think. It's a bit fuzzy."

"It was a good night, wasn't it?"

"Yes. What was that stuff Hagger and Rosey were drinking after the Old Man's Boots ran out?"

"I don't know, but it smelled like you could run the bikes on it."

“I hope they remembered the hangover pills.”

“Yes, they did, I spotted Rosey getting them out just before we had ours.”

“Cool, you ready for breakfast?”

“Sure. I wonder what they do?”

They headed out the door and down to the restaurant. It was looking a lot better now. The kabab machine had disappeared and the tables had been straightened up also the carpet had been cleaned. Datch seemed to remember the cleaners turning up as they were going to bed.

They found a table, sat down and started looking at the menu. After a couple of minutes, a waiter came over.

“Good morning, Sir and Mam. What can I get for you?”

“Good morning. We would like two fried breakfasts please.”

“Certainly, would you like coffee, tea or juice with that?”

“Err… What sort of tea?” Asked Carina.

“Our house tea is an aromatic blend of three types of shrubs. We also have a number of different varieties on offer including black tea, green tea, white tea, oolong tea and purple tea.”

“Hmm… I’m going to try the black tea but can I have milk with it?”

“Certainly, I’ll bring a jug over and you, Sir?”

“I think I’ll stick with coffee.”

“We have rich roast, dark roast and golden, all of which are freshly ground, Sir?”

“Err… I’ll have the golden one please.”

"Thank you, sir. Do you require anything else?"

"Yes, can we also have some fruit juice to go with the food please? Just surprise us with the type."

"Yes sir, is that all?"

"Yes, thank you."

The waiter headed back into the kitchen.

They were just finishing off their food when Tank and Clax came walking in. After saying good morning, Carina went to sit with them while Datch headed off to move the Raven. It was only a short flight and didn't need a co-pilot.

He went over to the reception and asked if they could sort out some local currency for the taxi. Then after getting directions from the doorman, Datch headed off up the street towards the plaza. It was a nice walk in the fresh air and the sun was warm. The city now had a relaxed feel about it and people were going about their normal business. A small group waved at him as he walked past a small café, he waved back and they smiled.

The streets were clean and tidy with a number of small shops selling freshly made bread and cakes. He called in at one and got a selection to put in stasis onboard the Raven. That way, they could have fresh food on the way between gigs. He turned up another street which had a lot more traffic on it. In the distance he could see the plaza. It took another couple of minutes for him to reach the top of the street. He walked onto the plaza and was greeted by a hive of activity with people carrying things backwards and forwards, building this and erecting that.

In front of the citadel a large staged area was being constructed and to the side of that seating had been laid out ready for a large band. In front of the stage more seating was being laid out in rows and judging by the numbers they were expecting a large crowd. Also, around the edge of the plaza a number of catering stalls were setting up shop selling various foods and drinks along with some fairground rides.

He spotted Tinfa directing a group of workmen putting up the PA system and walked over to him.

“Good morning, Tinfa.”

“Morning Datch, how are you?”

“I’m good thanks, you?”

“Yes, I’m good. Have you come to move the Raven?”

“Yes, Err. Sorry to bother you, I can see you’re very busy but I can’t remember what time you wanted us here?”

“The event starts at four pm which I think is about thirteen fifty ish ship time. So, get here say half an hour before as we are having a small reception before the main event.”

“Ok, thanks, I’ll see you later.”

With that he headed over to the Raven and after telling everyone nearby to keep clear, he went inside and headed to the cockpit. It took him a couple of minutes to run through the pre-flight checks and then he brought all the systems online and put his headset on.

“Arcaneus Control, this is the Raven requesting clearance to fly from the citadel to the spaceport.”

There was a short pause and then the comms burst into life.

“Good morning, Raven. Flight path is clear for twelve minutes. You are cleared to navigate.”

“Thanks, Arcaneus control.”

Datch increased the power to the thrusters and the Raven rose slowly into the air. Datch looked out over the city. The carnage of the day before had been cleared away and most of the evidence of the Plantars had been removed only the odd vehicle remained which appeared to now being used by the locals for moving things about.

Datch levelled the Raven out at two hundred metres. He figured that way he wouldn't take any roofs off. It was also a very leisurely flight. The Raven flew over a large park with children playing on swings and roundabouts. People were sitting on benches and a vendor was selling refreshments near a small pond. A number of the children looked up as he flew over and waved.

Datch felt good. Because of them this place was free again and it gave him a nice warm feeling inside. He spotted the spaceport up ahead and opened the comms.

"Arcaneus control this is Raven. On approach to the spaceport now. Where do you want me to park?"

"Raven, this is Arcaneus control. Land on marker three seven. Please note we are currently unable to offer any services."

"No problem control, all systems are good. On final approach."

Datch spotted the landing pad. Well, it was a landing spot which had a big three and seven painted in a very large circle all of which had been done in very bright colours. He brought the Raven in for a soft landing and shut down the thrusters.

"Control, Raven has landed. Where do I exit and can I get a taxi from somewhere?"

"Thanks Raven. You can exit to the city through the gate just too your right. If you follow the road outside up to the main buildings, there are some taxis outside."

"Thanks control."

"You're welcome, have a great day, control out."

He got up and headed down to the storage room to place the cakes in the stasis unit before heading outside and back into the sunshine.

He looked across the landing area. All the landing pads appeared to be just circles painted in various places across a large concrete area. That was apart from a small passenger terminal that had proper docking ports. There were a few ships around the landing pads which were being unloaded. Most of them were transport ships bringing supplies and IPSF personnel from the ships in orbit.

He spotted the exit gate and headed over to it. There wasn't anyone there so after waiting a minute to see if anyone came, he pushed it and found it was open. He walked through closing it behind him and headed off up the road in search of a taxi rank.

The taxi rank was at the top of road in front of the main terminal building. Datch stood looking at the taxis. They all had wheels and no wings or thrusters that he could see. Datch walked up to the one at the front. Its driver was sitting on the front of it chatting to another driver.

"Hello, I'm after a taxi to take me to the Golden Crowns hotel?"

"No problem, Sir. Please, get in." Said the driver standing up.

The driver walked around to the other side of the vehicle and got in. Datch looked for a door handle and pulled it. The door opened and he got into the seat next to the driver. The vehicle had a number of knobs and a steering wheel along with a fury ball hanging down from a mirror in the middle of the windscreen. Datch watched as the driver turned something on his side and there was the noise of an engine starting up. The driver pressed a button on a display panel and a display lit up showing the cost. The vehicle started to move forwards and Datch waited for it to take off. It didn't, it just carried on down the road.

"First time on this planet?" Asked the driver.

"Yes, we arrived yesterday."

"I bet a brave lad like you was part of the invasion?"

"Yes, sort of. We were, err, a support ship."

"I bet. They said it was a big fleet that came to save us."

"Yes, it was quite big."

The small talk carried on then ten minutes later the taxi pulled into the car park of the hotel. Datch looked at the local currency the hotel had sorted out for him earlier and gave the taxi driver some.

"It's not that much. Look, this one's a five, that's a ten and these are ones. So, I want one five and three one's"

"Thanks." Said Datch and gave him a ten. "Keep the change." He added.

"Thank you, sir, I like the IPSF already." He said grinning.

Datch got out and headed inside. He found the others in the bar with Gilla, Widfab and his aid who had come with him.

"Hi folks." Said Datch walking up.

"Hi Datch. How was the flight?" Asked Clax.

"Ok, it was only a five-minute trip but the scenery was very nice. The spaceport was a bit odd though."

"Why?"

"When I got there, they told me where the taxi rank was and to let myself out a side gate."

"What about security?"

"Must have been on coffee break. Then the taxi had wheels and couldn't fly."

"Oh. Very odd."

"I think they are still trying to sort things out at the spaceport. I heard my dad on a call earlier. It sounds like the Plantars left it in a right mess." Said Gilla.

"Yes, my aid was talking to the IPSF commander and they said it was going to take months to get the planet back on its feet properly." Said Widfab.

"Hi Widfab, I didn't think I'd see you till later."

"Hi Datch, well, the parties always happen around you, so we thought it would be nice to hang out with you folks if that's ok?"

"Sure, no problem, dude." Said Datch.

"Did you remember to ask Tinfa when we're meant to be there?" asked Fred.

"Yes, err, the event starts at thirteen fifty ship time or four in the afternoon local. He wants us there half an hour before."

"Gilla what's the time now?"

She looked at her watch.

"About twelve thirty so you've got about three hours."

"Cool," Said Tank, "Waiter?"

They had another round of drinks before heading outside. Gilla had offered to take them to some of the sights before going to the event and this time without the crowds. The city was very beautiful and other than the mess that the Plantars had left behind the streets were very clean. Widfab was very interested in the buildings as he said he liked ornate stone work. They stopped for a drink outside a coffee shop and had some freshly made cakes. The three hours flew by and it wasn't long before they had to head to the party.

They arrived at the plaza with time to spare. There was a number of security offices standing at the entrance and asked who they were before scanning their implants. Then they were told to go to the citadel where the seating arrangements would be explained.

They headed off across the plaza. The workers had been busy. The stage area had seating across the back of it and a podium at the front. It was decorated in multi coloured flags and bunting. There was a brass band setting up next to it and a number of food stalls as well as four outdoor bars on the opposite side. In the centre of the plaza, a small fun fair was finishing setting up and all around the edge, coloured lights had been erected. Even the new IPSF offices had coloured bunting on the front and the IPSF flag was flying outside on a pole next to the Arcaneus flag.

They arrived at the citadel and went inside. The place was very busy with large number of staff and also some of the local security officers. It looked like they had been through the mill a bit with some having visible injures. A member of staff came over to greet them.

"Hello ladies and gentlemen. Please follow me to the reception room." he said.

They followed him over to a large room at the side.

"We have drinks and light refreshments available. Please help yourselves to the food. The events will be starting in about thirty minutes. When you go outside just head up the stairs and a steward will show you to your seats."

They entered the room and were confronted with a lot of people in very posh clothes. The council members were all there apart from Tinfa and Janus. There were a number of the planet's dignitaries and the IPSF commander and senior officers from the IPSF offices. Also, a number of captains from the ships in orbit including Don. The Pack wandered over to him getting a beer on route.

"Hi Don." Said Datch walking up.

"Hello folks. I see you've gone for the casual look."

"Well, my suite is at the cleaners. Anyway, it's a party."

Don laughed and then spotted Widfab behind them. He was also wearing a casual short sleeved shirt and knee length shorts.

"I see Welly Four is here as well. Good afternoon Minister Prime."

"Of course, we wouldn't want to miss a party. You'll have to excuse me though. I need to talk to the leader of the council if I can find him?"

"I know where he'll be Widfab, follow me." Said Gilla and led him away.

Don was starting to think he maybe overdressed when another officer came over and saluted. Don saluted him back.

"Ah commander Tracks let me introduce you to The Pack."

"Folks this is Commander Tracks, he is the commander who will be in charge of the planets security until they can sort out their own."

"Pleased to meet you." He said and was then introduced to each of them in turn.

Then a few minutes later a bell rang and a tall man next to the door said in a very loud voice.

"Ladies and gentlemen, the presentation will be starting shortly. Please can you head outside to the seating area. Stewards will be on hand to guide you to your seats."

They started to file out. Don went over to the other captains and commanders and headed out the door.

"Looks like it's time to move folks." Said Fred.

They joined the line and filed out through the door.

Outside the seating in front of the stage was full and people were standing behind it filling up the plaza. A lot of the population had come to join the party and there were two vid crews on the top of trucks to broadcast the spectacle across the planet. There was also a news crew from the galactic press and three small vid bots were hovering in front of the stage. The food trucks were doing a roaring trade and the outdoor bars looked packed.

They headed up the stairs at the side of the stage and a steward directed them along the front row to the seats at the far end. They passed the captains and commanders who were also on the front row before finding their seats. In between them and the captains were eleven seats with the centre seat behind the podium.

"Not a bad crowd." Said Tank sitting down.

"Yes, what do you think six thousand?" Asked Peebop.

"Hmm, I would go with five and a half." Said Fred.

"I think four." Said Rosey joining in.

"Nah, more like seven." Said Hagger.

"Well, I think six as well." Said Carina.

"hmm... eighteen." Said Jep.

"Eighteen?"

"Yes, eighteen. We only think big these days, most of the gigs are fifty thousand plus. So, we think everything else is small. Therefore, I think eighteen thousand."

Everyone turned and looked back at the crowd.

"I see what you mean." Said Datch.

He beckoned at a stewed and she came over.

"Yes, Sir?"

"Err, how many people are here this afternoon?" asked Datch.

"We currently have around twenty-two thousand people here as far as I know sir."

"Thank you. We were just trying to guess the numbers." he said.

"You're welcome, sir."

With that she went back to her position.

"Well, I win." Said Jep triumphantly.

"I haven't had a go yet and I say thirty thousand." Said Dapo triumphantly.

"What? I still win."

"How?"

"Eighteen is closer to twenty-two than thirty."

"Oh."

They all burst out laughing and a number of the captains turned to look. Don just shrugged his shoulders and sighed.

At this point the council members started to come to their seats. They were all dressed up in brightly coloured robes and all carried a golden staff. They arrived at their seats and stood waiting. Tinfa came up the stairs. He was dressed in a long red and white robe with gold edging and the symbol on the planetary flag embroidered on the right side. He stopped at the podium facing the crowd and banged his golden staff on the floor. The other council members now banged their staffs on the floor and the sound echoed around the plaza. They took a step back and sat down leaving Tinfa standing at the podium. The crowd went quiet.

"Fellow Arcaneiums, I stand here today a free man on this planet. I'm am going to tell you the story of how we are now free and safe from slavery." He paused and then continued.

"When the Plantars invaded our world, they imprisoned the council members in our own homes. We were brought out as their puppets and made to tell you what they wanted you to hear. I started to think that it was the end of our world and started to think the worst. It was then that I decided to save my daughter. I arranged for her to leave the planet and head to safety. The Plantars told me that she had been killed and the ship had been destroyed when leaving the planet. I lost all hope and believed only a miracle could save us. Then, one night my daughter appeared in my cellar with some friends. I was so happy to see her alive and well. They wanted to take me from this world but I insisted that enough council members came with me to sign the treaty with the IPSF. I could not leave you, my people defenceless. These new friends spirited us away to another world at great risk to themselves. We had a Plantar battleship on our tail all the way but they didn't count on the IPSF. The battleship was disabled as we dived down towards a new world..." Tinfa continued to tell the story and the crowd listened intently to the tale. It took ten minutes for Tinfa to get to the end.

"And so, ladies and gentlemen. We owe a great debt of gratitude to these people on the front row, especially The Pack for braving the Plantars to rescue us and therefore we have decided to award them for their outstanding bravery and give them the freedom of the planet."

He banged his staff again and turned to The Pack.

"Please stand up."

The Pack stood up and the crowd all clapped and cheered. An aid came on the stage with a box and followed Tinfa over to Datch. He got a small golden pin from the box and pinned it on to Datch's shirt and shook his hand.

"Thank you Datch."

There was a round of applause and then Tinfa moved to Carina and did the same. One by one he moved along the row. Each time giving them a pin and saying thank you and each time there was a round of applause. Tinfa then went to the podium again.

"Ladies and gentlemen, I would also like to introduce you to our new friends here on my left. These are the people who helped free our world from slavery."

He turned to the commanders and captains

"I would like to thank you and your crews for helping our planet and I would like to give you all freedom of the city as a token of our gratitude. Please stand up."

He went down the row of captains and commanders each of them got a silver pin.

"Thank you to all of you."

There was another round of applause.

"Ladies and Gentlemen, before we continue, I have another announcement to make. We have the leader of another world with us today. They have asked if they could open an embassy here in the capital and the council has agreed. They are also going to help us rebuild and get interstellar trade links going. Please put your hands together for the Minister Prime of Welly Four."

Tinfa took a step back. Widfab stood up and walked over to the podium to a round of applause. The band started to play the Welly Four anthem which considering they were a classical brass band it gave them a few issues. They really needed a rock guitarist and a lot more practice but it was passable. Widfab waited until they finished and then addressed the crowd.

"Ladies and Gentlemen, it gives us great pleasure to be the first alien race to open an interstellar embassy on your world. I hope that we can build a strong friendship and create great trade links between our worlds and many others. I have pledged help to rebuild your world and some of our crews will be here in around a month's time. We hope we can help your world to prosper and grow with our guidance. Thank you."

There was another round of applause and Widfab went back to his seat. Tinfa took to the podium again.

"Ladies and Gentlemen that concludes the formalities. Please enjoy the rest of the evening. We have music and entertainment till late. Thank you all."

There was a huge round of applause and the band started to play.

Tinfa led the council members off the stage and back into the citadel followed by everyone else. Outside the band played and people were laughing and dancing.

Inside after they had got their drinks Fred turned to the others.

"Do you think this planet is ready for a Welly Four embassy?"

"I'm not sure but I think we'll find out soon." Said Datch.

Jep gave them a long look.

Then Don came walking over.

“Hi folks, I was just talking to Widfab and we’ll need to leave at lunch time tomorrow to get you to Welly Four in time for your whatever it is.”

“God hood.” Said Hagger with a grin.

“Yes. that.” Said Don frowning.

“Ok, we’ll be ready.” Said Fred.

“Do we do the same as before?” Asked Datch.

“Yes, take the Raven into orbit and then contact us. We’ll do the rest.”

“Ok, no probs.”

“Do you mind bringing the Minister Prime with you as he seems to like following you about? It would save sending another shuttle down.”

“Yes, that will be fine.” Said Clax.

Datch looked around the room.

“Widfab?” He shouted.

He looked up and Datch waved at him. Don looked at Datch and then at Widfab as he came over. The Minister Prime had just walked away from a delegation of council members because Datch had called him.

“Yes, Datch. What’s up dude?”

“You’re with us tomorrow dude, ok?”

“Sure Datch, what we doing?”

“Going to the Carpaycus so they can take us the Welly Four.”

“Ok, cool.”

“Did you need anything else?”

“No, that’s it dude.”

“Ok, no problem, dude.”

He turned around and headed back to the council members.

Don just looked at him in amazement.

“Datch, how do you do that?” He asked.

“Do what?”

Don was about to say something and changed his mind.

“Never mind.”

They headed over to the table with the buffet. It had little sandwiches, various quiches, some posh looking Vol-au-vents full of rich fillings and also a number of bowls with crisps and other snacks. They had a plate full each before grabbing another round of drinks and heading outside to join the party.

Tank insisted that they all went on the fun fair which was fine until Hagger went on one of the roundabouts and then felt ill afterwards. The best thing was they didn’t have to pay for anything. People would see them getting a beer and want to buy it for them it. Same with the rides, they would just be let on. The population was so pleased to be free and looked on The Pack and the IPSF as their saviours. They partied on into the night but made a point of heading to the hotel around midnight as they needed to leave by the following lunchtime.

# Demigods

The next morning The Pack along with the Welly Four delegation headed to the spaceport. Five taxis dropped them off at the gate where Datch had exited the day before. There was now a security guard manning it and after a couple of checks and a salute they were let through and walked over to the Raven.

Widfab was given Fred's seat behind Clax and Fred took the rest of his aids to the rec room.

"Wow, this is amazing." he said.

"Yeh, it's a nice ship dude." Said Tank.

"Yes, but it's the Music Warriors ship."

"Widfab, it's us dude, chill and enjoy the ride." Said Datch.

"I'll try but it's very exciting."

After the pre-flight checks. Datch contacted Arcaneus control and after a brief pause for an inbound freighter the Raven was cleared to launch. Datch slowly increased speed and height allowing all those at the front of the cockpit to get a good view of the city below before he accelerated up through the clouds. As they reached orbit they had to wait as the carrier ship came out of interspace followed by the destroyer and the rest of the escort ships. They slowed to a stop and parked in a high orbit. Datch wondered if the Plantars still had a star system left or if it had joined the expanding clouds of gas in interstellar space. Once cleared to move again he opened a comms channel to the Carpaycus.

"Carpaycus, this is the Raven requesting docking."

"Good morning, Raven. Please lock on to beacon IP99745 and we will do the rest."

Datch pressed a few virtual buttons.

"Locked on to beacon Carpaycus. Raven is all yours."

The Raven flew past number of transport ships that were inbound to the planet and then another ship similar to the Carpaycus. Then, the Carpaycus came into view. The Raven headed along her side before entering into the rear landing bay.

The bay was full of shuttles and was a hive of activity with crates being moved and chained down. The Raven was guided to the side of the bay and Datch dropped her softly on to the landing pad. There was a clunk as the docking clamps engaged and he shut down the engines. They headed out of the Raven and were met by a number of the crew who then showed them to their quarters.

They put their bags in their rooms before heading to the forward lounge for food. The forward lounge was split into two levels. The restaurant was upstairs and the downstairs area was made up of a selection of bars separated by trellises and partitions. Each bar area had its own theme which varied from quiet and relaxed to loud and lively. They went upstairs first and had a meal in the restaurant before heading down to the bar area. After a bit of searching, they found a bar playing rock music with a number of free tables. They pushed them together to make a large table after which they stuck a sign on the end saying the 'Barbers Inn on tour' much to the entertainment of the barman and a number of the crew members.

It took a day and a half to get to Welly Four. The Carpaycus flew past the pleasure moon before entering orbit near to a very new looking space station. It was a lot bigger than the little one Datch remembered and he was pretty sure it didn't have any paint peeling off the walls either. Also, in view was Welly Fours new galactic destroyer which was parked in orbit around the pleasure moon. It wasn't quite as big as the IPSF destroyers but was still twice the size of the Carpaycus.

Widfab took a shuttle to the surface with his aids while The Pack headed to the Raven. Don was waiting for them.

“Hi Datch, I hope you enjoyed your detour?”

“Well, it’s been an experience and was very different that’s for sure.”

“Well, you have a safe journey down.”

Don shook Datch’s hand.

“Thank you and thanks for the lift.”

“No problem. I’m thinking of changing the ships name to Datch’s Taxi.” He said laughing, “You take care now folks.”

“We will.” Said Fred.

They went inside the Raven and headed up to the cockpit.

After the pre-fight checks the Raven was cleared for launch and left the landing bay heading for the planet.

“Welly control, this is Raven we’re on approach to the great desert. We have a landing reservation at the Oasis Spa complex.”

“Copy that Music Warriors, all traffic is being cleared for you.”

“Thanks Welly control – entering atmospheric interface in three minutes.”

“Raven you are clear to navigate at your discretion.”

“Thanks Welly control. Raven out.”

“Well, that’s new. Clearing all traffic for us.” Said Clax.

"Hey, they like us." Said Hagger.

The Raven dropped down into the atmosphere and then a fighter escort joined in next to them.

"Wow. We have company." Said Datch.

The comms burst into life.

"Music Warriors we are your escort down."

"Copy that. We're descending to ten thousand metres before heading across the great desert."

"We will follow your lead sir."

Datch turned to Clax.

"Wow, we have our own fighter escort."

"Yes, pretty damn cool." Said Clax.

Behind them Carina, Hagger and Tish craned over the seats so they could see the fighters out of the windows. There were four of them. Two on each side and all flying in formation.

Datch took the Raven down and flew across the desert. The sands were stretched out below and were going underneath them very fast. Datch started to slow the Raven down and dropped to five hundred metres.

"Quaki control, this is Raven on final approach to the Oasis Spar complex."

"Raven this is Quaki control. All traffic has been cleared for you. Welcome home Music Warriors."

"Thanks, Quaki control."

Out of the window Quaki started to appear on the horizon. The little town that was nothing more than a hand full of dusty streets outside the monastery a few years ago was now a sea of hotel complexes. The small town was lost in amongst the buildings and at the centre of it all was the obelisk with the gem sitting on the top. As the Raven came into land the gem gave off a burst of energy as if to welcome them back.

Datch brought the Raven in for a landing at the resorts landing area. There was a crowd of people waiting for them to land. The Raven hovered over a very clean looking landing pad and Datch slowly dropped the Raven onto the pad with the gentlest of bumps.

"Raven to fighter escort, thanks guys."

"You're welcome, Sir. It has been an honour."

The fighters turned and headed off back across the desert.

"Quaki control. Raven has landed."

"Enjoy your stay Music Warriors. Quaki control out."

Datch shut the Raven's systems down and got up.

"Well folks, it looks like we have a welcoming committee outside. Let's not keep them waiting."

"I think I'm going to be needing a beer after this." Said Tank.

"Yes, I have a feeling we all will." Added Fred.

They headed down to the cargo bay and dropped the ramp down before opening the door. The heat outside hit them and after twenty-two degrees on the Carpaycus it felt very hot. At the bottom of the ramp were Tajiquay, Faberfab, Dag and father Jamby along with a large number of staff and the town's mayor.

"Hi dudes." Said Datch walking down to them.

“Welcome Music Warriors. We are very pleased to have you with us again.” Said the mayor.

“Thank you. We are very pleased to be here.”

He signalled to a number of staff and they came forward and placed garlands of flowers around The Pack’s necks.

“Thank you very much.” Said Datch. “It’s a great honour you’re giving us.”

“The honour is all ours, Music Warriors.”

Faberfab stepped forward and spoke.

“Music Warriors, we have reserved the presidential suites for you I hope they are ok.” he said.

“Cool. That’s great thanks. We’ve had a bit of a busy trip so we could really do with an ice-cold beer before anything else.”

“I figured you might want one after I caught the galactic news channel yesterday. The beers are already being pulled as we speak.” Said Dag.

“It’s been on the news?” Asked Fred.

“Just a bit, saviours of another world. You are starting to get a rep for doing it. The galactic press is here now.” He said pointing up to a small vid bot.

“I’ve not done my hair yet.” Said Rosey.

“Rosey, you look fine.” Said Tank.

“Are you sure?”

“Yes, don’t worry.”

Datch turned to the monk.

“Hi Jamby how’s it going with you dude?” Asked Datch.

“Very well thanks. I understand that Minister Prime has told you what is going on.”

“Yes, he’s explained it all to us. It’s a very great honour. Thank you.”

“You deserve it. Not only for saving our world but you have saved others as well.”

“Err… sorry to butt in but it’s a bit warm out here and I don’t want my beer getting warm in the bar.” Said Clax.

“Yes, of course. Please follow me.” Said Faberfab.

A number of staff stepped forward and took their bags from them.

Faberfab led the way across the landing area and into the hotel. The vid bot flew off in the direction of a small crowd at the edge of the landing field. The hotel was huge and as well as its private landing area it had its own private spar along with seven pools, six restaurants and fifteen bars.

The lobby was very busy and there were a number of security staff dressed in suits standing by the entrance as well as milling about. Datch recognised two of them as Tajiquay’s men from the camp in the desert, except now they were wearing posh suits. They headed across to the main bar that was on the opposite side of the reception area.

Faberfab took them to a roped off area which had a big table with flowers and a miniature water feature in the centre. Flower petals had been scattered on the floor around it.

“Wow this is nice.” Said Carina sitting down.

“Thank you, my wife designed it.” Said Faberfab.

“Well, tell her it looks wonderful.”

They sat down and several waiters came out carrying large glasses of beer which had ice on the outside of the glass.

“This looks so good.” Said Datch picking up his beer.

He took a big gulp and a big smile spread across his face.

“This is Bellatrixian beer!”

“Wow, it is.” Added Tank.

“Yes, we are now brewing it here on Welly to the Bellatrixian recipe. I thought you might like it. It sells well too.” Said Dag.

“Cool. Well, there is a barrel of the real thing in the storeroom on the Raven. I’ll get it for you later.” Said Datch.

“Thanks. Do you guys want some snacks?”

“Sure.” Said Clax.

Dag waved at the bar and three waiters came over carrying four large buckets of fried chicken, a number of bowls of fries and two pizzas.

“That’s better.” Said Datch relaxing into the chair.

“You can say that again.” Said Dapo.

Hagger was about to say something when everyone turned to look at him.

“What!” he said.

Everyone laughed.

“So, dudes, what happened on Arcaneus?” Asked Tajiquay.

“Well, we could have done with you and your men there, that’s for sure. But here’s what happened…” Said Datch.

The Pack spent the next hour telling them all about Arcaneus.

Then, after another beer they headed to their rooms to get changed into swim wear before moving the party to the pool side. It was forty-three degrees outside and the pool was a nice relief from the heat. The next two days were spent chilling next to the pool and the occasional picture with their fans.

They also had a meeting with a group of their devoted followers who were dressing like them and learning to play music. Also, they always spoke in Bellatrixian and only ate Bellatrixian food. It was kind of strange to meet them as after each sentence they would bow and keep calling them 'The Holy Dudes'.

On the third day they had a trip to the monastery to meet with the head of the order, Father Tiki. He ran through the ceremony with them and it was decided that they would perform the songs they did when they found the gem. He then took them for a kabab in the bar that had been added to the monastery.

The bar had been very tastefully done with wooden beams and wooden tables like the ones in the monks dining room. Datch looked a bit closer and then corrected himself. They were the ones from the monks dining room. He asked why and the head of the order told him they gave a rustic feel to the bar and they had wanted new ones for their dining room. They were nice brightly coloured chairs with cushions designed for comfort and some bright coloured tables to match the pastel-coloured walls. At least the old tables and chairs looked great in the bar unlike the bar itself that looked more like a wooden version of the Barbers Inn rather than something you would find in a monastery. Datch started to wonder if they were going to start painting the outside of the monastery, he then thought better of it in case next time they came it was bright pink.

The day of the ceremony arrived and The Pack were dressed up in long flowing robes which were bright green with a golden trim. They had to walk from the hotel to the monastery as a type of pilgrimage.

“This robe is a bit on the warm side.” Said Tank.

“Yes, I know what you mean. We only need to wear them until the end of the ceremony and they have promised a lot of cold beer afterwards.” Said Fred.

“Ok folks just remember we’re about to become gods.” Said Datch.

“Demigods.” Corrected Fred.

“Ok, Demigods. So, let’s make sure we look good.”

Datch held his hand out. The rest put their hands in.

“One, two, three lets party!”

They all broke hands and formed up in two rows.

Datch went in front with Carina. They headed out of the hotel and on to the main street. Vid bots circled overhead and the street was lined with people all wanting to see their new gods, sorry, demigods. The streets were hot with the sun beating down but because the robes were so bright, a lot of the heat was reflected away. As they passed by, people would cheer them on. It took about fifteen minutes to get to the monastery and all the way people packed the streets. They stopped outside the monastery door and banged loudly on it with a staff that Datch had been given.

Father Jamby opened the door. He was dressed in a golden robe with an image of the gem on its front.

“Why have you come here?” He asked.

“We seek to be enlightened and have come from across the stars to be one with the gem.”

“Please, enter, and follow.”

He turned and started to walk up to the courtyard. The route was lined with monks and they all bowed as The Pack walked past.

They arrived at the main hall and father Jamby banged on the door. It opened and a monk stood blocking the way.

“Why are you here?”

“I bring those that wish to be enlightened.”

“Bring them forth.” he said and stood to the side.

Father Jamby led them outside and onto the large open platform in front of the obelisk. The vid bots were flying above it.  They stopped in the centre of the platform and Father Jamby stepped to the side.

Father Tiki, head of the order of the gem stood there. He was dressed in a long flowing robe of gold and green with a golden tabard that had an image of the gem on the front.

“Tell me why you have come?”

“We have come to be one with the gem and take our place as those who are enlightened.” Said Datch.

“Why do you deserve to become one of the enlightened?”

“We have saved this world. We have brought the gem back to its rightful place. We are the Warriors of sound and song. We guide the course of this world. We ask to be recognised as the enlightened.” Said Datch very loudly.

“I accept your deeds are great and your hearts are pure. Bow down and let the gem show us if you are worthy to become our Lords.”

They all bowed down and the monks all started to hum in different octaves, the sound got louder and lounder and reverberated around the platform. As the monks got louder the gems around The Pack's necks energised and beams of light shot across to the four gems in the corners of the platform. The monk's tones harmonised and the four small gems sent beams of light up to the gem on top of the obelisk. Then the gem then let out a very bright pulse of light that shot out across the sky. The monks all became columns of green light along with The Pack.

"Stand enlightened." Commanded father Tiki.

The rest of the monks were now all bowing towards them.

"The gem has accepted your deeds and you are now our lords and masters. Please accept out blessings and take your weapons to show us your power."

The Pack bowed to father Tiki and then to the rest of the monks before walking to the stage at the foot of the obelisk. They stepped onto the stage and turned to face the monks and dignitaries. They dropped their robes revealing their normal stage clothes. They took a step back and were handed their instruments. Datch looked at the others at nodded. Tish hit the drums and Star Lovers blasted out across the town. The gem got brighter and brighter until it started releasing huge waves of energy across the sky. They played the songs and at the end the gem gave out a massive pulse of energy which encircled the planet.

The monks all bowed again. Father Tiki stepped forward and bowed again before taking The Pack to a line of dignitaries. Widfab was at the front of the line and bowed as they arrived. They bowed back and then one by one they worked their way down the line. Each time Father Tiki would introduce the person and they would do a deep bow looking down at the ground and then when they straightened up The Pack would bow. It seemed to take forever but finally they got to the end of the row and father Tiki gestured for them to turn around. Everyone now bowed to them.

“Rise!” Commanded Datch.

Father Tiki waited for everyone to straighten up and then cleared his throat.

“Now let’s celebrate our new spiritual leaders the Music Warriors. Let the music play and the partying commence.”

Music started to play from the sound system.

“Father Tiki. Any chance of a beer?” Asked Datch.

“Why certainly.”

He clapped his hands and a number of monks came walking out with tankards of beer on golden trays. They stopped in front of them and bowed their heads.

Father Tiki nodded for them to take the beer. They did and the monks lifted their heads before turning and heading back the way they came.

They took a large gulp of beer and Hagger let out a big burp.

“Did you have to?” Asked Carina.

“Err. Pardon me. I just had a bit of gas.”

“I’m not sure gods are meant to burp.” Said Rosey.

“Well now they do.” Said Datch grinning.

They all started laughing and a number people nearby did as well.

“Ok, Let’s party.”

“Yea, I need to let my hair down.” Said Tish.

"I need the bathroom." Said Dapo.

"I'll get one on the monks to bless it before you go in." Said Father Tiki.

They turned to look at him.

"Are the toilets that bad?" Asked Jep.

"Err. No. we've had them cleaned and they even have disco balls in the cubicles."

"Why the blessing thing then?"

"Well, it just seems to be the right thing to do."

"Well, if they're going to bless them, tell them to hurry up as I really need a pee." Said Dapo.

Father Tiki shouted at a monk who came running over, stopped and then bowed. Father Tiki whispered in the monk's ear and the monk went running off in a hurry.

"He's going to do the quick, quick, version. Please follow him."

"Cool." Said Dapo and headed off after the monk.

Dapo arrived at the bathroom and opened the door. Flower petals were falling through the air on their way to the floor and the monk was standing there chanting something very fast. Dapo smiled at him and gave him a thumbs up. The monk stopped and looked at him and bowed before leaving the room.

Five minutes later Dapo came back to join the rest of them followed by the monk.

"How was it?" Asked Datch.

"What? The pee or the blessing?" Asked Dapo.

"Err. The blessing, we can tell the pee was good by the relieved look on your face."

"Well, I think it was ok but I have a feeling the flower petals may become a trip hazard by the end of the night."

"What flower petals?"

"The ones the monk scattered on the floor."

"Oh, don't worry. We plan to put fresh ones down every time you need to go." Said Father Tiki politely butting in.

"So, we've got to wait each time we need to go?" Asked Clax.

"Err… We didn't think about the time aspect bit."

"Ok. Thank you for the blessing thing. We really appreciate it but, taking into account there are twelve of us the monks are going to be spending a lot of time in the toilets. May I suggest you just do a general one that lasts the night."

Father Tiki thought about this for a moment.

"I see your point. I'll get them to do a purification ritual in there. If that's ok?"

"Yes, and maybe loose the flower petals? Trip hazard, health and safety and all."

"I'll get right on it."

"Cool, are you going to be blessing anything else?"

Father Tiki looked at them for a moment.

"I think we'll be good with that. The food was blessed before we started along with the barrels of beer."

Dapo looked in his beer just in case there were flowers floating in it.

"Ok, cool. Let's mingle."

It took The Pack a good two or three hours to mingle as everyone they came to, bowed and then waited to be told to stop. The first few attempts resulted in The Pack standing looking at the person in a bowed position and waiting which in one case went on for over a minute. Then there were red faces all round before they got to grips with it.

It got a bit later in the evening and The Pack decided to do another couple of numbers. Then to get away from all the bowing at the end of the songs Datch had an idea.

"Ladies and gentlemen, thank you for the great honour that you have bestowed on us. I would like to propose something in the interest of your health and wellbeing. We are all concerned about your backs and ours too for that matter. So, if you would all like to take a big bow now, we'll count that as done for the rest of the night. Ok?"

Everyone looked at him.

"OK, Are you ready? Bow."

Everyone one bowed and The Pack bowed back.

"Right, we're all good now. No more bowing tonight. Ok?"

There was a lot of nodding from the crowd and a lot of relieved smiles.

"Cool, what do you think guys, what about Supernova for an encore?"

Tish hit the drums and the music blasted out.

The rest of the night went a lot better now that the bowing had stopped and ended off with a conga line heading down through the town back to the hotel were the remaining party goers continued in the bar with an impromptu karaoke session until the guests started falling asleep or ended up getting a taxi back to their own hotel. In most cases it was both.

The next morning Datch opened his eyes to a bright green glow. He blinked and there was Carina. They had found out that the glow while being bright could be filtered out by blinking. You could still see the aura but the brightness was somehow muted. Jep reckoned it was something to do with the psychic nature of the gem.

Datch gave her a kiss on the shoulder and she turned him.

“Morning my goddess.”

“Morning my god.” She said and they both laughed.

“So, what’s the plan for today?” she asked.

“The Pool, I think.”

“Sounds good. What about breakfast? Pancakes?”

“I can go with that.”

They had a shower and headed down to the restaurant for breakfast. There were still a couple of people sleeping on the sofas in the bar as they walked past. They went to their designated table. In other words, the big one in the corner with flower petals all around it. They sat down and a waiter came over to take their orders and then bowed before leaving. The food came out and the conversation turned to the joining.

“I’ve been thinking about the joining.” Said Carina.

“Yes, it’s been on my mind too. What were you thinking?”

“I think it’s going to have to be a big event.”

"Err... what do you mean?"

"Well, while you went to bathroom last night Rosey asked me about the rings and Widfab over heard her and then asked me about it."

"Oh, that's why he said congratulations when I came back. I thought he was on about the god thing."

"No, anyway, he wants to come."

"Well, if we invite him, we'll have to invite Coola. Maybe even Tinfa."

"Wow, the security for it will be a nightmare."

"Yes, and I think we had better do it sooner than later."

Datch looked at her for a moment with a strange look on his face.

"Err... you're not err... I mean we're not expecting... I mean are you pregnant?"

She burst out laughing.

"No. you're not going to be a daddy just yet. No, I just mean if we take too long planning it. Word is going to get out and we'll be hounded by the press."

Datch let out a sigh.

"Good, I'm not sure I'm ready to be a dad just yet."

"Me neither."

"Ok. Let's talk to the others. We're going to need all the help we can get. Any ideas where to have it?"

"Hmm... It's got to be a big venue but somewhere nice."

"Well, it's going to be getting towards summer when we get back so, outside would be good."

They stopped and thought for a moment. Then Carina spoke.

“What about up at Traxsent. It won’t be too hot up there and the mountains would make a great back drop for it?”

“Yes, that’s a great idea, I’ll request data on secure venues in Traxsent and the mountains. It may take a while to get here though.”

“We have plenty of time to look at them, it’s going to be another six weeks before we get back.”

A waiter came over.

“Would Sir and Mam like more coffee?”

“Yes please.”

He filled up their cups and then bowed before heading to the next table.

Carina took another sip of coffee.

“So, let’s think about this. We need to invite Coola, Widfab, Tajiquay, Dag, Father Jamby, Tinfa, Don and Alex.”

“Don’t forget Fizz as well. What about Jim and Joni Jabi?”

“Yes, sounds good. We can probably get Joni to do the media side. He would like that.”

“We’ll have to sit down with both our parents and make a proper list.”

“Maybe we should try and organise it for a week or so after we get back. We’ve just got four gigs at the Barbers planned and two gigs down south, that’s it then for the next eight weeks at the moment.”

“Yeh. Ok we have a plan.”

They finished their coffees before heading off to the pool.

During the following week they had two gigs on Welly Four. The down side with playing gigs on Welly now was that everyone wanted to bow before the gig and after it. So, with a bit of planning, Datch walked up to the mic and waited. The population then bowed to them and then The Pack bowed back. They had one gig in the capital and one at an ancient volcano that had formed the most incredible amphitheatre. The sound was amazing and the crater was lined with tiny gems. When they played the walls lit up like they were on fire.

They were also asked to do a blessing and play a few songs to officially open the pleasure moon which turned out to be really fun as they went in the low gravity water park afterwards.

The next six weeks flew by with gigs and interviews. Word was getting around now about Arcaneus and them becoming spiritual leaders. The press was digging for all the details. They finished their final gig on Hamel four. They had offered to give Dydinyon, Datch's brother a lift home and after a couple days relaxing at one of their favourite resorts. The morning arrived for their departure and Dydinyon turned up with his luggage. They put his rucksack in the cargo hold next to the bikes before heading up to the cockpit.

Datch directed him to the seat on the opposite side to Carina. He had been shown around the Raven before but not actually flown in her. Fred had said as it was his first flight, he could have his seat. Datch sat down in the pilot's seat and started going through the pre-flight checks. Clax came and joined him and started doing his check.

"You ready for the last bit then?" He asked.

"Yea, I can't wait to get in the pool at home and just relax."

"It's been one heck of a trip, hasn't it?"

"Yeh. Still, only eight more hours to go."

"We could do it in two if you like?"

“Nah, the Ravens been through a lot on this trip. I’m going to give her a deluxe service when we get home.”

“How much does that cost?”

“About twenty thousand credits but they go through her and check everything. If they find something that’s even slightly out of spec it gets replaced.”

“Wow. Now that’s a service.”

“Ok, I’m good over here, how’s that side?”

“I think we’re good to go.”

Datch turned to the others.

“Ok folks everyone ready?”

There was a round of nodding. Datch put on his headset.

“Hamel control this is the Raven ready to depart from Jafuler VIP area on route to Bellatrix Five.”

“Good morning, Raven. Please lock on to beacon 34264 and hover at two hundred metres until beacon shows clear. Traffic is light at the moment.”

“Thanks Hamel control. Lifting off and holding at two hundred.”

Datch increased thrust and the Raven slowly rose into the air. He brought her to a hover and held her there until the beacon turned green in his heads-up display. He turned the Raven to the beacon and increased thrust. The Raven accelerated into the sky. Outside the sky was blue apart from a few light clouds. Datch fell in behind a freighter and followed it up through the atmosphere. Outside the sky started to get darker and then turned to black. Datch banked the ship to the right giving a great view of the planet.

"Hamel control. This is the Raven. We are clear of the beacon and about to jump to interspace."

"Raven, this is Hamel control. Have a safe trip."

"Thanks Hamel control. Raven out."

"Computer set course for Bellatrix five, interspace fifteen."

"Course laid in; do you wish an alarm thirty minutes before arrival?"

"Yes please. Engage interspace."

"Alarm has been set engaging interspace drive."

The star outside vanished and then started to flicker.

"Ok folks, let's go and chill." Datch said getting up.

"Err, don't you need to stay here?" Asked Dydinyon.

"No, the computer's got it."

"Oh, so what do we do?"

"Well, a beer sounds good." Said Tank heading for the stairs.

"Yes. we have eight hours to kill. Also, I've checked we'll arrive around lunch time at the ranch."

"Don't we have to go to the space port first?"

"Nah, Datch gives the authorities all our ID's and they are happy for us to land at the ranch. The Raven is registered at Bellatrix central so it's our home world." Said Clax following along behind.

Seven and a half hours later the ships alarm sounded followed by the computer announcing that it was thirty minutes until arrival. Datch and Clax headed up to the cockpit. Over the next twenty minutes the others came up and sat down.

Datch put his headset on and pressed the comms button.

“Bellatrix control this is the Raven on course for Yuland city.”

“Good morning, Raven. Welcome home. Please follow beacon 97 on exit from interspace. Please send ID’s and cargo manifests.”

“Bellatrix Control copy that. No Cargo but one extra passenger. Sending information now.”

Datch pressed a couple of virtual buttons and the system beeped.

“Thanks Raven, data received. Follow beacon and contact Yuland city control on orbital interface.”

“Copy that Bellatrix control. Raven out.”

The planet appeared as a small flickering spot of light in the darkness of space and then started to get bigger. Soon it started to fill the whole of the view outside. Datch dropped the Raven out of interspace and the bright glare lit up the cockpit.

“Yuland city control. This is Raven on approach to orbital interface requesting vector to landing area YUL2759.”

“Good morning, Raven. You’re cleared to descend on beacon 45634. Weather is good and traffic is light. At fifty kilometres out, you’re cleared to leave traffic and head to landing area.”

“Copy that Yuland city control.”

Datch locked on to the beacon and descended through the atmosphere following a large shuttle from the space station. Below they could see the desert and then city. The Raven levelled out.

“Yuland city control this is Raven about to leave beacon.”

“Raven you are clear to do so.”

“Thanks, Yuland city control.”

The Raven turned to the left and exited the main traffic corridor. Up ahead the desert turned to scrubland and then fields. Datch slowed the Raven down to a hundred KMPH and then the ranch appeared in the distance with the landing beacon flashing. The Raven slowed down more as it started to pass over the scrubland. Datch positioned the ship over the landing pad and turned the ship so she was facing towards the desert. Then he slowly dropped her down on to the ground.

Datch let out a sigh and shut down the engines.

“Yuland City Control, Raven has landed.”

“Have a great day, Raven. Yuland city control out.”

Datch turned to the rest as he got up.

“Ok folks. We’re home, lets hit the pool.”

They headed down the ramp from the cargo bay and back on to home ground. Dechow and Tansya came walking over from the pool.

“Welcome back folks.” Said Tansya coming over and giving Datch and Carina a hug.

“Hi Mum. It’s good to be back.” Said Datch.

A lot of hellos followed.

“It’s been a bit of a busy trip with one thing and another.” Said Datch.

“Yes, I had a very large email from Don. Sounds like you had fun.” Said Dechow.

"Yes. It was, err… busy."

"We're now gods too." Said Hagger grinning.

"Demigods not gods." Corrected Tank.

"Yes, we know. That was on the galactic news channels as well! Come on, you can tell us about it next to the pool. I bet you need a drink." Said Tansya.

"We sure do." Said Datch.

They headed over to the bar and after grabbing various drinks went outside next to the pool.

After two hours going through the story of the trip Dechow went and started a barbeque.

"So," Said Tansya, "Have you two decided on a date for your joining?"

"We were thinking maybe four months time? It will be towards the end of the summer then and we have spotted a nice resort in the mountains near Traxsent. We checked on the way back and there are a couple of weekends free."

"It will cost a bit up there?"

"We just earnt three and a half million credits each so credits are not an issue. We just want it to be right." Said Datch.

"We also have a couple of planetary presidents coming as well." Added Carina.

"You do?" Said Dechow raising an eyebrow.

"Yes, Widfab has said he wants to come and Coola will come because Widfab is coming and we now have to invite Tinfa, the Arcaneus president as well." Said Datch

"Err… and how is that going to work?"

“The resort we’re looking at is in the mountains with its own landing site. It is also able to provide a secure venue for visiting VIP’s. Look.” Datch got out his vid com and pulled up a page to show his mum.

“It looks very nice. But what about the price?”

“Err… it’s just over a hundred thousand for a week and we think we should book it for two. But that’s not a problem.”

Dechow nearly choked on his beer.

“Ok, what about rings?” Said Tansya changing the subject before Dechow needed medical attention.

“We want some iridium rings with star patterns on them and they will have a small gem from Welly Four as well. Widfab has given us two gems to be fitted into the rings. We now just need to talk to a jeweller in the city.”

“Can I see?”

“Sure.” Said Carina and looked into space for a moment before looking at Tansya.

Tansya was deep in thought for a minute before turning back to them.

“Yes, they look great but they might cost a bit.”

“We think about two thousand a piece.”

“Wow.”

“Rosey and Fred are coming to the jewellery quarter with us the day after tomorrow.”

“Do you want me to come as well?”

“Yeh, if you want to, it would be great!”

“I’d love to.”

“We also need a hand with the invites. We want to get my mum and dad over and have a proper meeting with Rosey and Fred as well if that’s ok?” Asked Carina.

“Sure, when were you thinking?”

“Next weekend if that’s ok?”

“I don’t see a problem with that.”

They carried on discussing things till the sun started to set. The rest of The Pack headed off home leaving just Carina, Datch, Dydinyon, Tansya and Dechow. The sun set over the desert and there was a chirping in the air from the little critters in the grass.

Carina and Tansya went into the bar to sort out a couple of light snacks and Dydinyon was snoring in a chair near the pool. Dechow turned to Datch

“Are you sure you’re ready to look after Carina?”

“Yes, dad. I already look after her and will do forever. I will see stars fall before I let her down.”

For no apparent reason Dechow started to worry about various star systems and their futures.

“That’s good, what about kids?” He asked changing the subject away from any stellar catastrophises that could happen in the future.

“Err… we’re not planning any just yet.”

“Good, you have a lot of life to have fun with before you make me a grandad again.”

They turned to look out across the desert. The three moons sat in the sky hanging over the sands bathing them in moon light.

"You know dad, I always wondered why you would look out across the desert at night. Now I know. This is home but that is adventure."

Dechow looked at the stars and then at his son.

"I couldn't put that any better myself!" he said.

They sat with a beer in their hands watching the sky and thinking about the universe. It was a few minutes before Dechow spoke.

"Have you thought about a honeymoon yet?"

"We've talked about it and I think we're just going to take the Raven out there and see what we can find."

"What just the two of you?"

"Yes, the Raven's easy enough to fly solo. Everything is automated so we'll pick a world in range and go to see what it's like."

"Sounds like fun. I understand that Qwots took a look at the Raven while you were on board the Carpaycus?"

"Yes, he tweaked the engines and shields a bit. Apparently, she can do interspace seventeen now and has an extra twenty tera watts of shielding."

"That will come in handy. Have you tried the engines out yet?"

"No, not yet. We didn't need to and she had a rough time on Arcaneus so I didn't want to push things until she's had a deluxe service."

"That's going to cost you a bit."

"Yes, twenty thousand plus parts. I've booked her in for it in two weeks time. She'll be out of action for up to three weeks while they complete it. I had to fill in a document listing all the modifications she's had so they don't mess with them."

"Wow. Well at least she'll be in good shape afterwards."

"Yes. Just like new as they say."

Just then Carina came back out with Tansya.

"What are you two chatting about?" Asked Tansya sitting down.

"Just stars and spaceships." Said Dechow.

"So, Datch said you're just going to point the ship at a star and go for your honeymoon?"

"Yeh, it's going to be fun. We're going to take camping gear as well so we can go off grid."

"Well, you be careful doing that. Make sure you have an emergency kit with you won't you."

"We will."

The conversation turned to the tour and then after a few hours Datch and Carina headed to their house for an early night. They had been up for nearly twenty-four hours by this point.

After they had gone Tansya turned to Dechow.

"Did you ever imagen he would turnout like this?"

"No, I sort of hoped he would join the fleet and help save a few lives but judging by his current record I don't think he needs the fleet. He seems to be doing a better job by himself."

"Yes, He doesn't seem to worry about the red tape instead he just does it. Just like a young commander I used to know." She smiled at him and he laughed.

“I did have a knack for just doing things and worrying about the consequences afterwards.”

They chatted some more before going and waking Dydinyon up and heading inside.

# The Arrangements

The following week before the gig in the Barbers. Datch, Carina and Tansya arranged to meet up with Fred and Rosey in the city for a coffee and to start discussing things as well as the trip to the jewellery quarter to sort out the rings.

When they arrived at the pancake shop, Fred and Rosey were already there waiting for them.

"Hi folks." Said Datch walking up.

After a round of hellos there followed the acquisition of a number of coffees along with three cookies and two cream cakes. They then finally got down to business.

"So, we have arranged to see the head jeweller in Jackson Jewellery." Said Datch "They came highly recommended and after speaking to one of the staff they have assured me that they can fit the gems into the rings."

"Cool, what about the venue?" asked Fred.

"I've spoken to the manager of the Twin Peaks hotel and Spa. They have their own landing area and can secure the whole valley if required as there is only one way in or out. They also have two free weeks about a month apart. I've asked them to mark them as reserved until we can get up there in four weeks time. If that's ok with you?"

"Yes. that sounds ok."

"We thought we could go up there for the weekend, my mum and dad are coming as well as Datch's."

"Sure. Can I bring Hagger?"

"Yes. We thought you would want to. So, do you want us to book it?"

“Yes, go for it.” Said Fred.

Datch got out his vid comm and pressed a few keys on the screen.

“Hello, I am Datch Thome, I spoke to your manager earlier. I would like to book five suites in four weeks time for the weekend.”

“One moment please.”

There was a pause and then a man appeared on the screen. It was the manager.

“Hello, Sir.”

“Hello, I would like to book five suites for a long weekend in four weeks time so we can discuss the event.”

“I can certainly sort it out for you. I take it you would like a full tour?”

“Yes please.”

“We can also supply you with catering for the event should you require it. We can discus that along with everything else when you're here.”

“That's wonderful. Also, can you cater for alien races?”

“Yes, we can as long as their requirements are not too diverse. I'll send you a full list of what we can do.”

“Cool, that's great thanks.”

“Will you need to use our security or will you be supplying your own.”

“I'm not sure but I expect it will be our own as the president is being invited.”

“Oh, I see. This will be a state event then, Sir?”

“Well, we’re expecting at least one planetary leader and maybe two more so I expect it’s going to get a bit complicated.”

“I see, Sir, I totally understand. We have hosted similar events in the past. So please feel free to ask our advice.”

“Ok thanks. We’ll see you in four weeks.”

“Yes, indeed. Thank you, sir.”

With that the channel closed.

“So, how are we going to do the security?” Asked Fred.

“Hmm, I’m not sure. Maybe I need to talk to Coola. But I suppose we need to nail the date down.”

“Sure, when were you thinking?”

“Babes, which do you think? The 34.11 or 27.12?

“Hmm, let’s go for the 27.12 that way it will be cooling down by then.”

Datch pressed a few keys on his vid comm.

“It looks like it will be around 27C around at that time of year, so not too hot.”

“Ok, let’s go with that.”

“Fred, can you tell our agent not to book anything two weeks before and until four weeks after that date.”

“No problem Datch. I’ll sort it out as soon as we’re done with jewellers. I’m assuming we’re finishing in the Barbers?”

“Yes.” Datch paused, “I had better break the news to Jim come to think of it.”

“That’s a good idea but you had better tell him to keep his mouth shut about it as well.”

"I will."

"Right, time for the Jewellers."

They finished their coffees and headed off towards the Jewellery quarter.

The Jewellery quarter was not a quarter more like a large circle with a park in the middle. They stood in the centre looking around at the shops. They all had gleaming windows at the front with racks and racks of jewellery on display. The gems glittered and shone as the sunlight struck them.

After a couple of minutes looking around, they spotted Jackson Jewellery. It was a large two-story shop and had a flight of steps leading up to the doors in the centre with two large windows on either side. They walked across the park and headed up the steps and through the doors.

Inside, the shop had a large number of display cases all brightly lit. Some had rings while others had necklaces. They did just about every precious gem you could think of and a lot of the rings were one of a kind. At the far end of the shop was a long display case with a holographic ring spinning above it and standing behind it was a shop assistant. They walked over to him.

"Good afternoon, how may I help you?" He asked as they approached.

"Hello, my names Datch Thome, we have an appointment with Mr Pride."

"One moment please." the assistant tapped a couple of keys on the console in front of him.

The console beeped.

"Mr Pride will be with you in a few moments. Can I get you a drink while you wait?"

"No, we're good thanks."

A few moments later the door behind the assistant opened and a middle-aged man came out.

"Good afternoon." He said walking over to them, "I'm Mr Pride."

"Hello, I'm Datch, this is my wife to be Carina, My Mum and this is Rosey the maid of honour and this is Fred the man of honour."

"You wish to discuss a set of custom rings I believe?"

"Yes, Sir."

"What sort of price are you looking at?"

"We're not. Price does not matter. We can pay whatever the price is. We just want them to be right."

"Oh, I see. I just need to scan you to ensure you have the funds before continuing if you don't mind. Sort of a security thing you understand."

"Sure. no problem."

The shop assistant pressed a couple of keys and the console beeped. Mr Pride went over and looked at the unit's screen and raised an eyebrow before coming back to them with a big smile on his face.

"Well, that's all good. Let's go into the room over there to discuss your requirements."

They followed him over to a room at the back and went in. They sat down in front of a low desk. It had a number of holo emitters on the top of it and Mr Pride sat down behind it.

"So, have you thought about what you would like?"

"Yes. Can I send an implant file to you?" Asked Datch.

“This system here can read it directly. Just tell your implant to send the file to local terminal.”

Datch did and the holo emitters started to display five rings.

“These are all iridium correct?”

“Yes, iridium bands. We also require a gem stone placed in each.”

“What sort of gem were you thinking about?”

“I have them here.” Said Carina fetching a small envelope out of her pocket.

“These are from Welly Four and they have been pre-cut so all you need to do is mount them in a small clasp. We have been told to make sure they are mounted as is. You must not alter them in anyway.”

“I completely understand. Please let me see.”

Carina handed them over to him and he carefully placed them on a small dish before getting out a magnifier.

“These are very exquisite gems, what are they?”

“We’re not sure but they react with us. It’s very important that they are mounted properly.”

“Oh of course, I totally understand.”

“So, we have five rings here.” he said turning back to the holograms. “Which is the front runner?”

“Well, we sort of want this bit here,” Said Carina pointing at the first ring, “and that bit there…” she went along the rings pointing at different bits.

“Ok, let me see what I can do.”

He started to move parts of the rings around and then fitted them together like a jigsaw puzzle. Then he scanned the gems and added them into the mix.

"How's that." He said as a ring appeared in the centre of the display.

They looked at it.

"Hmm... can you make the scrolly bit a little bigger and make that bit a bit wider." Said Carina.

"Yes, and can you just bring this bit over here a little more." added Datch.

Mr Pride worked his magic and after fifteen minutes a ring was rotating in front of them.

"How does that look?"

"Hmm...I like it, what do you think babes?" Asked Datch.

"It looks great."

"Ok. That's the one. How long will they take?"

Mr Pride looked at it.

"Err... They will take about two months."

He pressed a few buttons on the console and then it beeped.

"The cost will be eighteen hundred credits each."

"That's great. We'll leave the gems with you."

"I just need you both to put your fingers on here so I can get the sizes."

Datch and Carina moved forwards and put their hands in the scanner and it measured their fingers.

“Ok, I just need your authorisation for payment before I proceed.”

“Sure, go ahead.”

He scanned Datch’s implant and a box popped up in his head asking for authorisation. He accepted it.

“I’ll give you a call when they are ready so you can come in for a fitting.”

“Ok, we do have a busy schedule though so we’ll need a few days notice.”

“Certainly sir. No trouble at all.”

They thanked him and left the store before heading across the city to the Barbers Inn. They could have taken the transport tubes but it was a nice afternoon so they decided to walk. It took them about an hour to get there and they called in at the cookie shop on the way.

The Barbers Inn was its sleepy afternoon self. It was around half full with people, some of which were having food. When they walked in the sports channel was playing on the vid at the back of the bar and Jim was leaning against the bar watching it. He turned to look at the door when he heard it open. Datch pointed upstairs and Jim nodded. They headed up the stairs to the big table. It was gig night so it was reserved for them from lunch time. They sat down and two minutes later Jim came up the stairs with the beers.

“Hi folks, you’re a bit early.”

“Yes, we have been shopping. Jim, sit down please.”

“Sure, what’s up?” He asked sitting down.

“We have some news for you but you need to keep it to yourself, no one can know, ok?”

"Sure, no problem. mum's the word."

"We are going to be joined." Said Datch.

Jim looked at them.

"Wow. Congratulations."

"Thank you."

"When is the happy day?"

"27.12 and it's going to be in Traxsent. We would be very pleased if you could come."

"Oh, I wouldn't miss it for the world. I take it the press don't know?"

"No and that's the way it's got to stay. We have at least one planetary president coming and there maybe three, so things need to stay very hush hush. Ok?"

"Ok, not a word will pass my lips. We can't go drinking beer with this news. I'll be right back."

He got up and headed for the stairs. A minute later he came back up the stairs carrying a tray with a bottle of sparkling wine on ice and six glasses.

"Here we go folks, we need to celebrate the news properly."

He opened the bottle with a loud pop and poured out the wine giving everyone a glass.

"Well, here's to the happy couple."

They all picked up their glasses and took a sip.

"So, who's coming?"

"Widfab who you know to start with and maybe the Arcaneus Prime Minister Tinfa and Coola hopefully. Also,

Father Jamby, Tajiquay and Dag. But we need to send out the invites first."

"Oh, so it's going to be a big do then?"

"Yes, we're hoping Joni Jabi can come as well."

They talked a bit more and then Jim had to go and start sorting things out for the evening. When Timbo arrived, they told him the date and asked him to start sorting out security for the event. The evenings gig was a big success as normal and across the city in the jewellers safe the tiny gems started to glow.

Two days later Carina's mum and dad came to the ranch along with Rosey and Fred.

After a bit of catch up they started talking numbers. It took a while but they finally got it down to eight hundred people. There were a number of relatives who just wouldn't get there in time as they lived in distant parts of the galaxy or even in other ones and the transit times was months not weeks. Even on the Trans-galactic ships it still took six months to get between galaxies. This meant that the normal thing to do was to record the proceedings and then send them a copy of the vid. They went through a number of different styles of invitations before they decided on the final format.

"Ok. We're all booked in at the Twin Peaks hotel and spa in four weeks time for the weekend so we can have a look around." Said Datch.

"Did you say it's in Traxsent?" Asked Pabi, Carina's mum.

"Yes, it's just outside in the mountains."

"That's a long way by the continental shuttle."

"It is a bit of a way so we're taking the Raven. It will only take twenty minutes or maybe thirty if we hit traffic."

"Wow, that's quick we don't need to race there." Said Jata, Carina's dad.

"No, dad, Datch will be taking it easy, the Raven goes a lot faster than that when we want it too. It is a spaceship."

He turned and looked over his shoulder. The Raven sat on its pad near the barn looking very big and very black.

"Oh, I suppose it is."

"We'll come and pick you up on route if that's ok?"

"Sure."

"Fred, Rosey, can you two meet us here. I think I might get told off if I tried to park the Raven in the city."

"Sure, no problem."

Dechow turned to Datch.

"Datch, I think you need to contact Coola. You need to invite him and also tell him about the other heads of state. He'll need to know."

"Ok, I'll call him."

He picked up his vid and pressed a few buttons.

The display lit up and Coola's face appeared.

"Hi Datch, what can I do for you?"

"Hi Coola, I'm calling to invite you to mine and Carina's joining."

"Oh wow, congratulations."

"Thank you. We would be very honoured if you could come. It's on 27-12 in Traxsent. We have a very private hotel lined up and also Widfab and maybe Tinfa is coming."

“I know Widfab, who’s Tinfa?”

“He’s the Arcaneus Prime Minister.”

“Oh, Yes, I heard you guys had been busy again.”

“We just wanted to help.”

“Yes. Ok, it looks like I’m free that weekend so I should be able to come.”

“That’s great. I’ll get a formal invite to you today and Timbo can talk to your people about security.”

“Sounds good. I would love to chat but I have a delegation from Sigma Four coming tomorrow and I need to do some prep work.”

“Ok, Coola, Have a great day.”

“You too Datch and congratulations again.”

With that the comms channel closed.

“Ok, that’s him sorted, so we had better get all the invites off.”

Dechow sat looking at him.

“Dad, what’s up?”

“You have the president of the planet on speed dial.”

“Yes, why?”

“No, never mind.” he said slowly shaking his head.

“So, how do you want to do this?” Asked Tansya.

“Err…” Said Datch and looked thought full for a moment, “Ok, Fred you use my vid to record it. Pabi, Jata, if you stand here next to me. Mum, dad. If you stand here next to Carina. Then me and Carina will be in the middle.”

There was a lot of shuffling about and then Fred decided that the background didn't look right and they all moved across to the other veranda and tried again. This time Fred and Rosey were happy.

"It sounded a lot easier a few minutes ago." Said Datch.

"Ok, go for it." Said Fred.

"For what?" asked Pabi.

"No, I meant start. Never mind. OK after three. One, two, three."

"Hello, myself and Carina would like to invite you to our Joining. It will be taking place on the 27 of 12 86221 in Traxsent at the Twin Peaks hotel. We would be very pleased if you could come and celebrate with us. Hotel accommodation will be provided. Please reply with the number in your party if you can attend. We look forward to seeing you. Datch and Carina."

"Ok, not bad just a couple of little things. Mums and Dads, please smile more. It's joining not a funeral. Can we do another take please."

They did and then another as a fly landed on Carina's nose, then again because Dechow broke wind and then on take five Fred was finally happy. They all sat and watched it before agreeing it was ok.

Afterwards, they sat and entered the list into Datch's vid com. It took an hour before they were all entered. Then, when they were happy, Datch pressed the send button. The vid com took a good five minutes to send all the invites out.

"Right. That's that bit done."

"Yes, now have you thought about a celebration cake?" Asked Pabi.

"Hmm... not yet." Said Carina.

"Wow, there's a lot to think about." Added Datch.

"You have to think about your joining clothes, The entertainment, Food, Drinks and not to forget the seating plan." Said Tansya.

"Oh." Said Datch.

"Ok, cake first. I think something with a light sponge cake. Maybe five tiers?" Said Carina.

"Five what?" Asked Datch.

"Tiers, the number of levels the cake has."

"Do we need five?" Said Datch still a bit puzzled.

"Good point, we have eight hundred guests so better make it seven tiers." Added Carina.

"Yes, that would be a good idea." Added Tansya.

"That's a lot of cake." Said Datch.

"Yes, but you want to make sure everyone gets a decent sized piece. Now what about decorations?" asked Tansya.

"Err, well I think lots of balloons and golden drapes." Said Datch.

"What on the cake?" asked Carina.

"We're still on the cake. Sorry, I got a bit confused."

"Well, you want to have the two of you on the top. That's traditional." Said Pabi.

"Hmm, I would like a flower type design." Said Carina.

"What sort?" Asked Rosey.

They sat and thought for a while, then Datch had a thought.

“I know this may sound silly but what if we had a green creeper winding its way up the cake?”

“That’s not a bad idea.” Said Carina thinking about it, “It could have a bright yellow flowers and light green leaves. We would need to think about the cake colours. What do you think Rosey?”

“It sounds ok. Is it ok if I can get Tish to help me with the designs?”

“Sure, both you and Fred can do whatever you need to do. That’s your jobs. Oh, and the speeches.” Said Datch.

“Cool, we’ll draw up a few ideas. Then when you are both happy, we can find a cake designer to do the hard bit. Wait, Speech, what speech?”

“Fred gives a speech for Datch and you give one for me.” Said Carina.

“Oh. I do? What is it about?”

“You can look up sample speeches with your implant.”

“Ok, one sec. I’ll look it up.”

“I’ll go and get another round of drinks while you do that. Everyone want one?” asked Dechow.

They all nodded and he headed off into the bar with Jata to fetch them. Back on the veranda Rosey had a look of concentration on her face and so did Fred.

“Oh, I see, that’s ok. I can do that.” Said Rosey

Fred switched back to reality.

“Yes, should be ok, No problem.”

Just then Dechow and Jata came back with the drinks and handed them round.

"Right, so rings, invites and cake sort of done. What's next?" asked Datch.

"Dress code. The men normally wear suits and ladies were dresses." Said Tansya.

"Any particular type?" Asked Datch.

"No, you just need to make sure they all match. Carina, do you have any ideas?" Asked Tansya.

"Hmm… something light, maybe a cream or light pink?"

"We can go and have a look in some of the shops in the city if you like?" Asked Pabi.

"We could all go." Said Datch.

"No Datch. This is a lady's thing. You go with you dad and Fred to sort out the men's suits. You'll just have to wait until Carina chooses the colours so they don't clash, ok?" Said Tansya.

"Oh, ok."

"So, what else is there to do?" Asked Rosey.

"I'm not sure we can do much more before we see the venue. We need to know the layout before we can do much more planning. Then we'll be waiting on people responding to the invites." Said Tansya.

"What about the decorations?" Asked Datch.

"Can we do them tomorrow. My brain's starting to hurt." Said Carina.

"Sure babes."

“Ok. I’ll go and start some food. Barbeque ok everyone?” asked Dechow.

There was another round of nodding and the rest of the weekend was spent talking and coming up with an idea or two before everyone went home.

The following week the Raven was taken to the servicing area near the spaceport for its service. Timbo contacted planetary security services about the event and started to work out the best to way to do things all of which seemed to be giving him a head ache. Joni Jabi was roped in to do the media side of the joining and was given exclusive rights to the event.

For the next couple of weeks, they did gigs at the Barbers and started working on a new song called ‘Stars on Fire’.

Then, Datch got a call from the service centre to go and fetch the Raven.

It came back with a clean bill of health. Apparently, the only things that needed changing were one of the external spotlights and a toilet seat that had a damaged hinge on one side. Datch sat on the veranda looking at the report on his vid com when his dad came walking out of the bar.

“Everything ok?” He asked.

“Yes, looks like I got my credits worth from the service. They went through everything and all they found was a blown light and broken toilet.”

“They can cause real problems in deep space.”

“What? The spotlight.”

“No, the toilet. Just imagen being ten light years from the nearest planet and you find out the toilet doesn’t work.”

They both started to laugh and then after Dechow asked.

“What about the drive systems?”

“All have triple A’s next to them with a small note stating they are working better than when they were made and a question mark after it.”

“That will be Qwots and his little adjustments.”

“Can I have a look?”

“Sure dad, here.” Datch passed his vid com to his dad.

Dechow started to browse through the list.

“Wow, they really do check everything. They even checked Tanks teddy bear.”

“Yes, I wonder what for though?”

“Probably stuffing or something.”

He finally came to the end of the list.

“Looking at this, I can’t think of anything they missed.”

“No, me neither. Dad, what’s a quantum flux inversion controller?”

“I think it’s inside the interspace drive but I’m not sure. You could always ask Qwots next time you see him.”

“Hmm, I might do.”

“So, we all set for next weekend?”

“Yes. I’m quite looking forward to it.”

“I know your mum is. She packed her bikini for the spa.”

“I’ll tell Carina, she might want to try it.”

“I’m sure she will. Err… when you have a spare minute can you come and give me a hand with the roof on the barn around the back. I need to replace a couple of the solar converters."

"Sure dad, do you want to do it now?"

"Yes, why not."

Datch got up and followed his dad outside.

# Twin Peaks Hotel

The following weekend arrived and it was time to head to Twin Peaks hotel.

Datch and Carina were up early and were very excited about the trip. Datch was sitting down at the breakfast bar drinking his coffee.

“Datch, did you pick up the list of things we need to ask about?”

“Yes, it’s in the rucksack’s front pocket.”

“I need to check if I packed our swimwear.”

“You have, Three times!”

“Cool, did we say ten thirty pick up for my mum and dad?”

“No, that is when Fred and Rosey are going. We said we would call your mum and dad just before we left here.”

“Oh yes. I forgot that bit. Did you say you had the list?”

“Yes. Now sit down and drink your coffee.”

She walked over and sat next to him.

“I’m very excited.” Carina said.

“Yes, I can tell.”

“What do you mean?”

“You’re jumping about like a cat on a hot tin roof.”

“Am I? Oh. well, I’m excited.”

Datch sighed.

“I am as well, but I’m trying to keep calm so we don’t forget something.”

“Good, because I keep forgetting things.”

“I had three more replies last night.” Said Datch trying to change the subject.

“Oh yes, who from?”

“One from Widfab saying thanks and he wouldn’t miss it for the galaxy. He also added that Father Jamby, Dag and Tajiquay plus families are coming with him, that way it won’t take them three weeks to get here. They need ten family rooms.”

“Wow. How are they getting here then? On the Carpaycus?”

“No. Widfab is bringing Welly Four’s destroyer. He said it will give it a good work out. Anyway, I think the Carpaycus is still at Arcaneus.”

“Why?”

“Well, I’ve received Don’s response at the same time as Tinfa’s and they both took the same time to get here according to the time transfer stamps.”

“Oh, did anyone else respond?”

“Yes, one of my relatives has said yes and is sorting out transport.”

“So how many is that so far?”

“Err… one sec, five hundred and eighty-seven.”

“Wow. Cool. Did I ask you about the list?”

“Yes.”

“Good.”

They carried on chatting and moved outside to the pool after putting their bags in the Raven.

Around mid-morning, bikes could be heard in the distance. Then over the village Fred's and Hagger's bikes appeared.

"Looks like it's time to go. I'll fetch your dad." Said Tansya who had come out to join them.

The bikes landed at the back of the Raven and the riders pushed the bikes inside before coming over to them.

"Are we ready folks?" asked Fred walking up.

"Yes, just about. Mum has just gone to find Dad and then we're good."

"I'll call my mum." Said Carina.

"Let her know, we'll be about twenty minutes. We have the city restrictions to deal with."

"Ok."

They headed over to the Raven and went up to the cockpit. Datch sat down and his dad was going to sit in the co-pilot's seat but Carina beat him to it.

"Err..." he said.

She smiled at him with puppy dog eyes. He gave up and sat behind Datch.

The Raven took off and headed for the city and then south to Carina's mum and dad's farm. They had to fly around the edge of the city in a narrow flight corridor to avoid the traffic at the spaceport and speed was restricted to one hundred KMPH.

Datch landed the Raven at the end of the drive with it facing towards the city. Carina went to fetch her mum and dad. Dechow was going to get in the co-pilots seat before Datch stopped him.

“Sorry dad, Carina wants to see where we're going.”

He looked at Datch and sat back down. It was the first time that his dad had just done as Datch said. No questions, no buts, just did. Datch said thanks and after a couple of minutes Carina came up the stairs followed by Pabi and Jata. She showed them to their seats next to Dechow and Tansya.

“I've put their things in Jep's room.” said Carina sitting down.

“No probs.” Said Datch.

“This is a very nice err... ship.” Said Jata.

“Yes, very big too.” Added Pabi.

“Thanks. If you like, we can give you the full tour on the way out.”

“That would be lovely thanks.” Said Pabi.

“Ok folks, everyone ready?”

“Err, is it like a shuttle?” Asked Pabi.

“Not quite.” Said Datch grinning and turned to the front.

“Yuland city control. This is the Raven, ready for take-off on route to Traxsent.”

“Raven cleared to launch. Follow beacon 819538 for Traxsent cruising height ten thousand metres. Be advised that traffic for the spaceport will be on your right and is currently heavy.”

“Copy that control.”

Datch brought the thruster online and the Raven lifted off. Datch started to increase speed and height. The sky started to look a darker green as they reached cruising height.

"This is very nice. I thought it would be a bit more bumpy. Did you say we were going to go fast?" Asked Jata.

Carina turned to look at him.

"We are, our speed is currently eight thousand kilometres per hour."

"Oh wow. That's fast."

Datch pressed a few virtual buttons and the vid screen above him stared displaying the view outside with speed and heading.

"There you go. That's the view from the front of the Raven"

"Everything looks so small."

"We are ten kilometres up in the air mum." Said Carina.

Carina's mum and dad were transfixed by the view on the screen.

"Raven. This is Yuland city control. We are about to transfer you to Traxsent control."

"Copy that Yuland city control." Answered Datch.

"Have a great day. Yuland city out."

"Traxsent Control, this is the Raven inbound from Yuland city. Requesting landing at Twin Peaks Resort landing area."

"Good morning, Raven. Traffic is very light. Please head on a vector of 263.3 17.3 and reduce hight to three thousand metres. Speed five hundred KMPH."

"Copy that Traxsent. Descending to three thousand."

Datch took the Raven down and below them the mountains came into view. Some of the peaks were still covered with snow.

"Raven. This is Traxsent control please slow to two hundred KMPH and turn on vector 193.4, 71.3 as you come over the city. Air space is currently clear."

"Copy that control."

As they got closer to Traxsent the falls came into view. Millions of gallons of water pouring over the edge of a cliff and falling two kilometres to the river below.

"Look at the falls. They look amazing." Said Pabi.

"Yes, if we get chance, I'll try to sort a trip out to see them." Said Datch.

The Raven flew over Traxsent and headed towards the mountains.

"Raven. Landing area is twenty kilometres ahead. Air is clear and navigation is now at your discretion."

"Thanks, Traxsent control."

Datch slowed the Raven down to a hundred KMPH and dropped down lower.

Up ahead was a small valley with mountains on either side. Large forests covered the sides and a small lake sat in the centre. Here and there were open areas that ran down the mountains to the valley bottom with ski lifts and little cabins dotted about. At the end of the valley was a large hotel nestled in the hillside. It had a large outdoor pool and a large seating area next to it looking out across the valley. Just to the left of it was a landing area hidden in the trees.

Datch slowed down even more bringing the ship in slow over the trees before landing on pad number seventeen.

“Traxsent control. This is the Raven. We have landed.”

“Ok Raven, Have a great stay. Control out.”

Datch shut the system down and then after showing Pabi and Jata around the ship they headed outside.

At the bottom of the ramp were two staff members. One was a tall woman with brown hair and the second was a man with a moustache. Both were wearing smart dark red suits.

The tall woman stepped forward.

“Welcome to The Twin Peaks Hotel and Spa. I am Caroline your concierge for the length of your stay and this is Serg, He will take your bags for you.”

“Hi I’m Datch and this is my wife to be Carina.”

“Please to meet you.”

“Does your ship need any services?”

“No. It’s good thanks.”

“Ok. If you would like to follow me, we will get you checked in.”

“Thank you.” Said Datch.

“The manger has arranged for a tour this afternoon around 1pm if that is, ok?”

“Yes, that will be fine thanks.”

They followed Caroline through a small wooded area full of Bellatrixian pines. They emerged from the trees into a large tarmacked area with a pond in the centre and a very ornate fountain. Behind it was the main hotel. It was four stories high and had two large glass doors at the front. The building looked like it had been made out of wooden logs and timbers. It all looked very rustic.

They went inside and were greeted with a very modem reception area. Datch was led over to the desk.

“This is Datch Thome.” Said Caroline to the receptionist.

“Hello, Sir, we have five suites booked for you. Please can you step forward in groups so you can be scanned for door entry.”

Carina stepped up next to Datch and they were scanned.

Then one after another they were all checked in.

“This is very nice.” Said Pabi looking around.

“Yes, it took three weeks of looking to find it.” Said Carina.

“Is it expensive?” She asked.

“Yes, very. It’s the sort of place that if you need to ask, you can’t afford it.”

“Oh!”

“Don’t worry mum, we can afford it.”

Caroline turned to them.

“If you would like to follow me, I’ll escort you to your suites.”

“Thank you.”

They headed to their rooms and arranged to meet up in the bar afterwards.

Datch and Carina looked around their suite. It was all tastefully done in wooden timbers and pine panels. There was an artificial log fire burning in a large fire place. However, it was not currently giving off any heat. Also, there was a glass coffee table with two very large sofas and a mini bar in the corner. The obligatory pamphlets were in a little rack on a small table between the sofas. It had a large sliding door that opened onto a balcony that looked out across the valley and had a small table with chairs so that you could sit and enjoy the view. The main room had a door leading to the bedroom.

The bedroom had an on-suite bathroom with his and hers sinks, bidet and a very large spa bath with a separate shower cubical. The bed itself was an extra-large king size double with enough room to sleep an entire family. The floor was fitted with a light cream deep pile carpet. It had a large vid screen opposite to the bed and a large sliding door that opened onto the balcony. The whole suite stated that this was a hotel for the rich.

They put their bits away and headed to find the bar.

The bar had a very large imitation log fire burning away but as it was the start of summer it was not giving off heat either. It did look really cool though. They found a table and sat down. A few minutes later Dechow came in followed by Fred and Tansya. Then Pabi and Jata came in and stood looking at the fire for a minute before coming to join them.

"Our room is amazing." Pabi said sitting down.

"Yes, the bath is huge." Added Jata.

"Well, this is a five star plus hotel." Said Carina.

Datch put his hand up and a waiter came over.

"Who wants what to drink?"

They ordered their drinks and the waiter went off to fetch them. Pabi kept looking around at the fire.

"Mum, It's not real." Said Carina noticing her.

"I couldn't work out if it was or not."

"It does look very good, doesn't it?"

Just then the waiter came back with the drinks and shortly after Hagger and Rosey came in.

They chatted for a while and had a light snack for lunch.

The hotel manager came over and introduced himself

"Hi, I'm Gorge the hotel manager."

It was then time for the tour. They were taken around the hotel including the grounds and spa. They finally came to the main function room which had a capacity of one thousand people. It had its own bars and a stage at the end. The left-hand side had a number of large sliding doors that opened out on to a very large lawn overlooking the valley.

Gorge sat them down at one of the tables.

"So, what do you think?"

Datch looked at Carina. She nodded.

"We like it. Therefore, we would like to go ahead with the 27/12. We will be booking the whole hotel for the week prior to and week after the main event."

"Excellent. What are your requirements?" he asked.

"Well, we have three planetary leaders coming to start with and we are expecting around eight hundred people in total."

"I take it the valley will need to be secured?"

"Yes, we are currently in talks with the planetary security services. Timbo our tour manager will be contacting you with the arrangements concerning that shortly." Said Datch.

"Are all of your staff vetted?" Asked Dechow.

"Yes, they all have security clearance as you would expect from an establishment such as ours. We have catered for a number of other events similar to yours in the past including a couple of presidential joining's."

"That's great." Said Datch.

"Will you be supplying your own catering for the main event or do you wish us to handle it? We can cater for various alien races."

"Yes, it would be easier if you could do it. I have a list for you to look over. It's not a complete list yet but pretty close." Said Fred.

He handed the manager a list.

"Just one second please." He said and put his hand up.

A member of staff came running over to them.

"Could you get the head chef for me please." He said and turned to Datch. "Would you all like a drink?"

There was a round agreement and the manager turned back to the staff member.

"And can you get a large bottle of the good sparkling wine and ten glasses please."

The staff member went running off.

"Are you having a cake?" asked the manager.

"Yes, we will be having a seven-tier cake. Rosey, have you got the drawings?"

"Yes." she got out her vid comm and pulled up a number of images.

"That is a bit more intricate than we are able to do."

"Do you know anyone local to do it. We can get it made in Yuland city but then we would need to get it here."

"There is a custom baker in Traxsent that specialises in cakes. One moment." he started to flick through his vid com.

"Ahh, there it is. If you wish I can call them and arrange a meeting while you're here?"

"That would be great thanks."

"OK, on the day itself. Where were you thinking of having the ceremony?"

"We were thinking outside on the lawn with the mountains as a backdrop."

"Yes, that is quite a popular choice. We can arrange a raised area with a podium for the official carrying out the ceremony. There should be enough room for the seating out there. We can also put up some large vid screens so the folks at the back can see everything."

"That sounds like a great idea." Said Tansya and then added "We wouldn't want anyone to miss anything."

At that moment the staff member who it turned out was the assistant manager came back with a chef and a waiter pushing a trolly with glasses and a large bottle in a bucket of ice.

"Ah, Claud. Ladies and gentlemen this is our head chef Claud."

There was a round of hello's and then he was given the list.

"Hmm. Yes, I think I can do all this. What's Arcaneus cuisine?"

"Err, we're not sure but I've sent a message asking them what they would like to eat. I think it's just normal food. That's what we had when we were there."

"Ok. That shouldn't be a problem."

"Also, the Minister Prime of Welly Four is coming."

"Ahh. That will be kababs then."

"Yes, they will have normal food to start with and then they like kababs in the evening. If they don't get them, they carry an emergency kabab machine with them that comes out."

"They do?"

"Yes, it's apparently part of the emergency kit on all of their ships."

"Well, you learn something new every day." Said the manager.

"Ok, I'll make sure kababs are available in the evening then. Also, I see you have put ice-cream down."

"Yes, it's my favourite." Said Datch.

"What sort would you like?"

"Chocolate, Mint and Renar Berry if you can."

"Yes, no problem. I'm sure we can supply everything."

"Excellent. Ok. Thank you, Claud." Said the Manager.

The chief nodded and left them.

"The next thing is entertainment."

"Yes, we are going to have the Snowmen perform in the evening with a disco afterwards."

"Right, so what we would normally do is set this room up with the tables so that they leave an area at the front for a dance floor. The DJ's booth will go at the side of the stage over there." He said pointing. "Also, we can set out a buffet in the evening along that side. Where were you thinking about having the set meal?"

"Hmm... will there be enough room outside for a marquee?" asked Carina.

"Yes, we should be able to do that. Ok. Gifts, Will you be receiving them?"

"Err," Said Datch.

"Yes, there will be gifts." Said Tansya stepping in.

"Ok. In which case, will you be wanting to display them?"

"I'm not sure we'll have time to open them." Said Carina.

"We can sort out a table at the back over there to place them on. We can even place a small force field up to keep them safe and a person to help point them out to guests."

"That sounds like a good idea." Said Pabi.

"Excellent. I think that just about covers everything for now. I'm not sure if a told you but the cost of the resort for two weeks will two hundred and fifty thousand credits."

"That's fine. Will there be any costs on top of that?"

"I don't think so at the moment. If anything, comes up, I'll contact you. Also, please note. As you are booking the whole resort, we can only refund fifty percent of the price if you cancel. Now I'm required to take a fifty percent deposit."

"Can we pay in full?" asked Datch.

"Yes, certainly. One second while I put the details in my vid com."

He started to enter the information in his vid com and after a couple of minutes he turned back to them.

"So, who is paying?"

"I am." Said Datch.

“Ok, if you would just like to press here and except the prompt from your implant.”

Datch pressed the accept button on the vid com and a little box appeared in his mind saying ‘Please verify transaction for 250,000 credits to Twin Peaks Hotel?’

Datch agreed and the implant said processing and then after a moment it said Transaction complete.”

“Ok, all done.”

The manager looked at his vid com.

“Thank You. Is there anything else I can do for you while I’m here?”

“Yes. Is it possible to get a trip to the falls organised for tomorrow followed by a trip to the Dancing Jaxx?”

“Yes, let me see if the baker is available tomorrow morning. Then we can fit it all in together if that’s, ok?”

“Yes, that would be great, thanks.”

The manager called the bakers and they arranged to meet her in the morning.

“Ok, so if we arrange the tour for say forty-five minutes after your meeting with the baker, Will that be enough time?”

“Yes, I would think so.”

“Ok, I’ll get Caroline to arrange it for you.”

“If you can contact Fred with anything else you need, He is my man of honour and will be dealing with organisation of it all.” Said Datch.

“That’s great. Please, finish your drinks and feel free to have a good look around the room before you head back to the main hotel. I would love to stay and chat but unfortunately, I need to sort out some matters in the office. I look forward to seeing you on the 19/12."

"No problem. Thank you and we'll see you then."

The manager got up and he shook everyone's hand before heading out of the room.

Pabi turned to Datch.

"Did you just pay him a quarter of a million credits?"

"Yes, why?"

"Our whole farm is worth less than that."

"Well, our last tour has netted us three and a half million each."

"Wow, I knew you were making a lot of money but that is incredible."

"Mum, my account stands at seven and a half million credits."

Jata nearly choked on his drink.

"Are you ok dad?"

"Yes, I think so."

"We also have the Ice-cream business bringing in money as well."

"Well, we know where to come for a loan then." Said Jata getting his breath back.

They all laughed and then after a good look around headed back to the main hotel.

The next morning a limo turned up to take them to the bakers. Pabi and Jata looked at the inside of it. It was the height of luxury and they sat down carefully on the seats. Datch and Carina sat next to the drinks unit and promptly started to get a drink.

“Does anyone else want a drink?” Asked Datch.

Pabi and Jata were looking at them. To them this was so posh they were almost scared to breath on it, whereas Datch and Carina were in their normal environment. Dechow smiled.

“I’ll have a light beer if there is one?”

“Sure dad. Mum?”

“No. I’m good thanks.”

“Mum, Dad?” Asked Carina.

“We’re good thank you.” Said Pabi.

They all sat back and relaxed in their seats for the twenty-minute trip into Traxsent.

The bakers was a small building with a shop at the front. The shop had a large selection of cakes and cookies on display. They went inside and met with the confectionary engineer (baker). They tried a few small cakes to work out which was best type of sponge for the filling. After which Rosey showed the design to the baker. After a few adjustments it was all agreed and they had some cookies to celebrate.

They went outside and were taken to the shuttle port where a shuttle took them to the falls. It circled above them before slowly dropping to the bottom of the falls. Water crashed off of a deflection shield which was over the top of the shuttle as it descended. It reached the bottom and landed next to a viewing platform. They stepped outside the shuttle onto the platform. They stood and watched as the water hit the base of the falls. The noise was incredible as tonnes of falling water hit the lake at the bottom of the cliff. A force field was in place to protect the tourists from the falling water and anything else that came over the top of the falls. As they looked up the sky was full of rainbows. Afterwards, the shuttle took them back to the shuttle port and they headed out into the city.

They wandered through the streets to the Dancing Jaxx where they had arranged to meet the Snowmen and have something to eat. When they entered Talia and Jarna were sitting near one of the windows on a large table. They crossed the room and headed over to it.

After a round of hellos and introductions for Carina's parents they got down to business.

"So, how many numbers do you want us to do and are there any songs that you would like in particular?" Asked Talia.

"We were thinking eight songs. Also, I know it's our song but is there any chance of Star Lovers to start with for our first dance?" Asked Carina.

"I'm sure we can do it. Any chance of getting the bikers for backing singers during it?"

"I'll sort that, no problem." Said Fred.

"Great, we'll make sure it's perfect for you."

"Cool. We have a DJ coming on after you so hopefully you won't miss much of the party. Fred will sort out the final details with you as things are still being worked out."

"We all feel very honoured that you've asked us to do it. I can't believe that the little Datch we first met in here is now getting joined. We're all really looking forward to it."

“We can’t wait ourselves.” Said Carina.

“I’ll give you Timbo’s ID so you can call him. The event will have a lot of security as there are at least two planetary presidents coming maybe three.”

“So, no pressure then.”

“No more than normal.” Said Datch and laughed.

“You will have to have a security check, but Timbo will sort that out for you.” Said Fred.

“I’m sure it will be fine.”

“So, I think after that we need another drink and some food.”

Datch put his hand up and a waiter came over and took their food and drinks orders.

They finalised the details as best they could while having some food and afterwards headed back to the hotel.

# The Last Days

The next few months flew past very quickly and everything came together ready for the joining. Their parents were going to the hotel at the beginning of the week to welcome the guests as they arrived. Whereas, Datch and Carina along with Fred and Rosey were going to arrive the day before the joining in time for the pre-joining party.

It was the week before when it happened. It was early evening and The Pack were in the Barbers Inn for the last gig before the joining. They were sitting on the balcony getting ready for the nights gig.

"Datch!" Said Fred loudly, "Look!"

They all stopped and looked where Fred was pointing. It was the vid screen.

A reporter was standing in the street outside the Barbers Inn. Jim spotted them looking and turned the sound up.

"I'm standing outside the Barbers Inn and a source has told us that very shortly Datch and Carina from The Pack are going to be joined. We're going to try to talk to them and find out if it is true."

The camera turned to look at the Barbers Inn.

"Jim, No!" shouted Datch from the balcony.

Jim nodded and shouted at the bouncers on the door.

"Well, we knew this would happen at some point. It's amazing it's taken this long. Do you want me to go and give them a statement?" asked Fred.

"Yes, if you can, it's going to get messy otherwise." Said Datch.

"What do you want me to say?"

"Just tell them that it's true and Joni Jabi has the rights to it."

"Ok. Back in a minute." He stood up and took a deep breath before heading for the stairs.

Down below there was a commotion at the door as the reporter tried to get inside. Fred walked down the steps and took another deep breath.

The vid screen was showing the outside of the bar and a number of bouncers blocking the reporter from getting in. The door opened behind the bouncers and Fred walked out.

"Let miss Jocks come forward please." he said.

The reporter stood right in front of Fred.

"If you would please stand back a little I'll give you a statement."

She waved at the news crew and they all stepped back.

"OK. Miss Jocks, you are correct. If you would like get ready."

He paused while Miss Jocks did her intro.

"We're here outside the Barbers Inn in Yuland city. Fred, a member of The Pack has agreed to give us a statement. Fred, please go ahead."

The vid turned to look at Fred.

"Hello everyone. I would like to formally announce that The Packs Datch and Carina are going to be joined within the next couple of weeks. They are both looking forward to it as are the rest of The Pack. I'm sure all of your viewers will join with me in wishing them all the happiness for the future. I cannot give you any more details about the event itself for security reasons." He paused and then continued. "Joni Jabi has exclusive rights to record the event and therefore any further information should come through him. Thank you."

"Can't you tell us the date and where it's happening?"

"Sorry miss Jocks, as I stated I cannot say for security reasons. That is the statement we are releasing. That is all. Thank you."

Fred turned and went back into the Barbers Inn.

"There you have it, folks. Datch and Carina from The Pack are to be joined. Remember you heard it first from channel 6 news."

The vid changed back to the news room.

Fred came walking up the stairs and as he reached the table Datch's vid com started ringing.

Datch looked at it, it was his mum.

"Hi mum."

"Hi Datch, are you folks ok? We were flicking through the news channels and happened to spot the Barbers Inn."

"Yes, we're ok. Fred looks a little flustered after the statement though."

"OK. Are you going to be able to get home alright?"

"Hmm… If they are still outside after the gig we'll stay over in the Barbers and then head back in the morning when it quietened down. Mum it maybe an idea if dad puts the shield up in case you get any unwelcome visitors."

"Your dad was already thinking about that. The whole planet will know in a few hours and the galaxy won't be far behind."

“Yes, I’m going to contact Joni in a minute and let him know it’s got out.”

“Well, if you need help, you know where we are.”

“Ok Mum, love you.”

“Love you too.”

The channel closed.

Datch pressed a few buttons on his vid com and after a moment Joni Jabi’s face appeared.

“Hi Joni.”

“Hi Datch, how’s it going?”

“Ok thanks, but the news is out. The press where just outside the Barbers trying to get to us.”

“Did they get in?”

“No. The bouncers were already here and stopped them. Fred went out and gave a statement confirming it and told them to come through you as you have exclusive rights to it.”

“I think they are trying already. I’ve got a call waiting from my boss at the station.”

“I better let you go then.”

“Ok, Thanks for the heads up.”

“No Problem. See you next week.”

“You take care and I’ll see you at The Twin Peaks.”

Datch put his vid com down.

“Ok folks, let’s get our heads in the game for tonight. I have a feeling they are going to be dancing in the street again. Oh, and we had better tell Jim he may need a lot more bouncers."

They headed down stairs and after telling Jim what was going on, they headed to the room behind the stage.

The bouncer re-enforcement worked and the gig went very well. The local security forces were deployed outside for safety reasons as well as a number of officers inside who also wanted autographs. The street was packed and the crowd just kept getting bigger until the beginning of the second set. The press didn't get a look in, that is apart from one vid operator who had snuck in and stood on the balcony. Datch let him record it as long as he left at the end of the gig.

The beginning of the week started with Datch flying most of The Pack and both sets parents to the hotel. Fred, Hagger and Rosey stayed with Datch and Carina at the ranch.

At the hotel Timbo was very busy along with a very large security force. People were starting to arrive and both the Welly Four and the Arcaneus delegations had arrived. In orbit above the planet were both the interstellar destroyer and three IPSF ships. One of which was the Carpaycus.

The president of Bellatrix, Coola was heading to the hotel mid-week as soon as the security services were all up and running. The Welly Four delegation now included a group of six monks who once the official Bellatrixian part of the ceremony was complete were going to perform a blessing with Father Jamby leading it. Father Jamby was also making use of the hotel bar along with Widfab and Tinfa.

The day before the joining arrived. Datch took a number of bags and cases to the Raven before going to sit with the others at the pool.

"How are you doing?" Asked Fred.

“I’m ok, just a bit nervous that’s all.”

“I think we all are. But it will be fine and I’m sure it’s all going to go to plan.” Said Fred who was trying to reassure himself as much as everyone else.

“I know.” Said Datch looking into the distance.

They all sat with their thoughts for a while and then Fred spoke again.

“Ok it’s getting close to departure time. Let’s have one last check around to make sure we’ve not forgot anything. Rosey, you go with Carina and I’ll take Datch.”

“What about me?” asked Hagger.

“Hmm... you can guard the drinks.” Said Fred.

“What from?”

“Insects. Just stay there and we’ll be back in a minute or two.” Said Rosey.

They headed off and did one more check. Fred checked he had got the rings and that all the suits were sorted. Rosey made sure that the Tiara’s and dresses were all on board the Raven. Datch and Carina checked all their luggage was ready for the honeymoon. Ten minutes later they headed back to finish their drinks.

Fred picked up his drink.

“Well folks. Here’s to a smooth joining.”

They all lifted their glasses and then took a big drink.

“Ok. Let’s get this show on the road as they say.”

They finished their drinks and headed to the Raven. Fred called Timbo to let him know they were on route.

Five minutes later the Raven was climbing high over the desert for the four-thousand-kilometre trip. Below the desert went by very quickly. In the cockpit it was very quiet. Everyone was lost in their own thoughts. The only person who wasn't was Hagger who sat playing a game on his vid com. Fifteen minutes later the mountains came into view and Datch brought the ship in over Traxsent before turning towards the hotel. The air space was showing a no-fly zone around the valley with the hotel. A number of small security ships were patrolling the area. Datch got clearance to enter the restricted zone and brought the Raven in for a slightly bumpy landing.

"Err... sorry folks, touch of nerves."

"You're good Datch."

Datch shut down the systems and they all got up.

"Ok Folks. This is it. Let's go."

They went to the cargo bay and opened the door.

Three porters were standing at the back of the ship waiting for them along with Caroline the concierge.

"Welcome back." she said stepping forward.

"I'm here to escort you to your rooms and then your pre joining party. If you require anything while you're here, I'm on twenty-four hour call for you."

"Thank you." Said Datch. "Hagger, can you sort out the bags for us?"

"Sure Datch." He turned to the porters, "if you would like to follow me."

They waited until the porters came back with all the bags and then followed Caroline, this time she took them in through a back door and up to their rooms.

Timbo was waiting at the end of the corridor and walked over when they came out of the lift.

"Hi Timbo, how's it going?" Asked Datch.

"All is good thanks. The guests are waiting for you in the main bar for your pre-joining. When you're ready to go down to the party I will let the staff know. They have been briefed about what you like and will have drinks ready for you."

"Thanks, Timbo, you're a star." Said Carina.

"Yes, thanks Timbo." Added Datch.

They put their things in their rooms and Rosey and Fred helped Datch and Carina get ready."

Thirty minutes later they headed down towards the main bar. They stopped just before the landing at the top of the stairs.

"Are you folks ready?"

"Yes. I think so." Said Carina.

"Yes, me too." Said Datch.

"Please wait here until you hear me start to announce you and then come walking down the stairs." Said Caroline.

"Ok. One second though." Said Fred.

Fred put his hand out Datch looked at it then put his hand on the top followed by Carina and Rosey.

"One, Two, Three. Let's Party!" He said and nodded to Caroline.

She walked halfway down the steps and stopped. Then she clapped her hands three times very loudly.

The room below went very quiet and then Caroline announced in a very loud voice.

“Ladies, Gentlemen and Aliens. Please welcome Datch and Carina.”

Datch and Carina started to walk down the stairs with Fred and Rosey flanking them. The room below erupted in applause.

They stopped just past Caroline. Datch cleared his throat. The room went quiet.

“On behalf of myself and Carina, welcome to our joining celebration. It is our great pleasure to have you all here to witness our two souls becoming one. Thank you all. Now please enjoy the party.”

Everyone applauded.

Datch and Carina carried on down the stairs and joined the party. Caroline escorted them across the room to a big table in the bar. It took a while as a lot of people wanted to say hello. When they arrived, their parents and the rest of The Pack were standing at it waiting for them.

They sat down between their parents.

“You got here in one piece then?” Asked Tansya.

“Yes, it was quite a good flight.”

“Is the Raven ready for the honeymoon?” Asked Dechow.

“Yes, it’s refuelled and the systems are all good. Oh, and I cleaned the fluffy dice.” Said Datch grinning.

“What fluffy dice?”

Datch started to laugh and everyone else joined in.

“So, let’s get this party started.” Said Datch.

Fred nodded at Caroline who was standing near the bar. She turned and said something to the barman and music start to play and a round of champaign came out to the table.

"Here's to the joining of your souls."

After Datch and Carina had finished their champaign and been equipped with a couple of pints of beer, they got up and started to work themselves around the guests welcoming them to the party. Fred and Rosey followed them around making sure they had everything they wanted. The rest of the day flew by and after a karaoke session in the bar in the evening it was time to go to bed.

# The Joining

The morning of the joining arrived and after breakfast that was served in bed. Datch and Carina went to separate rooms.

They both had their own hair dresser and makeup team to help them to get ready. It took two hours to prepare them and then it was time.

Outside, the large gardens had been transformed. There was a huge marquee filled with tables and chairs. An external bar had been built next to it along with a staff area for the food to be taken out from. The main grass area had a large number of white chairs laid out in rows separated by three aisles. The two outside isles each had a small white tent at the end and the centre one led to the main marquee at the back. Each of the aisles were lined with white and yellow flowers with bright green stems and green leaves. At the front was a small stage with a podium in the centre. The stage was also covered in white and yellow flowers running up a number of poles and across the top which was in the shape of a pyramid.

Fred walked along the corridor to the room where Datch was getting ready. He was dressed in a ceremonial suit with long sweeping back tails and large lapels. It was a traditional dark green colour and had two flowers, one in each lapel signifying the two to be joined. He stopped and knocked on the door before going in.

Datch was sitting having the last bit of makeup added. He was wearing a white ceremonial robe with gold and light green symbols embroidered on it. A towel was currently draped over it while they finished things off.

"How you doing?" Fred asked.

“I’m ok apart from my stomach is doing summersaults and I feel like my legs are going to turn to jelly.”

“Well, that sounds normal for you.”

They both laughed.

“Right. Here, have this.”

Fred poured some brown liquid out into two small glasses and handed one to Datch.

“What is it?”

“Just a shot of whisky to steady your nerves and also mine. Here’s to the both of you.”

They touched glasses and necked the drinks. Datch shook his head as he swallowed it.

“Wow. That’s good stuff.”

“It should be, that was a fifty-credit shot of Dark Forest malt.”

The makeup artist finished and removed the towel. Datch stood up.

“What do you think?” he asked.

“Well, you look the part, that’s for sure. Let’s go and get you joined.”

They headed down the stairs and out of a side door. As they came to the garden some of the guests were starting to take their seats. It was another thirty minutes until the ceremony but both the parties to be joined had to be in their tents before it started. Datch and Fred walked over to the tent to the left. The other tent had the cover pulled down signifying that Carina was in there.”

Datch and Fred entered the other tent and closed the front cover. Inside there were two chairs. They sat down.

“Well, Datch, this is it. Time for you two to become one. And don’t worry, I’m right behind you.”

“Thanks Fred. To be honest I’m shaking a bit.”

“Here, have another one of these.”

Fred handed him another shot of the whisky.

“Thanks.”

They sat in the tent chatting about how Fred had helped them get together at the beginning and how they got to where they were now. Then a gong sounded outside.

“Ok. looks like we’re up. Come and stand in front of the door next to me.” Said Fred standing up.

They stood up and moved to the door.

Outside another gong sounded twice. A little slot opened and a set of eyes looked through. Fred turned to the eyes and nodded.

Moments later the gong sounded three times and then the cover over the door dropped to the ground.

“OK. Let’s go.”

Datch and Fred came out into the sunlight. The chairs were now full of people all looking at them. Up on the stage behind the podium was the official who was carrying out the ceremony. On the opposite side Carina and Rosey had emerged from the tent. Carina was in a long flowing white and gold dress with flowers in her hair. To say she looked stunning was an understatement.

They both walked slowly to the stage and as they did white flower petals were scattered in front of them.

They reached the front and Datch offered his hand to Carina and helped her onto the stage. They stood either side of the small podium and then turned to face each other.

The official then spoke.

“Ladies, Gentlemen and Aliens. We are here today to join together these two souls. They have asked to become one with each other.” He stopped and waited.

The gong rang out twice.

“Datch Thome. Do you wish to become one with Carina?” he asked.

“Yes, I do.”

“Carina Ganta. Do you wish to become one with Datch?”

“Yes. I do.”

“Does anyone here know of any reason why they should not become one?”

The gong rang out threes time with a pause between each strike. Then the official paused for a moment before continuing.

“Datch please hold out your left hand.”

Datch put his hand out and the official took it with one hand.

“Carina please hold out your left hand.”

Carina put her hand out and the official took it with his other hand.

“We now bring your hands together to show unity of your beings.”

He moved their hands together and then reached down and picked up a silvery white cord.

The gong sounded again.

"We now bind your hands to join your souls."

He placed the cord around their wrists and tied them together.

"Datch please give your pledge."

Datch looked straight into Carina's eyes.

"Carina, I promise to take care of you. I promise to love you. I promise to keep you in my heart forever. I promise to support you and treasure you for all of time."

The gong sounded.

"Carina, please give your pledge."

"Datch, I promise to take care of you. I promise to love you. I promise to keep you in my heart forever. I promise to support you and treasure you for all of time."

The gong sounded.

"Datch, please repeat after me. 'I Datch Thome willingly give my heart and soul to Carina Ganta.'"

"I Datch Thome willingly give my heart and soul to Carina Ganta." Datch's voice was starting to tremble a little.

"I wish to become one with her and become soul mates from this day forward." Said the official.

"I wish to become one with her and become soul mates from this day forward." Repeated Datch and then smiled at her.

The gong sounded twice.

The official turned to Carina.

“Carina, please repeat after me. ‘I Carina Ganta willingly give my heart and soul to Datch Thome.’”

“I Carina Ganta willingly give my heart and soul to Datch Thome.” Datch could feel Carina’s hand shaking slightly.

“I wish to become one with him and become soul mates from this day forward.” Said the official.

“I wish to become one with him and become soul mates from this day forward.” She smiled at him.

The gong sounded twice.

“Can I have the rings please.”

Fred and Rosey stepped forward.

First, he took the ring from Fred.

“Now the ring that signifies Datch’s soul.”

He gave it to Datch who with his free hand placed it on Carina’s finger and at the same time said.

“Carina, I give you, my soul.”

The official then took the ring from Rosey.

“Now the ring that signifies Carina’s soul.”

He gave it to Carina who with her free hand placed it on Datch’s finger and at the same time said.

“Datch, I give you, my soul.”

“Please step together.”

Datch and Carina came together almost to a close embrace with only the tied hands between them.

The official took hold of the end of the knot.

"I hereby announce to everyone within the sound of my voice that Carina and Datch are now soul mates and shall be known from now onwards as husband and wife."

The gong sounded three times.

He pulled the cord and it dropped away allowing Datch and Carina to kiss. Everyone clapped. When it had quietened down, he spoke again.

"Now the Monks from Welly Four will perform their blessing."

He stepped backwards and left the platform. Father Jamby was standing at the back of the chairs with six other monks. They walked down the centre aisle and stepped up on the platform.

Father Jamby stepped up to the podium and the six monks spread out around Carina and Datch. Three behind Datch and three behind Carina.

"Ladies, Gentlemen and Aliens. I am very honored to be able to give our blessing not only to these two wonderful people but also to our spiritual leaders."

The monks bowed their head.

"Datch and Carina, I'm here to make you one in the eyes of the universe. May the blessing of the gods shine down on you and may you have strong and healthy children. May the mountains smile on you and may the stars light your way."

He bowed his head and started humming a low tone. The other six monks started to hum as well and then the humming started to turn into chanting. A green glow started to appear around the monks and then Datch's and Carina's ring started to glow brightly. Two columns of green appeared around Datch and Carina. The chant got louder and louder as monks entered some form of trance. The glow became an almost blinding light. Then, Datch and Carina's two columns expanded into each other and merged forming one continuous column with Datch and Carina in the centre. Datch could see Carina's thoughts and she could see his. Their two minds became one, he could see her memories and feel her love for him, they became one entity. At the same time everyone watched as Datch and Carina lifted half a metre into the air above the stage before slowly floating back down. They were both staring into each other's eyes transfixed by each other's thoughts. They landed back on the stage and the chanting slowed down to a stop. Datch and Carina blinked at each other.

Father Jamby lifted his head and snapped back into reality.

"The blessing is now complete."

Datch kissed Carina and the column of light exploded across the valley. They turned to Father Jamby.

"Thank you and may you live many times over." They both said together.

He bowed to them as did the other monks and they all stepped back. Datch and Carina turned to face the front.

They stepped off the stage and everyone cheered.

Slowly they made their way to the Marquee with Fred and Rosey behind them. Then their parents filed in behind. Caroline was waiting at the door standing in front of a line of waiters.

"May I offer my congratulation to you both."

"Thank you." Said Datch.

"If you would please follow me to the top table."

She led the way across the marquee to a table that had been placed on a platform so everyone could see the happy couple. All the other guests filed in behind and sat down.

The food came out and afterwards it was speeches time. The final speech was Datch's. He stood up and cleared his throat.

"I'm sure you're all glad to know that this is the last speech of the day. I'll try and keep it short as I know you all want to party."

There were a few titters from the room.

"On behalf of myself and my wife. We would like to thank both of our parents for guiding us through life to now. We would also like to thank Fred, Rosey and Timbo who have all worked very hard to make this day come together. Now please raise a glass for them." He paused while everyone got up.

"Cheers all."

Everyone took a sip of their drink and there was a round of applause.

"We would also like to thank all of you, our friends and family for coming to celebrate with us. Today is a new chapter in our lives and I think it's going to be a good one. Thank you all."

There was a round of applause.

"We would also like to thank all of you for the lovely grifts that you have given us. Thank You. Well folks, that's the end of the speech. So, let's get this party going."

There was a round of applause and a lot of cheering. Datch sat back down and turned to Carina and said.

"Yes, I thought so to."

Dechow gave Datch a funny look.

They finished off their drinks and headed to the function room. Caroline escorted them to a table down near the dancefloor and people slowly made their way over. They sat having another drink before heading to mingle with the guests.

Datch finished his drink and got up.

“Yes. It will.” he said to Carina.

Both Fred and Dechow this time looked at him.

Fred got up with him as did Rosey.

“Err Datch?” Asked Fred.

“Yes?”

“What happened when the blessing took place?”

“Err, it was pretty amazing we were in each other’s minds.”

“I think you still are.”

“Why?”

“Well, you keep answering Carina’s questions before she has asked them.”

“I do?”

“I don’t know either.” Said Carina.

“You just did it then as well.” Said Rosey looking at Carina.

“Oh wow, let’s try something.”

“Blue.”

"Yes! your turn."

"Beer."

"Yes."

"Wow, this is really cool."

"What are you two doing?"

"When I think of a question for Carina" Said Datch.

"I hear it in my head." Said Carina.

"Oh boy. This is going to get really confusing. I think we had better talk to Father Jamby before we go around the room."

"Yes, that sounds like a good idea." Said Rosey.

"I like it too." Said Carina.

They headed across the room to Father Jamby who was standing at the bar getting a beer.

"Hi folks, congratulations."

"Thank you. Err, we need to asked you something."

"The telepathy?"

"Yes, The..." Datch stopped and looked at him.

"It's your rings. The blessing synchronised the gems you have on and connected them to your minds. When you think about asking or telling Carina something she will hear it in her mind and vis versa."

"Wow, is it forever?"

"No. It will only work when the gems are energised. So, it will last for a few weeks and then stop working until your next gig energises them again."

"Yes, what a gift." Added Datch.

"I take it Carina thinks it a great gift then?"

"Oh, sorry, yes I do."

"Right, this is going to take some getting used to." Said Fred.

"At least you're going to be on honeymoon for a couple of weeks. It will give them a chance to discharge." Said Rosey.

"We both like singing though."

"Ok, just try and not do it or if you do just answer the question in your mind instead of speaking it."

Datch and Carina looked at each other and started to giggle.

Fred sighed.

"Thanks Father Jamby, we love it." Said Datch.

"Yes, it's really cool." Added Carina.

"Come on you pair. Let's do the rounds. I think it maybe a long night." Said Fred.

They worked their way slowly around the room stopping at each table and thanking people for coming and their kind gifts. It took till early evening before they got to table with the rest of The Pack on.

"How are you two doing?" Asked Tank.

"We're good guys, Yes, mine too babes. Both our feet are aching a bit." Said Datch.

"Err... maybe I should explain about the ring thing?" Said Fred.

"Yes... that maybe a good idea." Said Rosey

“What ring thing?” Said Jep.

Fred went on to explain about the telepathy thing and then after a lot of testing by Tish and Dapo they headed back to the table where their parents were sitting.

Fred then explained to their mum’s and dad’s what was going on and that then involved more testing by them.

“So, let’s get this straight now. You both have telepathic rings is that correct?”

“Yes.” Said Datch.

“Hmm... I wonder...” Said Dechow but was then cut off in mid ponder as Don walked up with Widfab.

“Sorry to interrupt but we have a surprise for you outside.” he said and nodded at Caroline who stood at the front of the stage holding a mic.

“Ladies, Gentlemen and Aliens. Please could you follow Datch and Carina outside.”

Datch and Carina got up and headed outside into the darkness that had descended over the valley.

Datch and Carina followed Don to a spot half way across the lawn and as soon as everyone had come out Don gave Datch a comm link.

“Look up and press it.”

Datch handed it to Carina. She looked at it and pressed the button.

The Sky exploded in colour as both the Carpaycus and Welly destroyer lit up the sky with energy explosions. The valley was lit up like daytime as volley after volley streaked across the sky. They watched as showers of shimmering light cascaded down through the atmosphere. The lake acted as a mirror reflecting the rainbow of coloured explosions. Great showers of light cascaded through the heavens and then an image of Datch and Carina appeared in the sky surrounded by golden explosions. As it faded the words 'Congratulations Datch and Carina' appeared in the sky. Then after one final huge explosion the sky returned to darkness.

Don turned to face everyone.

"Thank you all. If you would like to head back in, I believe the band is going to start shortly."

Datch and Carina turned to Don and Widfab.

"Thank you both. That was wonderful."

"You're welcome. It was our pleasure. Now I believe it's your turn to entertain us." Said Don.

"Yes, I suppose it is."

They headed back inside and grabbed a quick drink at their table while the bikers and the Snowmen got set up.

Caroline was standing on the stage and waited until everyone was back inside and then looked across to Datch and Carina to make sure they were ready before picking up the mic.

"Ladies, Gentlemen and Aliens. Please put your hands together for the Snowmen."

There was a round of applause and the Snowmen came running on to the stage with the bikers.

Talia trotted up to the mic.

"Good evening, Twin Peaks!"

There was a cheer from the room.

“First, we would like to say a big congratulations to Datch and Carina. We hope you have a great life together and give you our best of wishes for the future.”

There was another cheer from the room.

“Datch, Carina, would you please take to the floor for the first dance.”

They got up and walked to the centre of the dancefloor.

“Ladies, Gentlemen and Aliens. This is their song, Star Lovers!”

They started to play and as they danced around the room their glow increased but instead of two columns of light there was just one large one surrounding them both. The intensity got brighter and brighter until they kissed. Then the column of energy that was surrounding them exploded across the room with a bright explosion of green energy. Outside the animals in the forest all looked at the sky as a wave of energy lit up the valley as the wave expanded outward. Above the hotel a pulse of energy vanished into the depths of space heading across a thousand light years towards welly four. The song came to the end and Datch and Carina walked back to their seat with a very bright glow around them.

The dancefloor now filled up with all the guests who now also sparkling and very big smiles. The party now shifted into high gear with everyone having a great time and of course the kababs came out along with burgers and a light buffet.

It was three in the morning before Datch and Carina finally got back to their room. They walked in and shut the door then just looked at each other, smiled and ran for the bedroom.

The next morning breakfast was served in the bedroom and afterwards, they both had showers and put on their holiday clothes. Not that their holiday clothes were much different to their normal clothes but it was a holiday ritual for them. It was almost lunchtime before they were ready to go downstairs.

They called Caroline who sent a porter up to get their things and then they headed to the bar.

Both of their parents were there waiting along with most of the guests.

They all clapped when they walked in. Dechow walked over with a drink for each of them and they followed him back to a big table. Tansya was there along with Carina's mum and dad and The Pack.

"Well Mr and Mrs Thome, how does it feel to be husband and wife?" Asked Clax smiling.

Carina looked at Datch.

"Yes." he said and paused before continuing,

"About the same, we think? But we're both loving this telepathy thing, it's great."

"And we can just think of something and," added Carina,

"the other one knows what it is without," added Datch,

"having to talk about it." Finished Carina.

"Oh boy, this is really going to take some getting used to." Said Fred.

"You can say that again." Said Clax.

Datch and Carina finished their drinks and then turned to the rest.

"Well, I think it's time to go." Said Datch.

"I hope both of you have a great time." Said Tansya.

"I'm sure we will." Said Carina.

They both got up headed across the bar stopping at the entrance leading to the landing area.

"See you all in three weeks folks." Shouted Datch.

Everyone cheered.

They turned and headed to the Raven through the pine tree that lined the route to the landing area.

Five minutes later they were sitting in the cockpit. Datch in the pilot's seat and Carina in the co-pilot's seat.

Datch contacted Traxsent control before turning to Carina

"Are you ready my wife?"

"Yes, my husband."

He brought the thrusters online, pointed the Raven's nose towards the sky and they headed for the stars.

# The End

Other Books in the series.

Datch – The Great Adventure.

The Datch Pack.

The Mystical Gem.

The Quest for Earthly Delights.

Hunting Jackars.

The Orphaned World.

www.ingramcontent.com/pod-product-compliance
Lightning Source LLC
Chambersburg PA
CBHW070428170726
48291CB00002B/404

* 9 7 8 1 9 1 7 2 3 8 1 6 8 *